Mile Marker Zero

Benny Sims

Contents

Bluecat Press
Second Edition

Softcover ISBN 979-8-9994824-2-6
eBook ISBN 979-8-9994824-3-3

First edition published by Pandamoon Publishing

Library of Congress Cataloging-in-Publication Data is on file at the Library of Congress,
Washington, DC

Jacket design and illustrations © Pandamoon Publishing
Art Direction by Don Kramer: Pandamoon Publishing
Illustrations by Don Kramer: Pandamoon Publishing
Editing by Zara Kramer, Kathleen Bosman, and Rachel Schoenbauer: Pandamoon Publishing

All rights reserved under International and Pan-American Copyright Conventions. Library of
Congress Cataloging-in-Publication Data is on file at the Library of Congress, Washington,
DC

Reviews

A dark, fast-paced thriller, *Mile Marker Zero* gives new meaning to the term "to-do list." Terrifying and unforgettable.
— **Bruce Robert Coffin, award-winning author of the Detective Byron Mysteries**

Benny Sims' latest thriller, *Marker Mile Zero*, does everything a thriller is meant to do – shock – and build anxiety and a growing fear in the reader's mind. The best thrillers are constructed so those feelings continue post-read and lend a new perspective about how dangerous the world really is (or could be). Sims' tale had me worried and anxious from page one... and after I turned the last page and put the book down, I did find myself reacting to every happenstance encounter with new suspicions. This is a scary and fascinating window into the mind of a man who has no reason to live...
— **Jule Selbo, Silver Falchion award-winning author of *10 DAYS, A Dee Rommel Mystery* and its sequel *9 DAYS***

Benny Sims has a smooth writing style and from page one he pulls the reader into Mile Marker Zero, making it effortless for the reader to immerse themselves in the world of John Doe, serial killer. The reader sees all facets of John thanks to Benny's portrayal of this desperate and complex man, who is at a pivotal point in his life. When John is faced with a chance of

redemption and possible happiness, I found myself saying out loud, "Oh no," at one of many unexpected plot twists. Benny writes about the human condition, and through John's revelations, handling our problems with violence. Benny's depiction of characters had me anxious for John, as well as anxious for his victims. Great imagery, excellent dialogue, this book is hard to put down.
— **Joanna Vander Vlugt, podcaster and author of the Jade & Sage thrillers *The Unravelling* and *Dealer's Child*.**

A burned-out factory worker who has nothing left to live for sets out on a mission to make one kill a week for a year. Will he succeed? A page turner until the heart-stopping climax!
— **Stacy Lucas**

Mile Marker Zero is the literary opposite of *"A wonderful life"*. A deadly travel blog, the writing is sharp and every bit a thriller. The suspense doesn't ever stop as the reader waits for the inevitable ending. At its core, Mile Marker Zero is a what-if exploration of the failures of society as you watch the mind of a man that's been dealt nothing but lemons finally struggling to leave a legacy of blood.
— **Tony Ollivier, author of the David Knight thrillers *The Amsterdam Deception* and *The Tokyo Diversion***

A funny and depraved satire, putting the lie to the contemporary true-crime glorification of violence. Sims' tale reminds me of that other great naked open-road novel of Americana, Going Native by Stephen Wright.
— **Seth Augenstein, author of *Project 137* and *Llama With A Gun***

I received an advanced review copy (ARC) of Mile Marker Zero thinking it would be a run of the mill mystery. This is a book that no matter what time of the day you start reading it, you know you're going to finish it that day. In the beginning a guy is getting ready to have his traditional Sunday breakfast, one he has after accomplishing an as yet unknown deed until the next page details his worry over getting rid of the body in the car trunk; a murder duly marked off on his calendar. You soon learn that this "murder" will fit into his life accomplishment enshrining him forever In History. The goal of someone who has gotten close to the goal line but never crossed it. You

might think it's a gruesome goal but it should be easily accomplished in this day and age - after all people are murdered, disappearing without an eyebrow lifted or the case solved. And so, in a casual, thoughtful manner, this aging guy travels the country in rental cars, selecting his victims at random while Karma quietly starts adding sand to the gears of his plan. You'll enjoy this book, asking questions while you read, getting to an ending you won't forget.
— **Richard Kwasniewski**

In an intriguing departure from the usual murder novel narrative, Benny Sims takes the reader on an unexpected journey in his newest novel, Mile Marker Zero. This is a gripping tale not of finding the murderer(s), but an exploration of human emotions, cause and effects, and the fragility of life. It will be difficult to put down once started, and challenging to not ponder the events as they unfold (and their possible ramifications) once finished. In a surprising departure from the style of Code Gray, Benny Sims definitely proves his talents as a first-rate author!
— **Lydia Bosse**

This book is dedicated to Jesse and Aliyah, Conner and Hannah, and, as always, to Tammy

Part One
THE SIGHT OF BLOOD

Chapter One

I STARTED MY SUNDAY THE SAME WAY I'VE STARTED EVERY Sunday so far this year, with a stack of pancakes, a cup of coffee, a calendar, and another dead body added to my list.

Last Sunday at 7 a.m., I was in a Cracker Barrel somewhere outside of Columbia, South Carolina. But today I'm in a little roadside greasy spoon diner in southern Illinois. I walked through the door at exactly seven o'clock, according to the brownish-whitish grease-stained clock mounted on the wall above the grill.

Most mornings during the week I wouldn't even eat breakfast. Unless a pastry and a Styrofoam cup of coffee from a convenience store counted as breakfast. I never considered that as a real breakfast, though. To me, a real breakfast involves sitting down and using utensils to eat your food. There's something more civilized about that, in my opinion.

But come Sunday, it was a real breakfast. I figured it was the perfect way of rewarding myself for hitting another milestone. The first thing I did every Sunday after ordering my pancakes was pull the rolled-up calendar from my back pocket and open it up.

I used salt and pepper shakers to hold down the curled corners, then I flipped through the pages until I found the next blank square beneath Sunday, and I drew a red X, top corners to bottom corners.

I looked at today's date. April 24. Then I swallowed my first mouthful of coffee. Man, that stuff tasted awesome. Nectar of the gods, my old man used to call it. I don't know whether that's true or not, but I do know I'm usually as nice as a bear with a toothache until I get the first cup in me. Maybe it ought to be called the "Nectar of the Grumpy Bastards." I finished my first cup in about four swallows.

I caught the eye of the waitress and held up my cup, signaling I needed a fresh refill. As she walked over with a steaming pitcher, I counted the number of red marks on my calendar, starting from January 3. Today made seventeen. I was still on schedule, and I was beginning to get really good at this. Finally, something in this shitty life that I was good at.

The calendar was just a little fold-up, dollar store kind of thing that I bought this past Christmas, with a picture of an old rickety barn above the days of each month. Twelve pages, twelve pictures in all, not including the picture on the cover since it was the same picture used for January. The big white squares made it easy to count, and for somebody as old as me, that's a huge plus. I need reading glasses for the newspaper and magazines and the diner menu, but not for my calendar. It was ready for me whenever I needed it.

"Whatcha got there, sweetie?" asked the waitress after she finished pouring. She was probably a redhead once upon a time, but the gray had pretty much taken over her teased and sprayed hair. But you gotta love Midwestern women. They're friendly and down-to-earth, more so than just about anywhere else in the country, and it seemed she had never met a stranger. She was a perfect fit for the job of a diner waitress.

"That's my countdown clock," I told her as I lifted my full cup. The coffee was hot again, and it was awesome.

"Countdown to what?"

"Retirement," I said. "Just keeping count of the weeks I have left."

"How many ya got left?"

I tried doing the math in my head, but I was never good at math, so I just made something up. "Twenty," I said. "Twenty more weeks and I'm done." It was a lie, but the number didn't matter, anyhow. She was never going to see me again.

She shook her head, partly due to jealousy and partly due to surprise.

"I sure wish I was that close. I never would have thought you were old enough to retire," she said as she walked away to fill another cup on the other side of the diner.

Three minutes later she brought my pancakes, and I dug in. I had to get finished with my Sunday ritual before moving on, and the final stage of that ritual involved getting rid of the body stuffed in the trunk of my rental car.

It was a teenage girl this time, probably about seventeen or so. Dark hair, about five-four and thin. Her piece-of-crap car had given up the ghost on an unlit two-lane last night, and I happened to drive past while she stood under her raised hood. She wore a uniform like they wear at fast-food restaurants. I couldn't tell what color it was because it was very dark, and the only light came from my taillights. Her cell phone had no service out in the boondocks, she had told me, and asked if I could give her a lift home.

It's easy to trust a gray-haired older man who looks like someone's uncle, especially when you're desperate, and she was desperate. The road was totally deserted, and there were no lights showing across the flat Midwestern landscape. I had asked her if she wanted to try my cell phone, and while she was figuring out how to dial it, I stepped behind her, grabbed her chin with my left hand and the back of her head with my right, and gave her skull a violent twist.

She crumpled to the ground as if her bones had instantly turned to sawdust. No scream of fear or pain, no flailing of her arms, just instant death. Also, no blood, which is the way I prefer it. It's too messy, and it's a guaranteed way of getting caught. Cops today are so sophisticated they can track down a killer by using a single drop of blood.

The girl was light, maybe a shade over a hundred pounds. Picking her up required only a little more effort than snapping her neck. I laid her on the plastic tarp I had earlier spread out in the trunk, then rolled her up like a homemade cigarette. She fit into the far recess of the trunk quite easily, and a carpeted cardboard barrier propped up in front of her kept her completely hidden.

My car was now parked in the diner's gravel lot only a few feet outside the door, and I knew that it wouldn't be long before the smell would be strong enough to escape the trunk, especially now that the weather was starting to warm up.

I left enough money on the table to pay for my breakfast, plus a nice little tip for the waitress, then walked out and got in the car. Before I started the engine, I inhaled a large breath through my nose. No smell yet. She would be covered with dirt or thirty feet underwater within an hour, so I didn't have anything to worry about.

I pulled away from the diner and drove the back roads for a few miles, looking for a good place to get rid of her. Some people might think I'm crazy for doing this in broad daylight, but I actually think it's pretty smart. Doing things at night require lights, and lights can be seen from a long way off. Somebody walking through the woods at two o'clock in the morning attracts a lot of attention when they've got a flashlight, and vehicles driving down old dirt roads or through pastures in the middle of the night are easy to spot. Not so much during the day, though. People mill about during daylight hours and nobody really pays any attention to them. Think about it. Would you be concerned if you saw a car driving down an old country road during the day?

After about thirty minutes, I came to a bridge that crossed a lazy, muddy river. Because it was moving so slow, I figured it was deep enough to dump her. It wouldn't matter if she floated to the surface a couple of days later, because I would be two states away by then.

I pulled to the side of the road right next to the guardrail and opened the trunk. I moved my duffel bag containing my clothes over to one side, then pulled out a small tackle box and a telescoping fishing pole and leaned it against the car's bumper. That was going to be my alibi in case someone drove by. I was just some old man getting ready to do a little fishing.

The side of the road was rocky, with chunks of chert and limestone nearly as big as my hand. I picked up four of them and laid them off to the side in the trunk, then lowered the carpeted cardboard and moved the girl towards me. The tarp unrolled all the way, and she ended face up against the rear edge of the trunk, looking at the sky and the raised trunk lid. For the first time, I noticed her name tag pinned to her uniform. *Amy.* Her eyes were both half open, and so was her mouth. Strands of her hair were stuck to her lips. She probably had been quite pretty once, maybe the girlfriend of the high school quarterback, but now she was only number seventeen.

A seventeen-year-old for number seventeen. A happy little accident. I love it when that happens. At this point in my life, I'll take any kind of little victory I can get.

I shoved the rocks into her uniform pockets, just enough to weigh her down for a few minutes. All I needed was enough time to get out of the county. I gave a look down the road in both directions and saw nothing. I didn't hear anyone coming, either. I scanned the riverbanks for hikers or someone fishing. I was the only person around. This early on a Sunday, most people around here were getting ready to head to church, not out enjoying nature. That would happen later this afternoon.

I scooped her up in my arms and lifted her out of the trunk. She was a little heavier than last night because of the rocks in her pockets, but not by much. I turned a half-turn and dropped her over the guardrail and into the brown water.

She hit with a large splash, which surprised me considering her small size. The expanding circles where she hit the water moved downstream with the current, growing larger as they got further away. I waited for about half a minute, but her body didn't float to the surface. The rocks had done their job.

I rolled up the tarp and shoved it into a pocket of my duffel bag, then put my tackle box and fishing pole over to one side where I always kept them. Then I drove away like an old man out for a Sunday drive.

Two hours later I turned in my rental car at the St. Louis airport Avis lot, my seventeenth one-way rental of the year. Then I walked over to the Hertz counter and paid for another one-way rental. I shoved my luggage into the trunk, and less than an hour after arriving in St. Louis, I drove out of town on my way to El Paso, Texas.

Chapter Two

I probably should have been a trucker, since I enjoy long drives on the open road. There's something about an endless stretch of highway that calms me and allows my mind to think without all the clutter that comes from being cooped up all the time. You spend your life in a box made of concrete and steel, working to pay the rent and keep the family fed, and after a few decades those concrete and steel walls begin to feel more like a prison. You breathe the same stale air that smells like machine oil, sweat, and dust every day for that many years, and that box starts to mess with your mind. It can convince you that you're not the hero to your kids you'd hoped to be, that the pinnacle of your career is right where you are now, and that you should scale back your definition of self-worth so that it's determined only by how well your favorite college football team does.

I should know. That's what happened to me. Thirty-five of the best years of my life pissed down the drain while I helped some fat cat CEO become a millionaire. Actually, during those thirty-five years, I helped *seven* of those bastards get rich enough to afford their own private jets, more houses than they had fingers, and vacations in the south of France every two months. Me, I managed to get rich enough to own a 1,200-square-foot house, two cars, an aluminum fishing boat, and a riding lawn mower. But those CEOs were always trying to scale back my paycheck. I never understood that. How in the hell can a millionaire accuse some poor sap of making too much money and still manage to sleep at night? Millionaires telling their employees that they pay them too much...Jesus H. Christ.

Yeah, I should have been a trucker. That way, if some rich CEO tried to cut my pay, I could just run his ass over and claim that the throttle stuck.

Sorry, rich boy. Too bad all that money couldn't buy you a suit of armor.

I don't know why my mind sometimes wanders back to those years. The memories are like demons that wake up from a long nap and scratch at old wounds until they bleed again. And because of that, I get on the road and drive. Yeah, those memories might come and go while I'm behind the wheel, but they don't last long. The highway wipes them away.

I can honestly say that I haven't let those thoughts bother me since about a month ago. I was halfway between Baltimore and Indianapolis, just after sunset, somewhere in southeastern Ohio when they hit, and I let them get to me. Before I knew it, I was in the middle of a full-on, teeth-clenching, white-knuckle rage. I had to do something about it, so I pulled into a truck stop and looked for a place to park. The lot was full of cars, so I pulled around back where all the truckers parked. I had intended to go inside and grab a cup of coffee to calm down, but I stopped the car when I noticed a woman with one foot on the passenger-side steps of a semi, her hand gripping the door handle.

She noticed me, too. She let go of the door handle and sauntered over to my open window. She wore a dirty denim jacket and tight jeans, and she smelled like a combination of two-dollar cologne and cigarette smoke. I had interrupted her while she was about to negotiate with the trucker for a half-hour in the motel next door, but apparently she thought I was a better prospect. Must have been my gray hair.

She said her name was Rene and asked if I wanted a little company. I nodded my head at the passenger seat, and she walked around the car and got in.

There was a narrow alley about a hundred yards long between the dozens of parked semis that allowed a car to pass through and out of the parking lot, and before we'd made it fifty yards, she was unconscious from a punch to the jaw and had slumped over with her head in my lap. I squeezed her windpipe with my right hand while my left steered. Less than a mile down the road, she had no pulse. Two miles after that, I dumped her in a deep ditch full of three-foot-high bushes, along a rural road with no traffic at all.

She was number thirteen.

It amazes me that in a country with hundreds of millions of people, it's often easy to find empty roads only a couple of miles from a busy truck stop next to an interstate highway. But I'm not complaining. Not one bit.

By the time I got to Indianapolis the next day, and after I had my pancakes, coffee, and made my red X on my calendar, I felt a whole lot better. The demons and those asshole CEOs haven't been back since.

Ten miles past Oklahoma City, I stopped for a bite of supper and more coffee at a fast food joint. It was sandwiched between a movie theater and a strip mall, and the area was crawling with potential victims, but sometimes too many choices mean there aren't any choices at all. Most of them were under the age of twenty. There were a few under twelve years old, but I didn't consider them potential victims. That's where I drew the line. No children. Adults and older teens only. I might be a murderer, but at least I'm not a monster.

I ignored them all and focused on getting some food. It was still Sunday, and I had a full seven days to find number eighteen. With all that open space between Oklahoma City and El Paso, I wouldn't have a problem finding somebody. That was one of the great things about my new life. I wasn't under a difficult time schedule. Seven days to find, kill, and dispose of one person. One victim a week for an entire year.

Fifty-two victims. It was a goal I should be able to reach without any problems. Unless I got caught, of course. Getting nabbed by the FBI for being a serial killer would pretty much finish off any hope I might have of setting a goal and achieving it.

All the other goals in my life had failed miserably. I had hoped to climb the ladder at my job, and that never happened. I went nowhere for thirty-five years. I once heard somebody say that the only thing worse than going nowhere fast was going nowhere slow. That described my career perfectly. I was going nowhere slow. So, I called it quits and retired, but that was after a few other goals had failed.

I wanted to have a marriage everybody could admire, and I did for a little while, until the bitch ran off with her high school sweetheart. I came home after work one day to find a note on the kitchen counter, and all her clothes gone from the closet. Her lawyer mailed divorce papers to me a month later, and I signed them and mailed them back. What the hell. If she didn't want to stay, I sure didn't want to force her. Anyway, it was another notch on my failure belt.

Looking back to the beginning of my new hobby, I probably should have made her my first victim, and I would have, except for the little voice in my head that kept telling me I would have been the dumbest serial killer in the whole history of history. How could I be a serial killer if I got caught right after my first murder? That automatically knocks the word "serial" off the name. I would have been just a murderer, caught because I was the ex-husband of the deceased. Current and former husbands are instant suspects when a woman dies, even if she accidentally steps in front of a train or something. And even if they didn't do it, the cops sure give them a long, hard look before they let them go.

So, all in all, I guess my inability to kill her could be labeled a failure, too.

I wanted to raise a son or daughter that I could be proud of, and they could be proud of me. Instead, I ended up with a moody, anti-social, parent-hating son who was now a moody, anti-social, parent-hating thirty-something-year-old who moved an entire continent away from his parents so he wouldn't have to spend time with them on holidays. Last I heard, Ethan was working as a tattoo artist somewhere in Oregon. I haven't seen him or spoken with him since his mother and I got divorced.

I'm a failure at my career. I'm a failure at marriage. I'm a failure as a parent. And all these failures tore at my psyche. I desperately needed something that would give me a feeling of accomplishment, that made people sit up and take notice of me. So I took a couple of days off work and did nothing but think about what to do. There were a lot of discussions between the devil on my right shoulder and the angel on my left, but in the end, the devil won. He convinced me my plan would give me a sense of accomplishment, even if I didn't get caught, or it would send shockwaves across the country if I was.

Either way, it would end with, "Look what I did."

Isn't that basically the definition of a goal? Isn't it being able to say "Look what I did" after the goal is reached? A goal isn't just the next fence post you pass while you're walking down the road of life. It's an end to a means.

Of course, the angel on my shoulder wasn't very happy with the path I decided to take, but screw him. He never really helped me during my life, anyway.

I decided on killing people for different reasons. Primarily, it was my anger at being such a failure, and I wanted to take it out on somebody. Secondly, it would be extremely difficult, but achievable. Tough goals are the most rewarding when they're reached. Third, it was unique. I don't know of anyone else who intended on killing one person a week for an entire year. It would be the first time in history, as far as I knew.

A fourth reason is one I don't want to admit, but it's probably true. I think I'm a little bit insane. If I'm totally honest with myself, I have to admit that no sane person would do what I'm doing.

A normal-looking, middle-aged man sitting in a fast food restaurant chewing on a burger, and he's got a screw loose. You couldn't tell by looking that I'm crazy. What does crazy look like, anyway? Should I look like the cartoon version of insanity, with wild eyes and hair that looks like it was combed with a pair of jumper cables?

It's been said that crazy people don't know that they're crazy. Well, sometimes we do.

As I sat there chewing my hamburger with my crazy teeth, holding my soda with my crazy hands, propping my crazy elbows on the table, I saw with my crazy eyes a police cruiser pull into the parking lot, into the space right beside my rental car.

I'm not sure why, but at that instant my heart started to beat a lot faster.

The cop was alone. No partner in the passenger seat. He got out, then looked at my car. He walked behind it and looked at the license plate. Then he moved to the driver's side and peered through the window. He looked around, then got the attention of a teenage boy who was walking out of the restaurant. I could see the cop saying something to him, then the boy twisted his torso and pointed right at me. The cop followed the boy's finger and looked me right in the face.

Oh, shit.

My heartbeat pounded, and a million thoughts raced through my head at once. Did someone see me dump the girl into the river? Did I make a mistake somewhere during the past four months, and the cops were just now catching up to me?

He walked into the restaurant and headed straight for me. I pretended to be busy eating, but I could feel him getting closer. He stopped right next to my table.

"Excuse me, sir. Sorry to bother you, but is that your car right there?" He was pointing to the parking lot.

I put down my burger, took a moment to swallow, and looked outside with a slight frown.

"Which one?" I asked.

"Right there," he said, pointing again. "The one beside my car. The blue one."

I nodded and looked up at him. "Yes, that's mine."

"You probably didn't realize it, but that's a handicapped spot, and I didn't see a handicapped sign on your car. Do you think you could move to another spot?"

"You're right. I didn't know it was a handicapped spot. I'm sorry. I'll, uh..." I started to get up, then sat back down and looked at my tray of food. I fumbled with it, picked it up, sat it down, started to stand again, then sat, all with the intention of acting confused and not knowing what to do.

The cop put a hand on my shoulder. "Tell you what. Don't worry about it. It's not that big a deal. Just try not to leave it there too long," he told me.

"Okay, thank you. I'll be done here in a minute or two," I said. I tried to keep my voice from sounding shaky.

He gave me a smile and a nod, then headed back to his car and pulled away.

I took a deep breath and picked up my half-eaten burger, then put it back. I decided I needed to wet my dry mouth before taking a bite. I reached for the soda, then stopped before grabbing it.

My hands were trembling.

Chapter Three

I was back on the road the next morning by seven o'clock. Normally, I would have preferred to sleep in until around eight or so, then take my time getting out of the hotel, since I didn't have a job to go to or a Sunday breakfast to eat. This morning was different, though. I wanted to be out of that town as quickly as I could, so I took a shower around six, threw my duffel bag into the trunk, and peeled out of the parking lot of the little mom-and-pop hotel I was in last night.

It would be a stretch to say that I got a good night's sleep.

Actually, it would be an outright lie. I didn't sleep a wink, even though I tried. I tossed and turned all night because my brain wouldn't slow down long enough for sleep to catch up with me. That encounter with the cop was a wakeup call...literally.

Parking in the handicapped spot was an act of carelessness that I can't afford to make again. I was just lucky this time. Next time, I might end up in the back seat of a squad car with adjustable bracelets on both wrists, and that would be the end of my little hobby.

I let out a long, head-shaking yawn that nearly made me dizzy. I was sleepy, and I hadn't had my customary unhealthy snack of convenience-store food and coffee. My car's gas gauge showed over half a tank. That was enough to get me far enough out of town to make me feel more at ease before I had to stop and fill up.

Monday morning traffic on the back roads of central Oklahoma was surprisingly heavy, and that made for slow going. I decided to avoid the interstates. I used them only if I was in a hurry, and that rarely happened. I wanted to see the country from the small towns and two-lane highways. Plus, I was more likely to pass through some sleepy little town and find an easy victim.

At a stoplight, I pulled my wallet out of my hip pocket and checked my funds. I still had well over nine-hundred dollars with me. I tried to have at least a thousand bucks on me at the beginning of each leg of my trip. That would have been more than enough for a week's worth of hotel rooms, food, gas, and any supplies that I might need along the way.

All I can say is, thank goodness for ATM machines. Withdrawing a thousand dollars is no big deal anymore. Not like it used to be, anyway, when you were limited to about three hundred dollars a day.

The only bad thing now about ATM machines is they only give you twenties. That leaves me with a huge stack of money. I usually stop at a bank and swap about half the twenties for hundreds to make the pile a lot more manageable.

I eat on the cheap. I sleep in small, nondescript hotels. I use rental cars. There's nothing about me that's elaborate or fancy. No expensive clothes, no expensive shoes.

I stay in a hotel for as long as four days in a row, depending on the abundance of potential victims, and sometimes I stay just one night and move on. I wear blue jeans, denim work shirts, and leather boots. I have one baseball cap that I wear whenever I decide not to shower that day. It's just a plain navy blue, with no logo or any other identifying features, that I bought at Wal-Mart.

If you want to blend in, you can't stick out like a sore thumb. And I wanted to blend in. I wanted to be the kind of person nobody would remember. This whole thing was just for me, just so I could say, "Look what I did" to myself.

That's the way I lived, from one week to the next, paying cash for everything so I wouldn't leave a trail. But doing this for an entire year was going to take a lot of money. Fifty-two thousand dollars minimum, to be exact. I normally wouldn't have had that kind of money just lying around, so before my new life started, I had to come up with a way to make it happen.

After my wife divorced me, I decided that I wanted a divorce from my job. I crunched the numbers of my retirement pension, plus my savings fund that I had been building since the day I started my job, and I decided that it would be doable, but barely. To stay within the margin of error, I was going to need more money.

But I went ahead and retired anyway. Then I spent the next six months getting into shape. Well, as good a shape as a man in his fifties can manage. I weightlifted in my garage. I started running...if you can call a slow trot running. But most importantly, I started studying self-defense.

There was an ad in the local paper about martial arts classes, so I called the guy up. I figured I'd have to wear one of those karate pajama suits, like you see on television all the time. I also thought I would be taking classes with a bunch of other people. Turns out the guy gave private lessons in your home. He taught some kind of military style that I couldn't pronounce. It's not all that flashy stuff you see in the movies. It's basically just moves that kill people and keep them from killing you.

So, I paid him in advance for six months of lessons, and he came to my house twice a week for twenty-four weeks straight to show me how to disarm someone with a pistol or knife, or how to break someone's neck, or stab them in a place that didn't produce a lot of blood. I didn't tell him why I wanted to learn. I just acted like I was a middle-aged man who was afraid some terrorist would try to kill me one day while I'm grocery shopping, and I wanted to know how to protect myself.

I worked hard, and after six months I was pretty good, I think. I know I wasn't a world-class elite killer, but I could hold my own for somebody over fifty.

And man, it was fun. There's just something really awesome about knowing how to pop out an eyeball with your thumbs, or crush a windpipe, or break someone's neck with a sudden twist of their head. Call me crazy, but I just think that's some cool stuff to know. And I used some aspect of that knowledge on every one of my victims so far.

After the six months was over, I sold everything I had. Furniture, boat, lawnmower, most of my clothes, and finally, my house. I kept my truck because I needed a way to get to the first car rental place. As far as I knew, it was still sitting in the parking garage at the airport, running up a huge parking fee.

I took a hit on most of the stuff, but after it was all sold, I had over a hundred and fifty thousand dollars. Combined with my pension and savings fund, I had nearly three hundred thousand. Every dime of that went into a new account at my bank. That's where I was getting my money for my hobby. With that much money, I didn't have to worry where my next meal, my next hotel room, or my next rental car was going to come from.

A little over three hours after leaving the little mom-and-pop hotel, I crossed the Red River into Texas. The whole countryside was nothing but farmland as far as the eye could see. Flat, fertile fields produced from the floodwaters of the river had been turned into farms that grew the wheat for my Sunday pancakes, cotton for my blue jeans and shirts, and soybeans for my...well...whatever it is you make with soybeans.

One thing I knew they didn't grow here was coffee, and my foggy brain managed to convince me I needed a caffeine boost. The lack of sleep, the stress from the cop encounter last night, and my empty stomach were all ganging up on me. Plus, my car needed gas. A few miles past the river I came to a small town called Seymour, and I stopped at a corner convenience store to fill up.

"How far to El Paso from here?" I asked the store clerk when I placed my coffee, doughnuts, and sausage biscuit on the counter.

The clerk gave me a frown as if she didn't believe I was going to El Paso. She was about forty or so, and she had that look like she was one of those women who called out bullshit whenever she heard it.

"You driving to El Paso?" she asked. She gave me a winced look as if to say, "Better you than me, honey."

"Yeah, that's my plan," I said. "How long should it take me?"

"If you take the interstate, it'll be quicker, but it's still gonna be a full day of driving."

I let out a low whistle. I didn't want to drive all the way there in one day. I wanted to take my time and find my victims.

"Is there a hotel in town?" I asked.

She pointed down the street. "That way about a half-mile. It's on your left." Then she rang up my sale and put the doughnuts and biscuit in a small plastic bag.

And right then, a light bulb popped up in my foggy brain. I knew how I was going to kill my next victim.

Twenty minutes later, I was checked into a hotel room and sprawled out on the bed. The hotel clerk had been nice enough to let me have a room even though check-in time wasn't for another two hours. I was so tired, not even convenience store coffee could have kept me awake at that point. My half-empty coffee cup sat on the bedside table, getting cold. The doughnuts and biscuit were still in the plastic bag at the foot of the bed, sitting on my duffel bag. They could wait. Right now, I needed sleep. Within a minute after lying down, I was out like a light.

It was nearly dark when I woke up. And I would have stayed asleep if it hadn't been for a loud crash outside my door.

Chapter Four

You know that confused feeling you get when you suddenly wake up after being in a deep sleep? The one that makes you forget where you are and what day it is, and makes your motor skills completely disappear? Well, that's what happened to me when I heard that loud noise.

I jerked awake and swatted at the air like something was attacking me. I guess I had been dreaming a bad dream. It was almost completely dark in the room, the only light from streetlamps that seeped through the cheap curtains. It took a few seconds to figure out where I was, and when I reached to turn on the lamp, I knocked it completely off the table because my arm was asleep. I must have had it under me while I slept. It felt like someone else's arm when I grabbed it with my other hand and pulled it off the table.

When I tried to stand up, I nearly fell, and had to catch myself against the wall, because my left foot was asleep, too. Sometimes I think you could look up the phrase "hot mess" in the encyclopedia, and my picture would be there.

After I hobbled to the door and opened it just enough to peer outside, I saw what had made the noise.

It was horrible car crash. It looked like someone had run a stop sign and T-boned another car, flipping it over onto its roof. The driver's side of the upside-down car was caved in, and the front end of the other car was mashed back to where the tires should have been. I didn't know what the speed limit was on that street, but whatever it was, the car that caused the damage was certainly exceeding it.

The driver of the upside-down car appeared to be curled up in a fetal position, wrapped up in a cocoon of bent metal, broken car seats, and glass. I couldn't tell if it was a man or a woman. They weren't moving.

The driver of the other car was still in the driver's seat, their head nodded forward as if they were asleep. It appeared as if it was a young man with dark long hair.

I stomped my tingling foot on the floor a few times and slapped my dead arm to get the blood flowing faster, then opened the door all the way and stepped outside. I didn't hear any sirens. A few other drivers had stopped but were still sitting in their cars. When I looked left and right, I didn't see anybody running toward the wreck to check on the victims.

Was I the only person alive in the whole world right then, except for the other drivers who were still sitting behind their steering wheels? What the hell is wrong with people these days? Couldn't they see that people were hurt? One of the drivers who refused to get out of the car turned around in the middle of the road and sped off in the opposite direction.

It's that kind of bullshit that'll make you lose your faith in humanity, I swear.

I paced back and forth a few times in front of my room, trying to decide what to do. I didn't know anything about first aid, other than how to put a band-aid on a cut. But these injuries were certainly much worse than a cut. After about a minute of waiting for a good Samaritan to show up, I made up my mind. Screw it. I was going to do my best to help these people. I'd let somebody else call an ambulance.

My foot wasn't asleep any longer, and my arm was tingling enough to let me know it would be fully functional within a few moments. I trotted over to the driver of the car with the crumpled front end. The impact had popped open the doors on each side of the car. There was a round spider web of broken glass on the windshield right in front of the steering wheel. Apparently, this guy hadn't been wearing a seat belt, and the force of the impact threw him into the windshield. I didn't see a deflated airbag that would have prevented this. His face was shattered, and blood dripped out of what was left of his nose and mouth. But he was breathing, and with every ragged exhale I smelled alcohol on his breath.

For one brief moment, I considered being an angel of death and breaking this guy's neck. No one would have known, and it would have been an easy addition to my total, but I decided against it. Killing someone who's nearly dead is almost like cheating. Besides, there were people watching. So I walked away.

I decided to let someone else tend to him. The hell with him. If he's so stupid that he would get behind the wheel after drinking too much and put innocent lives in danger, then I didn't care if he lived or died. He deserved to suffer a little, either way.

Another reason I left him is because I don't like the sight of blood. Never have, never will.

I moved over to the upside-down car, on the driver's side, just as my stomach began to get a little queasy. I had to get down on my hands and knees to look into the car, which didn't help my stomach situation any. This was the same position I always found myself in when I was in high school and had too much to drink. It never failed that I would get down on my hands and knees and pray to the porcelain god.

Sometimes if I took really deep breaths, the sick feeling would go away for a little while, so I filled my lungs three times before leaning in to check on the driver. It helped a little, but I knew it wouldn't stay that way.

When I looked inside, I couldn't see anything but the driver's legs. It was definitely a woman. The sandals on her small feet and her painted toenails gave that away. She didn't move, and I couldn't see that she was breathing. Her head was closer to the other side of the car, so I stood up and took a few more deep breaths before walking around to the other side.

Off in the distance, I heard sirens. Help was on the way. Maybe I wouldn't have to stick around here much longer.

When I reached the rear of the car, a woman standing in the hotel parking lot yelled, "Sir, are you okay?"

I waved at her. "Yeah, I wasn't in the wreck."

Then I pointed at the first driver. "He needs some help, though."

I could see flashing lights several blocks away, coming towards the scene in a hurry. Blue lights of the cops, and red lights of an ambulance. Just one ambulance. By the looks of things, they were going to need more than that.

I moved around to the passenger side of the car and stopped dead in my tracks. There had been someone else in the car with the woman. A little boy who looked to be no older than five or six was lying face down on the pavement, five feet from the shattered passenger door window. The tumbling action of the car had thrown him out.

The scalp on the back of his head had been peeled away, and bloody, rope-like strands of his brain were draped across his cheek. He was lying in a massive pool of blood.

I couldn't take the time to check on the woman in the car, because a wave of nausea churned up from deep in my guts and overpowered me. There wasn't anything in my stomach but bile, but it was rushing its way into my throat like lava from a volcano. There was no stopping it this time. No amount of deep breathing would prevent me from puking.

But there was no way I was going to make the scene worse for everybody by making a puddle right next to the dead boy, so I started running, while fighting off abdominal spasms strong enough to make me nearly fall. I headed for a cluster of buildings across the street and ran behind the first one I came to. The bile jolted into my mouth before I got behind the building, and I spat it out as I ran. There were more waves still coming from my stomach.

A dumpster sat behind the building, and I slid open the door and leaned my head inside just as another spasm of bile flew out of my mouth. The smell inside the dumpster made things even worse. It was like someone had dumped a bunch of fish guts on top of month-old used kitty litter, which was mixed with maggot-filled roadkill carcasses. Flies buzzed all around my face, angry that I had disturbed their meal. It didn't matter, though, because there was no stopping now.

After about three minutes of dry-heaving, I pulled my head out of the dumpster and slid the door shut. I was a little dizzy, and my stomach was still queasy, though not as bad as before.

The blood had been bad enough, but seeing the extreme trauma that little boy went through was more than I could handle. This was yet another reason I decided not to have bloody murders. Keeping evidence out of my rental cars was a good enough reason by itself, but I refuse to put myself in a situation where my stomach contents are going to be all over the crime scene.

Who would have thought that a serial killer like me would end up being the world's biggest wuss who can't stand the sight of blood? That's not what I'd call conducive to achieving my goal. I can't even watch TV shows where doctors are performing surgeries. That's why I fish rather than hunt. I wouldn't be able to field dress a deer without blowing chunks everywhere.

Yeah, I'm a real badass killer, all right. Except for the badass part.

I sucked in some oxygen to clear my head, then I composed myself the best I could and walked back to the scene of the wreck. I kept my distance as I walked across the street because I didn't want to see any more blood and guts. But when I reached the hotel parking lot, I saw two EMTs pushing a gurney into an ambulance that was parked along the road. They didn't seem to be in a hurry, like most emergency workers would be if they were transporting to the hospital someone who was barely clinging to life. The gurney's white sheet covered a small lump, with a large, dark red spot that appeared to be the size of a child's head at one end of the lump.

You can't unsee what's already been seen, and apparently my stomach saw it first. A new batch of bile must have formed while I was walking back from the dumpster, because it was about to fly out of my throat again.

I covered my mouth with both hands and ran the remaining thirty yards to my still-open hotel room door. I cracked my shin on the wooden desk chair near the foot of the bed and limped into the bathroom, where I fell down on my knees and began praying to the porcelain god once more.

Yeah, badass at the highest level.

Chapter Five

I was still on my hands and knees, spitting the foul taste out of my mouth into the toilet, when I heard a woman's voice from outside my hotel room door, which was still open.

"Hello, sir! Are you in here?"

I grabbed a towel from the rack and dabbed my mouth, then stuck my head out of the bathroom to see who it was. It was a female police officer, standing in the doorway, a flashlight in one hand and a note pad in the other. She looked to be around thirty, with sandy brown hair and a uniform that didn't quite fit right. The pants were too long and bunched up on top of her shoes, and her shirt was too large. She looked more like a child playing dress-up than an adult dressed for her job.

Dammit. That's two cops in about twenty-four hours wanting to talk to me. It's probably nothing, like yesterday when I was parked in the handicapped spot, but it still made me nervous.

"Yeah, I'm in here. Sorry, but I'm not feeling well," I said as I continued to wipe at my mouth with the towel. "Hey, could you turn the light on, please? The switch is on the wall right there beside you."

She leaned in and flipped the switch, which made me immediately regret asking her to do it. Now she could see me plain as day. Not only did I look like death warmed over, but in a worst-case scenario she could provide a positive identification of me if the FBI managed to track me down.

"Yes sir, that's the guy right there. You know, I had a feeling about him the first time I saw him. He just looked like he was guilty of something."

"I understand you were a witness to the wreck. Mind if I ask you a few questions?" she said.

I sat down on the corner of the bed and motioned for her to have a seat in the chair at the desk. The one that I banged with my shin when I was running for the bathroom.

"No, I'm fine. Thanks," she said.

I shrugged and wiped at my mouth again. There wasn't anything to wipe off, but I still had the feeling that something else wanted to jump out of my stomach, and my only instinct was to wipe it away before it got there.

"The sight of blood kinda makes me sick," I said. "When I saw that boy..." My voice trailed off. I wasn't sure what else to say.

"I totally understand, sir. I can't blame you. Can you answer some questions for me?"

"I'll try."

She put the flashlight into its holder on her belt and flipped open her notepad. She pulled a pen from her shirt pocket and wrote something down.

"Your name, sir?"

Suddenly I panicked inside. See, I have five different driver's licenses, with five different names, from five different states, and I try to use a different one every time I rent a car. That makes it harder to track me. It also makes it harder for me to remember on the spur of the moment which one I've used.

It's amazing how easy it is to get an authentic-looking driver's license from the internet.

My mind raced through the last three or four transactions where I had to use my license. The rental car in St. Louis. The hotel room outside Oklahoma City. And now, this hotel. Which one did I use for this hotel? Was it Kenneth Raymond from Atlanta? Gerry Rogers from Albany, New York? Scott Williams from Naperville, Illinois? Darren McCarty from Missoula, Montana? Or did I use my real name...Jonathan Doe from Jackson, Mississippi?

Yeah, that's right. My real name is Jon Doe. My parents were real freaking comedians. They could have named me Thomas, but they gave my brother that name. They could have called me anything...Joey, Ralph, Kyle.

Hell, they could have named me Martha for all I care. But no, they named me Jon. I got a lot of teasing for that when I was a kid.

I realized that I had used my real ID when I checked in earlier today. The cop was surely going to raise her eyebrows when I told her my name, but I couldn't afford to tell her a lie about this. Knowing my luck, she would find out the truth, and that would open up a whole new can of worms.

"Jon Doe," I told her.

She wrote it down and didn't flinch. "Okay, Mister Doe. Do you remember what time the crash happened?"

Don't you hate it when you get all worked up over a potential problem, worrying about how it's going to turn out for you, and then when your blood pressure is about to pop a cork, it turns out to be nothing at all?

I mean, I was glad she didn't say anything about it, but I was pissed at myself because I worried about it too much. If I was going to make it all the way to fifty-two victims, I had to stop being so nervous. That's not to say that I had to go about things like a bull in a china shop, but a little confidence would surely go a long way.

I cleared my throat before answering her. "I didn't see what time it was. It woke me up, though."

She scribbled away at her notepad. "So, you were asleep?"

No, dummy. I was wide awake. That's what it means when somebody tells you they woke up.

"Yeah," I said. "I've been driving all day and I was tired."

"Did you hear any screeching tires or horns or anything like that?"

"Nope. Just a loud boom."

"How long after you heard the crash did you look outside?"

"I don't know. Maybe thirty seconds or so."

"Did you see anyone leaving the scene of the accident?"

"Well, a few other cars had stopped, and a couple of them drove off after a minute or two."

Her eyes moved from the notepad to me. "No, I mean, did you see anyone leave from the cars involved in the wreck?"

"Uh...no. Were there other people in the cars? I just saw the driver in the first car and the woman and her kid in the other one."

"We're pretty sure there was at least one other person in the first car. There was blood on the passenger seat, and we talked to a witness who said she saw somebody stumble away, but she was so far from the wreck that she couldn't tell if they came from inside the car or they were on the sidewalk when it happened. We searched the area and couldn't find anyone who might have been in the wreck."

"Well, I didn't see anybody else," I said. "It was all I could do to look at the people who were hurt. I didn't even go check on anyone until a minute or two after the crash, because I knew what I was going to see."

I paused for a second, then asked, "Was the driver drunk? I thought I smelled alcohol on him."

She didn't answer, but she gave me a look that told me I was right. "It doesn't matter now. He never made it to the ambulance. Neither did the other driver." She flipped her notepad shut, clicked her pen, and stuffed both of them into her shirt pocket. She reached into her other shirt pocket and pulled out a business card.

"Here's a number where you can reach me in case you happen to remember anything that might help us," she said as she offered the card to me. "Thank you for your help, Mister Doe. I hope you start feeling better."

"Have a good evening, Officer," I said as I took the card. *Officer Juanita Flores,* it said, with a phone number below. She gave me a nod and walked out of the room without closing the door.

I glanced at the clock on the bedside table. Nearly eleven o'clock. The wreck happened more than an hour ago. I had slept for nearly ten hours. But now, I was completely wide awake. My stomach felt better, except for the fact that I hadn't eaten since earlier this morning. The plastic bag with the biscuit and the doughnuts was still sitting on my duffel bag. I picked it up and pulled the biscuit out. It was harder than a hockey puck. I tossed it in the trash can without even attempting a bite. No sense breaking my teeth.

The doughnuts weren't as hard, but they were a long way from fresh. I ate one, anyway. I figured it would tide me over until I could get a regular meal. I washed it down with a glass of tap water from the sink. The rest of the doughnuts went into the trash along with the biscuit. I wadded up the plastic bag, shoved it into my back pocket, then walked back outside.

All the police cars and ambulances were already gone. The upside-down car was now right-side-up and sitting on a flatbed tow truck. The other car was gone, obviously on its way to the junkyard. A cleanup crew was sweeping the street with push brooms, clearing away the broken glass and bits of metal.

I stood on the sidewalk, picturing the crash scene in my head. Let's see...the upside-down car was over there to my left, and the first car was sitting in the middle of the street to my right. If I was a survivor of a wreck, and I wanted to get away as fast as possible, which way would I go? Across the street were the buildings I ran behind to throw up. That was one possibility. To the right past the intersection was a two-lane highway that faded off into the distance. There was nothing in that direction that could provide a hiding place. They didn't run towards the hotel, or I would have seen them, most likely.

The person who ran from the wreck was hurt. Blood on the passenger seat verified that. A hurt person can't make it very far if they're losing blood, so my guess was they made it no more than a mile before they had to stop and rest. But which way did they go?

Instead of overthinking it, I just took off walking in the direction my instinct pointed me. It was extremely dark on the side streets and behind the buildings lining the main street, and I didn't have a flashlight, so my instinct was all I had to rely on.

I crossed the street and down the alley between two buildings, back in the same general direction I had run when I got sick. I passed the same fly-infested dumpster, with the fish guts and roadkill now mixed with my spit and bile. I turned and gauged the distance between the dumpster and the crash site. A hundred yards or so. If the passenger ran this way, where did he go from here? How much farther could he have gone?

Another fifty yards beyond the dumpster was a streetlamp that illuminated a narrow road that disappeared into the darkness. Something told me to go that way. When I reached the circle of light below the lamp, I found a dark smudge on the aluminum post. It was hard to tell what it was with the bluish mercury-vapor light, but I had a pretty good idea. I touched it with a finger, and it was slightly tacky, like paint that hadn't dried all the way.

Blood does the same thing. It'll dry to a brownish color, but thicker globs of it stay damp longer. I rubbed the wetness between my thumb and forefinger. The more I rubbed, the drier it became, until it turned to tiny dark flakes that fell from my fingers to the ground. The smear on the post was at shoulder level, and it looked like a palm print from where someone had steadied themselves against the post while they paused there to catch their breath.

No doubt about it. It was definitely blood. Good thing there wasn't more of it, because that small smear made my stomach knot up a little.

The only place for an injured, scared person to go to avoid detection was down the dark road. The only other choice was back toward the main road where all the cops and EMTs were, or into an open field that provided no cover at all. I followed my instinct again and followed the road into the darkness.

A quarter mile from the streetlamp—which provided the only light this far away from the crash site—the road took a ninety-degree turn to the left. I slowed from a trot to a walk. Halfway through the turn, I heard the grass rustle in the ditch. Not loud, just a slight swish that sounded like it didn't belong there.

By now, my eyes had gotten accustomed to the dark, and I could make out the shape of a person lying on their side in the ditch, rocking slowly back and forth. That had to be the guy who ran, and he was obviously in a lot of pain.

I jumped into the ditch and placed a hand on his shoulder. He let out a soft moan and pulled away from my hand. I tried to calm him with quiet shushing sounds and by resting his head in the palm of my hand. He was breathing fast and shallow, and by feeling along his arms, torso, and legs, I could tell he had several broken bones and bad cuts. He had a caved-in spot on the side of his skull just above his right temple, and blood was trickling out of his ear. His right hand covered a gash on his stomach. That's where the smear on the light post had come from. His white T-shirt was mostly dark from the blood.

All that blood. All those injuries. My stomach twisted again, like it did earlier with the other victims. It's a good thing it was dark. I couldn't have done this in the light. I would have puked until my guts turned inside out.

He was in bad shape. His buddy had already died from his injuries, and now this guy didn't have much time left, either. Such a waste to die at such a young age.

"What's your name, son?" I asked him.

He stopped his rapid breathing long enough to answer. "Josh," he said.

"Don't you worry, Josh. I'm gonna take care of you."

"We...we were drinking. I'm sorry," he said. "I'm really sorry."

"Don't you worry about that now. Everything's going to be okay," I said.

From my back pocket, I pulled out the wadded-up plastic bag that once held the doughnuts and biscuit. This could be considered low-hanging fruit, making a victim out of someone who's already near death, but I considered it doing him a favor. I had a chance to be an angel of death with the driver of the first car, but I chose not to because I wanted him to suffer. Well, maybe *now* was the time to be that angel. This kid had suffered enough.

I pulled the bag over his head and cinched it tight against his neck. He tried to struggle, but with broken bones, torn muscles, and a huge loss of blood, he was no match for me. He bucked, kicked, and clawed at me for nearly a full minute, until I felt his strength leave him like water pouring from a cup. He eventually lost his ability to fight back, and his body relaxed as if he knew it was useless to resist. For the last ten seconds of his life, he was like a balloon that had lost all its air, lying there as limp and lifeless as the mother and son in the other car.

He was number eighteen.

After he had been completely still for half a minute, I pulled the bag off his head and wadded it up before stuffing it back into my pocket.

When the cops finally find him, maybe two days from now, they would assume he died from his injuries, not because of suffocation. They wouldn't need an autopsy.

I left him just as he was, lying on his side, nearly covered by tall grass, and I began walking back to the hotel. In a day or so, the buzzards would gather around his body, and then the cops would find him. I stopped under the lamp post to examine my clothes for blood spots. I couldn't find any. No trace evidence to convict me. As I passed the dumpster where I had puked earlier, I tossed the wadded-up plastic bag inside.

Back in my room, I grabbed my duffel bag and car keys, and climbed into my rental. My room was paid for, and I had already slept all I'd needed today, so I pulled out of town. Twenty miles down the road, at nearly one o'clock in the morning, I found an all-night diner, and for the first time in nearly eighteen hours, I ate.

Chapter Six

Early May in the Great Plains is a beautiful time of year, unless there are tornadoes. So far, my little hobby was going fine, except for a couple of minor blips, and I was enjoying the weather as much as I was enjoying my good luck.

My stop in El Paso had been relaxing. A few days sight-seeing, then my Sunday breakfast and a new rental car, and now I was on my way to Lincoln, Nebraska, passing through the panhandles of Texas and Oklahoma while hoping I wouldn't run into a huge thunderstorm capable of dropping hailstones bigger than a softball. A piece of ice slamming through your windshield could ruin anybody's day, and I certainly didn't want something like that. It's not that I was on a strict time schedule, but dealing with a rental company over a destroyed car could cause major delays. Besides, who needed that kind of drama in their life?

So, I kept my eyes on the skies, and every once in a while I would check the weather app on my phone. If I saw a line of thunderstorms, I'd either go around them somehow or wait until they were out of the way.

Man, the benefits of being retired and not having to worry about a time schedule were great.

I chose Lincoln almost totally at random, like all the other towns I visited. Almost. Except for one bit of that town's history that kinda intrigued me. There was a guy there in 1958 named Charles Starkweather who went on a two-month killing spree and killed eleven people, most of them with a shotgun. It was just a .410, a whole lot smaller than a 12-gauge, but it's enough to blow someone's face off. He dragged his fourteen-year-old girlfriend along with him, and he even killed her parents and two-year-old sister without telling her about it. Some claim the girlfriend might have killed some people, too. They went across Nebraska, all the way to Wyoming, where he killed another person. That's when they got caught.

Now, I'm sure there are people who might claim that I was just like that Starkweather guy, killing people for no reason, just to be mean. But I wasn't like him at all. First of all, he was an absolute amateur when it comes to killing. When you use a gun, there's too much of a mess and it's too loud. There are too many possibilities of getting caught. Plus, he didn't have a plan. He just started killing people and running, making it up as he went.

I wasn't like that. I planned things out. Maybe not all the way to December, but I had a plan a couple of weeks in advance at all times. Second of all, I didn't use a gun and I didn't plan to. Yeah, shooting somebody is quick and easy and probably gives you all kinds of goosebumps and shit, but that's not for me. I didn't see myself as one of those guys who thinks he's all macho badass because he has a pistol strapped to his waist. I could kill people with my bare hands without a sound. To me, that's better than a gun.

Plus, I hate the sight of blood, so there's that.

The other difference between me and Starkweather is that he didn't have a reason to kill all those people. I do. This was going to be a goal that I could finally reach. It's going to be something I can look back on and feel good about. It's definitely something that would capture people's attention. People notice violence faster than they notice anything else. They don't care about people who do good deeds or try to make the world a better place. They gravitate to the things that outrage them the most. Senseless murder tends to get the most outrage.

So, I'm heading to Nebraska to pay homage to Starkweather by committing just one murder, without any blood. He might have killed eleven people in just a few weeks, but I'm going to have way more than that by the time I'm finished.

The distance from El Paso to Lincoln is nearly a thousand miles. Depending on how often I stop, that would equal about sixteen hours of driving. Most of my trips were usually shorter than this, but going from St.

Louis to El Paso was even longer than this leg. I tried to keep the trips to more than three hundred miles and less than a thousand, but it didn't always work out like that.

I'm not sure why these last two trips were so long. Was I using the extra road time to do more thinking? That couldn't be it. They were planned out a couple of weeks ago. Maybe I was subconsciously thinking that I might be going a little crazy at this point and needed the extra solitude. I don't know.

Regardless, it didn't matter. Right now I was cruising along a two-lane highway in Kansas with the windows down and the radio blasting, and everything felt right with the world.

Kansas is flatter than a tabletop. I swear I could see the curve of the earth on the horizon. That's how flat it is. I remember reading once that it's actually not as flat as Florida or Louisiana or about seven other states, but right now, it would be hard to convince me that anywhere else in the world was more level. Maybe it's the miles and miles of farmland that seem to go on forever, without a house or building in sight. I looked right and left, and all I could see all the way to infinity was farmland.

But you know what? I prefer desolate places like this because in today's world, cameras are everywhere. Every store, warehouse, and residence have a security camera. Every phone is a video camera. Even stoplights have cameras on them now. That makes it tough on someone who wants to commit a crime and get away with it. That's why I'd rather not kill or abduct someone on a downtown street, where some blurry security camera belonging to Billy Ray's Bar and Grill and Transmission Repair could catch me in the act. Out here in the wide-open spaces, it was less likely to be seen by a camera or a person.

The bad thing about being out in the country like this is the lack of potential victims. In the city, they're everywhere, but on the back roads of this nation, it's hit and miss whether I might happen to run across a hitch-hiker or someone with car trouble, like girl number seventeen several days ago.

I realize that I won't be able to find all fifty-two victims in the country. I know that I'm going to take chances in a city somewhere because of necessity, or opportunity, or because my schedule for the week is getting closer to Sunday. I took enough of a chance the other night when I tracked down that boy who ran away from the wreck and finished him off just a few blocks off the main road.

I also realize that I won't always be able to choose easy victims, like the elderly, or the weak, or the small of frame. There will come a time when I'll have to deal with some big brute possibly twice my size. When that time comes, the only thing in my favor is the element of surprise. With smaller, weaker, and already-injured people, I could easily overpower them in a matter of seconds. But with somebody the size of Hulk Hogan, I'll only be able to get them by sneaking up from behind and popping them on the skull with a baseball bat.

Out of the fifty-two, there'll be at least one like that. I'll probably do it just to see if I can. You always need to challenge yourself, you know.

I crossed over I-70, heading north. Just after dark, I hit McCook, Nebraska. I decided to stay there for the night.

Following a good night's sleep and a breakfast of only coffee, I drove east toward Lincoln the next morning. The countryside was pretty much the same as Kansas. Still flat with a lot of farmland.

With this much wide-open land, how in the hell did Starkweather manage to get himself caught? What a freakin' loser. Anybody with any brains should have gotten away scott-free, but he was apparently as sharp as a pencil eraser, and he paid for his stupidity. They caught him, tried him for murder, and fried his brains out in the electric chair in 1959.

Three and a half hours after leaving McCook, I pulled into the outskirts of Lincoln. As I got closer to town, I could see a big stadium ahead. I decided to pull over there and stretch my legs for a bit.

I eased into the nearly-empty parking lot of the stadium and got out of my car, stretching my arms over my head as far as I could reach. The weather was perfect. A few puffy clouds in the sky, temperature in the high seventies, a gentle breeze blowing from the west.

I turned a full circle, getting a feel of the city, surprised that it was as big as it was. I never knew it was a town this size. I always knew the University of Nebraska was here, and I was standing on campus at this moment. They were the Cornhuskers, the guys who wore white football helmets with the red "N."

Somebody once told me the "N" stood for "knowledge," but I'm pretty sure they were wrong about that.

At this time of year, students were probably getting ready for finals. I didn't see very many of them milling around. I bet if I found my way to the library, they'd be everywhere, but there would also be cameras everywhere.

Besides, I wasn't in the mood for some co-ed. I wanted someone a little easier. Someone slower and older. In a town this size, I'm sure that person would be easy to find, and I had five days to find them.

While I was standing beside my car looking at the campus, I heard a train horn not a block away. I turned and saw a half-mile of boxcars crawling southwest past the stadium. Curiosity got the better of me, and I walked to the four-lane road running between the stadium and the tracks, trotted across while dodging traffic, and stood at the chain-link fence just off the shoulder of the road. I watched the last few cars crawl past, going no faster than fifteen miles per hour. It rolled along on one of four sets of tracks.

That many tracks combined with the extra-slow pace of the train could mean only one thing. There was a rail yard somewhere near where I stood.

And a rail yard meant vagrants. Tramps. Hobos. But I would never stoop to calling someone like that such a derogatory name. I called them potential victim number nineteen, instead.

I ran back across the highway, jumped in my car, and set off in search of a greasy spoon diner for lunch, and then a hotel. Then I would take a nap and wait for nightfall.

Chapter Seven

I waited until after eight o'clock to find my way to the rail yard. That way, the guys milling around would be getting somewhat settled for the night, and the workers, if there were any at all, would be inside the buildings watching TV or playing solitaire on their computers.

After I found a parking lot a few blocks away, I headed for the dozens of idle boxcars a few hundred yards away from the switch house. That's where the vagrants would be gathered. They would stay close to the shelter of the cars while staying as far away as possible from the eyes of the rail yard workers.

I came to a fence dividing the tracks from the rest of the world. It took about five minutes of searching, but I found a hole large enough to squeeze through. These hobos were resourceful, if nothing else. They would always find a way to get to their means of transportation.

I eased through the fence and assessed the situation. It was quiet as a graveyard. No trains were moving, no security guards wandering around with a flashlight, no nothing.

The rail yard must have had thirty sets of tracks, some with boxcars, some completely empty. I didn't know which way to go to find the hobos, so I just stood there beside the fence for a minute, thinking. What if nobody was around? Would I break into the switch house and kill one of the workers there? No, that would probably end up getting messy. If some strange guy came strolling into their office unannounced, they'd immediately be suspicious. They'd probably think I was there to rob them. Plus, if there happened to be more than one of them, they would gang up and beat the hell out of me, and I really wasn't in the mood to put up with cuts, bruises, and a possible concussion.

So I decided the rail yard workers had just earned themselves a free pass.

If there were no vagrants around, I still had several days left until Sunday. Plenty of time to find a victim.

I scanned the rail yard again, trying to see through the darkness. I could probably look in all the boxcars, in case someone was asleep inside, but that would take all freakin' night to look in every one of them. There must have been nearly a hundred cars on the tracks, or maybe there were a million. I don't really know. I'm not good at math.

My best plan of action was to walk to one end of the yard, then cross the tracks one by one while I looked between the lines of boxcars. Maybe some people were huddled around a small campfire in those narrow spaces. It would be a great place to hide from the rail yard security, and if they kept their fire small enough, they might never be seen.

I was about to move to the far end of the rail yard when I thought I heard laughter, like the aftermath of someone telling a joke. I stopped and stood completely still, listening for the sound to come back.

You ever notice that when you're concentrating on hearing a faint sound, every other sound in the world comes blaring through? I listened for laughter, but all I could hear was crickets, highway noise, a plane flying overheard, and an ambulance siren from somewhere downtown.

I stayed still for nearly three minutes, which is a really long time if you think about it. The laughter didn't happen again.

Did I imagine it? If I hadn't imagined it, did it come from the rail yard? Could it have come from several blocks away? Sound travels in strange patterns in a city, with it bouncing off buildings and echoing in all directions. Maybe it came from the switch house. I couldn't see the whole building from where I stood, just the roof barely visible over the top of the boxcars. Were the switch house workers standing outside taking a smoke break?

Being a serial killer is a tricky business. You have to be daring, but at the same time you can't take unnecessary chances. That's how you get caught. It's sort of an oxymoron. *Daringly cautious.* It's kinda like *almost exactly,* or *freezer burn,* or *same difference.* Or, in my case, *serial killer who's not a monster...not really.*

I gave up on hearing the laughter again and took a few steps toward the end of the rail yard when I heard it again. Laughing. Gut-busting laughing. Like three people had just heard the funniest thing in the world and couldn't control themselves. It went on for a good six or seven seconds, then it stopped. But that was long enough for me to get a bearing on where it came from. I looked in that direction, at the middle of the millions of boxcars, and I could make out a thin wisp of smoke rising from between them.

There were people down there. One of them was going to be my next victim. Number nineteen.

It took me less than five minutes to get near their location. I stood back about four boxcars from them, watching from the shadows. There were three men sitting on stacked railroad ties. They all looked to be about my age, but they had stubbly beards and ragged clothes. They were sitting around a car wheel that lay flat on the ground without its tire. There was a small fire burning inside it, and they had a makeshift spit over the fire with a small pot attached to it. Probably some kind of soup warming over the fire.

There was no time like the present, so I summoned up more bravery and strolled straight toward them. They heard me coming well before I got there because of my shoes crunching on the gravel, and they turned to look at me as I approached.

"Got room for one more?' I asked.

They looked at each other, as if getting permission to speak. Finally, the one closest to me said, "Help yourself." He didn't sound very enthusiastic.

I found an empty space on the wooden ties and plopped down.

"What's in the pot?" I asked.

They looked at each other again, then back at me. They didn't answer.

I held my hands up, palms out. "Whoa, whoa, whoa. I don't want any food, guys. I'm not hungry. I'm just looking to warm up by the fire for a bit."

The one who spoke earlier looked at me with a sideways glance. "It's May. It ain't really that cold."

"Yeah, I know. I'm just cold-natured," I said. "So, uh...where you boys headed?"

They didn't answer. Hobos seemed to be a strange bunch. They weren't friendly at all. Maybe that's why they ended up as hobos.

One of the men reached for the pot and pulled it away from the fire. He took a bent, rusty fork out of his pants pocket and stirred whatever was inside it, then shoveled a heaping pile of it into his mouth. I don't know what it was, but it looked like some kind of rice with chunks of meat or something in it.

He handed the pot and fork to the next man, who got a mouthful and then handed it to the third man. When he got his share, he handed it back to the first man. They kept going around and around until the food was gone. They never offered me any, and for some reason, this made me a little ticked off. Isn't it a common courtesy to offer a stranger food, even though he said he didn't want any?

That's what's wrong with our society today. Everybody thinking of themselves, not caring about their fellow man. Why can't people be nicer to each other? I nearly decided to kill all three of them over this, but my calmer side prevailed, and I elected to take out just one of them. Besides, killing three of them would throw my schedule way off, and I might never recover. This was not a time to be irrational. I had to stay focused.

When the food was gone, the first man scraped the pot with his fork, then put the fork back into his pants pocket. He pulled a small, worn-out backpack from behind the stacked ties and shoved the pot inside.

I guess hobos don't carry a knapsack tied to the end of a stick anymore. They use backpacks. You gotta love progress.

He stood up, slung the backpack over one shoulder, and trudged off without saying a word. The sound of gravel crunching got fainter as he walked away.

The other two stood up and stretched, then turned to walk off in the opposite direction.

"Hey, where you going?" I asked.

One of the men kept going without answering, but the other stopped, breathed a huge sigh, and turned to me. "What do you care, buddy?" he said.

"I don't, I guess. I was just trying to be friendly, that's all. I figure people like us need all the friends we can get."

He looked at me for a second, then turned toward his friend who was still walking away. "What do you mean by *people like us*? Hell, you ain't nothin' like us. We could tell that as soon as we saw you. You've got new shoes, clean clothes, and you shaved today. You probably ate two or three times today. Now, how exactly does that make you like us?"

I didn't say anything.

"Unless your ol' lady kicked you out of the house a few hours ago, you don't have to worry about a place to sleep tonight. We'll be lucky to get two hours in before one of those bulls comes and kicks us out. So, you can stop pretending to be one of us."

I shook my head and stood up.

"Yeah, you're right. I should have known better. I was going to offer you three a hot meal, but it looks like you don't need one. Or want one. Sorry about that. Have a good night. Best of luck to you."

He looked at me for another few seconds, then looked toward his disappearing friend. He seemed to want to say something else to me, but before the words escaped his mouth, he stopped. He then nodded at me and walked away, following his friend.

This was a first for me. A potential victim—heck, three potential victims—had gotten away. I was left back at the drawing board, still searching for victim number nineteen. I gave a sigh of resignation, then turned to walk back to my car.

That's when I saw the beam of a flashlight waving between the cars a hundred yards away. One of the security guards was making his rounds. The three hobos probably knew his schedule and had disappeared before he showed up.

I was about to jump over the couplings between the cars and take a shortcut back to my car when I saw a second light beam darting across the tracks in the other direction from the first security guard. There were two of them. With a rail yard this size, that wasn't surprising.

The two light beams were coming toward each other, and I was stuck in the middle between them.

The first security guard was now closer to me, maybe only eighty yards away. The second was much farther than that. If I stayed where I was, I would be caught. But, if I ran, they would hear my feet making noise on the gravel. I looked for a place to hide, and the only place I could find was inside one of the boxcars.

I jumped through the open door of the nearest car two seconds before the beam of light from the guard's flashlight swept across the very spot where I had been standing. I stumbled over a crisscrossed stack of planks piled on the floor. One nearly slid off the top of the pile, but I grabbed it before it could make more noise. Thirty seconds later, he arrived at the fading fire in the car wheel. I watched from beside the open door of the boxcar, leaning on the plank for stability.

He held his hand out to the fire, testing the amount of heat radiating from it. He then pointed his light around the area, between and beneath the cars, looking for the culprits.

I was no more than twenty feet away. If he found me, how was I going to explain myself? Would he believe me if I told him I was offering a meal to three vagrants, but they turned me down? My heart was racing, and I couldn't figure out if I was scared or excited. That's when I developed a new strategy.

He spoke into a radio microphone attached to his shoulder. "Hey, Adam, I got a campfire down here."

I assumed Adam was the other security guard at the opposite end of the yard. A muffled voice screeched out of the radio, but I couldn't understand what was said. Then the security guard at the fire waved his flashlight in the air, sending the light beam up to the sky like a searchlight. "You see me?" he said into the radio.

Adam's muffled voice answered, and it sounded like "Yeah, I see you now."

I had to make a decision. I could either stay hidden and risk being caught by these two guys, or I could run out of the other side of the boxcar and risk being heard, and then being caught, or I could create a diversion so I could escape.

The plank I had in my hands was old, dried-out wood, like barn wood. It was about four feet long, four inches wide and maybe an inch and a half thick. It would do the job.

I banged the board against the metal side of the boxcar, creating a loud *boom*. The flashlight beam filled the door of the boxcar, and I heard the guard say, "All right, I know you're there. Come on out."

I stayed still, waiting for him to get closer. I heard the gravel beneath his feet as he got closer, his flashlight beam getting more concentrated in the open doorway. When it seemed he was nearly at the door, I leaped out with the plank over my head like a lumberjack about to split firewood. Somehow, I managed to gauge my distance perfectly, because I landed five feet from him, and I swung the plank down on his skull just as my feet hit the ground. Not the wide part of the plank, but the narrow edge. I had to make sure it would do enough damage with one blow.

He wasn't wearing a hat, which was good. The plank split his scalp and he fell in a heap. He twitched a few times, and then he was still. I turned to find the other guard, and I could see his flashlight beam still a hundred yards away. The dead man's flashlight had switched off when he dropped it, luckily for me. A bright light sitting on the ground would have made it easier to find him.

I did my best to avoid looking at the blood pooling around his head as I reached to feel the pulse in his neck, and there wasn't one.

Victim number nineteen.

There wasn't enough time to dispose of his body, not with the other guard coming, so I tossed the plank back into the boxcar and crossed the coupling into the next space between the tracks. After being as quiet as I could be for several sets of tracks, I took off running.

I never heard the other guard arrive at the body. I was too busy getting out of there. Within ten minutes, I was in my rental car, driving back to the hotel.

On the way back, I felt my stomach growl. I needed to get something to eat. Those hobos had made me hungry, the bastards. But my adrenaline was pumping so hard, there was no way food was gonna stay down.

Chapter Eight

It took twenty minutes from the time the security guard fell until I walked into my hotel room. I almost didn't make it back, either. I was so fired up I nearly ran off the road a couple of times, and I'm sure I ran a few red lights. I couldn't help it. Something about killing that guard gave me renewed energy. Maybe it was because I made the decision to kill him thirty seconds before I did it, or maybe it was because I used a method I had never used before. I don't know.

If anyone had seen me driving back to the hotel, they would have seen a crazy person behind the wheel, whooping and shouting, pumping his fist, dancing to nonexistent music, and grinning like a maniac.

Things didn't slow down when I burst into my hotel room, either. I ripped off my jacket and threw it on the floor between the bed and the wall, then I sat on the bed to take off my shoes, but I was too hyper to sit still, so I jumped back up and shadowboxed. I threw punches at an imaginary opponent, hitting him with jabs, uppercuts, elbows, all kinds of moves I had learned from my training. I felt like Rocky Balboa after he had run up the steps, triumphant and ready to take on the whole world. Every once in a while, I would pause my punches long enough to raise my fists in victory, just like Rocky.

This was such an incredible feeling, like it was a drug and I was high on it. I danced and bobbed around the room for at least five minutes without slowing down, reliving the leap from the boxcar, the plank sinking into the guard's head, watching his lifeless body twitch on the ground.

When I worked in the factory, I used to love the feeling of getting a paycheck with lots of overtime on it. The extra work was always tough, but the reward was well worth it. There were times I worked Saturdays and Sundays and got a check that was twice the size of my regular take-home pay. Those usually made me feel like I could do no wrong, and that's how I felt now.

I felt strong. I felt vindicated by my choices in life. I felt...invincible.

But all good things must come to an end. All drugs eventually wear off. What goes up must come down.

It didn't happen all at once. It might have taken a couple of minutes or so, but my punches started losing their speed and snap. My bouncing and bobbing gave way to simply standing in place. My kicks stopped entirely.

I eventually dropped my hands and let them hang at the ends of my arms, my clenched fists loosened. I wiped the beads of sweat from my forehead with my shoulders because my arms were too tired. As I caught my breath, I looked around the room. It was a typical hotel room, with a bathroom at the opposite end from the door, a low-profile heater-slash-air conditioner below the window, a countertop against the wall that served both as a desk and a place to pile your belongings, and a bed with an ugly floral print bedspread. The place was only slightly better than a prison cell.

I was the only living, breathing thing in the room. I was the only person experiencing this moment. Nobody else shared my happiness right then. The reality of that fell on me like a ton of bricks. There was no one in the world who cared about me or who I cared about. This hadn't been a problem for five whole months, but now for some reason there were things about my present situation that I didn't like much.

I was lonely. It wasn't easy to admit to myself, but it was the truth.

But how could I go from being on top of the world one moment to feeling lonely the next? Is this how the brain of an insane person worked? Did their mind move so fast that the thoughts piled on top of each other, each thought burying the previous one before itself being buried? I know mad scientists were like that, but what about serial killers?

Maybe I was experiencing the crash after an adrenaline dump. Or maybe I was just hungry and my blood sugar was playing tricks on me. Or maybe a thousand other potential explanations.

Or maybe I was really lonely. Maybe I had reached that point in my life when being by myself had reached its full limit. But what could I possibly do about it now? I wasn't about to drive down to the local girlfriend store and find someone, and I was way too old to start hitting the local bars.

There was no way I would ever try to get my wife back, either. Not after what she did. I seriously doubted if Ethan...

Ethan. My son. What about him? What if he came back into my life?

I pulled my wallet from my back pocket and flipped it open. I dug through the whole thing, but I didn't find a picture, phone number, or address for him. It was almost like I had voluntarily wiped him from my world. And in a way, I guess I had.

He was a good kid when he was younger. He was happy and carefree, and we had a good time together. I used to take him fishing with me, and we would go hiking and camping, like dads and their sons are supposed to, but something happened when he turned thirteen. He started growing like a weed, and he went from being a normal-sized kid for his age to nearly six inches taller than the next tallest boy in his class. The pimple fairy showed up right around that same time, too. The bullies and their taunting started almost immediately.

I remember him coming home from school one day and going directly to his room. I knocked on his door a few minutes later, and he told me to leave him alone. From the sound of his voice, he sounded like he was crying. I wasn't exactly sure why at that time, but I had a pretty good idea. I ended up doing what I shouldn't have done. I left him alone.

From that day on, he transformed from a child who loved his parents and wanted to be around them all the time into a teenager who got smacked in the face with the reality of what the world was actually like. He totally withdrew from both of us, but especially me. I wasn't home as much as my wife, and he noticed that. When I was at home, he wouldn't talk to me, no matter how much I tried. He wore black clothes, let his hair grow long, and by his fifteenth birthday, had at least ten tattoos. His group of friends shrank to three or four others who looked just like him.

When he was away from home, I would go into his room and look around. His walls were covered in drawings he made, all of them depicting images of death, torture, and evil. He had a well-used bong sitting on his dresser. There were magazines on the floor with topics ranging from tattoos to freelance art to heavy metal music.

By the time he was a senior in high school, we were total strangers living in the same house. He didn't go to his graduation, and he let us know in no uncertain terms he wasn't going to college. By then, both his mom and I were beyond caring any longer. We had tried everything we could think of to reach him, but nothing worked.

One month after his last high school exam, he moved out of the house. He didn't say goodbye to his mom and me. He just left.

I came home and found his bedroom door open, which was out of the ordinary. I called his name and didn't get an answer, which was *not* out of the ordinary. I pushed the door open further and found his drawings had been removed from the wall, his bong was missing, and his closet was empty. He left while we were at work, without letting us know. Why would he say goodbye to someone he considered strangers?

It took us nearly a week to find out where he had gone. The parents of one of his friends called and told us their son and ours were in Pueblo, Colorado on their way to the West Coast. They had hitchhiked the whole way there and were doing odd jobs to get spending money. He didn't have a cell phone, so we had no way to contact him unless he called us.

We tried for years to find him, but it was like he was a ghost. He couldn't be found. No matter what we tried, the trail always came up empty. After a while, we simply gave up. We figured there was no reason to find him if he didn't want us to.

I never heard from him again until right around the time my wife and I divorced. He called me out of the blue one day, about a week before the papers were signed.

I didn't recognize the number, but I answered it anyway.

"So, you're finally getting rid of each other," the voice on the other end said.

It took me a moment before I recognized his voice. I had heard it so infrequently the past few years it sounded like someone I didn't know. I guess it *was* someone I didn't know, come to think of it.

"Ethan? Uh, yes, I guess you could say that," I answered. "How did you find out?"

"Word gets around, even this far away."

"Where are you, son? Are you doing okay?"

"I'm doing better than ever."

"But where are you?"

He paused before speaking, as if he was deciding whether or not to tell me.

"Oregon," he said.

"Where in Oregon?" I asked.

"Doesn't matter."

"Are you working?"

"About to be. Me and a couple of friends are starting a tattoo shop."

I was speechless. How was he able to start a business without any money? I was running that thought through my brain when he spoke again.

"Are you happy now that you're single?"

It took me a minute to answer, because I wasn't sure where he was headed with this.

"No. Not really."

"Good," he said, and then he hung up.

That was the last time I spoke with him, more than five years ago. He would have been about twenty-five then, which would make him right around thirty now.

The sweat was dried up on me, and my pulse had slowed to normal. My thinking slowed down, too. Sometimes, even insane people are able to think clearly, and my mind was as clear as it had ever been.

I dug through my duffel bag and found the road atlas. I counted the miles between Lincoln, Nebraska and the west coast of Oregon. It was more than seventeen hundred miles away. That was a lot of driving, especially with the Rocky Mountains between here and there. My son might not be on the west coast. He might be living in the eastern part of the state. Or he might be entirely somewhere else. It didn't matter to me. Oregon was a starting point. If I had to go somewhere else from there, then so be it. I had all the time in the world and plenty of money.

What I didn't have was someone in my life, and I was going to do everything in my power to change that. Starting tomorrow, I had a mission to go along with my hobby. Maybe I was insane to even try, but I was going to find my son and reconnect with him even if it killed me.

Chapter Nine

It's amazing. Sometimes a good night's sleep is the perfect remedy for a brain that's running at warp speed. It slows you down, throttles back the rapid-fire thoughts, and makes you actually process things before acting on them.

A bad night's sleep won't do that. You wake up tired with your brain in the same place it was when you fell asleep. The thoughts aren't any slower or fewer, and you feel like you have to rush to get things done, because doing them right now is what's important. Not doing things correctly.

I was lucky to have a good night's sleep, and I woke feeling calm, refreshed. I took a slow, hot shower, shaved, got dressed, and walked across the street to a Waffle House for breakfast. It wasn't Sunday, but I got pancakes anyway. Plus, my regular cup of coffee.

It was almost like I didn't know what to do with myself, sitting here with no calendar to mark. I wasn't used to having this kind of breakfast when it wasn't Sunday. Usually, I was still on the go during the week, figuring out how I was going to find my next victim, planning out my next destination. And I would have been like that today, but because I slept so well, I didn't feel a sense of urgency. So, I spent my time between bites deciding what to do about seeing my son again.

Oregon was a long way from Lincoln, Nebraska. Half the way across North America, as a matter of fact. I had just finished three very long trips, and I really didn't feel like making a fourth, especially when that involved driving through the Rocky Mountains. If I was going to travel through an area that magnificent, I was definitely going to take my sweet time.

Should I make a direct route with stops a hundred miles apart? Fifty miles apart? That would slow me down the way I wanted.

No, that wasn't feasible. There weren't likely to be car rental places that close together in the great wide-open west. And if I was going directly there, even if I made frequent stops, it wouldn't feel like I was taking my time.

Maybe if I went north and south, moving west a little at a time.

As I chewed on my last mouthful of pancakes, I decided to take a zig-zag route to Oregon, something that would put me there in about a month. It had already been years since I had spoken to Ethan, so what was another month going to hurt? I could spend the extra time gathering my thoughts and planning out what I was going to say to him when we finally met.

I would also have an additional three or four victims added to my list. If I was going to do this, and everything fell through with him, at least it wouldn't be a wasted trip.

I could do it in four or five stops, but I needed to look at my road atlas before deciding which way to go first.

My "waitress" was a young guy named Chad who was probably a college student working to make ends meet while he chased the American dream. He also looked like he wanted to be somewhere else but pouring coffee in a Waffle House at eight in the morning.

He walked over to refill my coffee cup, but I put my hand over it.

"I'm good," I said.

Chad shrugged and walked to the next booth without saying a word. The only thing he had said to me since I walked in was "Whatcha want?" He never looked me in the eye, and he never smiled. He definitely wasn't a good example of the typical Midwestern waitress who had never met a stranger. Maybe everybody was a stranger to him. Maybe he was just mad at the world.

I probably shouldn't call him a waitress, either, but people like him tend to bring out the worst in me.

If I hadn't already claimed my last victim, Chad would have been number nineteen. He needed somebody to put him out of his misery, but I had places to go and things to do. Where in the hell was Charles Stark-weather when you needed him? He could have done the job for free.

Bismarck, North Dakota is about a ten-hour drive from Lincoln, which is perfect for me. I could break it up into two days and take my time getting there. I wouldn't even have to kill somebody between here and there, since that security guard in the rail yard offered himself as a sacrifice. I would see the sights along the way and stop every now and then to simply smell the air.

My decision to find Ethan gave me new life. It became my purpose. Killing fifty-two people in a year was still my goal, but my son was my purpose. Goals and purposes are two different things. A goal is something you work toward. An end to the means. A purpose is what keeps you moving forward towards that goal. Even though my goal and my purpose had nothing to do with each other, seeing my son again would get me out of bed every morning, and staying on track to meet my goal would let me sleep at night.

Before I left Lincoln, I got a new rental car. A Chevy Impala with plenty of leg room and a big trunk in case I needed it. I probably wouldn't because of all the unpopulated areas in this part of the country. I could dump a body in a deep ditch or body of water in broad daylight without anyone seeing me. That was a good thing and bad thing. Good because small populations meant I stood a better chance of getting away. Bad because it meant the pool of potential victims was much smaller. In these areas, once I saw an opportunity to kill someone, I had better act on it instead of waiting for someone else. There might not be someone else, and that would throw my schedule off.

A two-day drive would put me in Bismarck, and once there I would get a new car and a hotel room. I planned on relaxing, seeing a movie, eating a nice big dinner, and sleeping like a log. When I woke up, I would have my typical Sunday breakfast, complete with plenty of coffee, pancakes, and my calendar. When I put victim number nineteen officially in the books, I would be leaving town.

I love it when a plan comes together.

Chapter Ten

I'VE ALWAYS WANTED TO SEE A BUFFALO, WHICH IS ANOTHER good reason to make a jaunt through the Dakotas. There's something about that animal that makes me feel connected to it. Generally, they seem fairly docile and want to do nothing but graze, chew their cud, and lay around all day. But they can turn nasty in a heartbeat. All you have to do is antagonize them, or just look at them the wrong way, and the next thing you know you've got a fifteen-hundred-pound missile of horns, hair, and muscle hurtling toward you at thirty miles an hour.

I'm a little bit like that, I think. I'm generally a nice guy, but whenever something or someone pisses me off, I can fly into a rage. A good example is my new hobby. I had one failure after another until I reached my nasty point, and now look at me. I'm spending almost all my time perfecting the art of killing without being caught. I'm not exactly doing it in a wild frenzy of anger, but the end result of fifty-two dead bodies could be considered rage.

Of course, a buffalo never had to worry about a wife and son leaving him without notice, so my life was probably a little more stressful than his. But then again, I never had to worry about some game hunter trying to shoot me so he could mount my head on a wall like a trophy.

Fine. We'll call it even.

Everybody knows there are lots of buffalo in the national parks of the plains states, especially in South Dakota, so I made the decision to drive through one or two of the parks on my way south from Bismarck. My first stop out of Lincoln was to spend the night in some little town along Interstate 90. The lady at the hotel's front desk told me I could take the interstate west to Badlands National Park or further on to Black Hills National Forest, and she guaranteed I would find buffalo along the way. But I wasn't going to deviate from my plan, so I saved the buffalo hunt for after my stop in Bismarck. Life has taught me that if you get distracted by shiny objects when you should be focused on a goal, the shiny objects eventually become the goal.

Not that I considered a buffalo a shiny object. It's just that I wanted to see one before I die, and I didn't know when that might be. I'd like to think I was going to live another forty or fifty years, but that's not very realistic. It's not *impossible.* It's just not likely. If I finished my hobby without getting killed, and I didn't get sick, or I didn't get gored to death by a buffalo, then I might live another thirty years.

But let's be real here. The odds of me making it all the way to victim number fifty-two were fairly steep. There was a good chance I'd choose a victim who was ready for an attack and would shoot me, stab me, or break my neck while I was trying to break theirs. You just never know. I mean, I prepared myself the best I could by working out, getting stronger, and learning some lethal moves, but no matter what I did, I couldn't keep the sands of time from falling into the bottom basin of that hourglass.

So before something happens to me, I want to see a buffalo, dammit. When I was growing up in the hills of Tennessee, the only place I could see one was on television. I was always infatuated with their majestic look, with their huge shoulders and thick mane, their sheer bulk, and their oversized head with horns that were just the right size to do the job without appearing overly dramatic.

To me, they looked powerful, confident.

Manly.

The hotel had a small room with computers for guests to use, and I decided to use one to look up information on areas where I could find buffalo. It was while I was typing "buffalo" into the search box that I was smacked in the face with a question.

Why wasn't I using my time to find my son?

I sat there and stared at the screen for a few moments. Well, why wasn't

I? Was I putting it off until I got closer to Oregon? Why would I want to do that? Wouldn't it be better to find out where he lives, then spend the rest of my time figuring out what I'm going to say to him?

There's one problem with searching for him on hotel computers, though. I would leave a trail if the FBI ever managed to connect me to my victims. When you do a public search on a public computer, everything you see, every link you click, becomes available.

So far, I had been using my cell phone to map out my routes and find rental cars, but it's not easy for a middle-aged man with middle-aged eyesight to navigate cyberspace on a small phone screen. I needed something that would solve both my eyesight problem and the confidentiality issue.

I typed "computer stores in Bismarck, North Dakota" into the search box.

Two days later, after eating my traditional Sunday breakfast and marking my calendar with victim number nineteen, I drove to a computer store to find myself a laptop. I needed something small enough to pack into my duffel bag and powerful enough to race across the internet at the speed of light. After browsing the different models without knowing what the hell I was looking at, I was approached by a girl wearing a blue polo shirt with the store's logo on the left side. She introduced herself as Melissa, and appeared to be college-aged, maybe twenty years old. She was most likely another college student working a dead-end job to pay her way through school. At least she had a better personality than Chad, my "waitress" in Lincoln. I told her what I was looking for, and she showed me three different models. I chose the one with the median price.

I could have chosen the expensive one, but it had more bells and whistles than I needed, and the cheaper of the three was a brand I had never heard of. Probably made on some island off the coast of Thailand or somewhere like that. I didn't trust it.

Besides, I've always heard you get what you pay for, which means if you pay a fairly high price, the merchandise is usually pretty good. But on the other hand, I've also heard that you pay for what you get, which means that the cheaper things might cnd up costing you more money in the long run.

It was going to take about an hour to get the laptop set up with all the programs I wanted, so instead of hanging around the store, I took a walk around Bismarck.

I wound up at the Missouri river, at a spot called Keelboat Park. The sun was warm, but a cool breeze out of the north made the air a little chilly. There were several people in the park, milling around with their families, looking at scale models of boats. The Missouri was tinged brown from spring rains, and it flowed like a slow stream of molasses past the park and under an old railroad bridge until it disappeared out of sight. The bridge was an old, traditional style, with skeletal beams and trusses forming three humps above the tracks, making it look like three turtles crossing the river nose-to-tail.

Even though this region experienced some of the most brutal weather anywhere—crippling blizzards in the winter and searing heat in the summer—it didn't take away from the fact that this was absolutely beautiful country. The wide-open grasslands along with the rock formations made me think I might want to live around here when I finally finish my project.

That is, if I finish it and live.

I strolled around the riverside for a half hour, watching people and playing mental games with myself, guessing which ones would be viable victims and which ones would beat the shit out of me.

A young mother holding hands with her toddler daughter while looking at the river would be an easy victim, but I would have a hard time killing her if I knew of her family situation. This pissed-off heart of mine still has some soft spots on it.

There was a man milling around the park's artwork, hands in his jacket pockets, glasses, somewhat pudgy-looking, with thinning hair. He looked to be around thirty-five or so. He was exactly the kind of person I would look for if I didn't want a challenge.

At the far end of the park was a tall, hulking man with long hair pulled back into a ponytail, a trimmed beard flecked with gray, a black T-shirt beneath a black leather vest with a large patch on the back. Apparently, the chilly wind didn't bother him at all. His arms were as thick as railroad ties. One of his legs was as large as both of mine. He was probably six-four or taller. He had his arm draped across the shoulders of a woman with bleached blonde hair. She looked like she spent most of her time in bars. As we used to say when I was a kid, she looked like she had been "rode hard and put up wet."

Yeah, he would probably beat the shit out of me. Or maybe I should leave "probably" out of that sentence. But one of these days, I was going to make somebody like him one of my victims. I may pay for it with a broken jaw and several stitches, but it's a challenge I couldn't resist. I had to be able to prove to myself that I could kill anybody if I wanted to be considered the world's most famous serial killer.

The biker guy must have seen me looking at him out of the corner of his eye, because he turned his head toward me and stared. I looked away as if I didn't see him, but I could feel him looking at me. It was a challenging stare, primal, daring me to look at him. I had driven all these miles, hoping to see a buffalo, a creature that could mangle you to death for no reason at all, but instead I was probably going to get killed by a two-legged buffalo in a park beside the Missouri River while my brand-new laptop computer sat waiting for me in a store a mile away.

Oh wow. My laptop. I nearly forgot about it. I looked at the time on my cell phone and saw I was due to pick it up in ten minutes. Or at least, that was a good excuse to get out of there. I turned and hurried my way out of Keelboat Park.

I could feel that biker's eyes burning a hole in my back the whole time. I figured if I didn't turn around, maybe he would forget about me and go back to grazing and chewing his cud.

Chapter Eleven

Thank goodness for barbed wire fences.

The next day, after nearly six hours of driving south, I made it to the outskirts of Badlands National Park, and I stopped when I saw large brown spots dotting the landscape beyond a fence. I was driving on a narrow two-lane, and I pulled over to the shoulder so I could get out of the car for a better look.

The buffalo were scattered across a pasture that sloped up from the road to the peak of a small hill. They were grazing, switching their tails back and forth to swat flies. A couple of them looked up at me as I got out of the car, but they didn't seem bothered. They watched me for several seconds as I walked to the fence and leaned against a post, then they went back to eating grass.

Magnificent animals. There's no other way to describe them. They looked more awesome in real life than they had in pictures and videos. The huge head. The thick mane. The muscles rippling beneath their skin.

And then there was their bellow. The nearest one to me let out a sound that was closer to a growl than anything else. Almost like what you would expect from some prehistoric dinosaur. It was a low, rattling noise that came from deep within their chest cavity, and it was intimidating. I had never wanted to get too close to one of these things, and now I *really* didn't want to.

I figured out the one bellowing was a female, because it looked like she had six or eight legs. I know that sounds strange, but that's the way it really looked. She was standing broadside to me, and she had more legs than she should have had.

After a few moments I figured out she had a newborn calf, and it was standing on the other side of her. She was using her body to shield me from her baby. Whenever she took a few steps, so did her calf, shadowing her in perfect unison.

I don't know whether it was instinct or just a mother buffalo being a mother, but she didn't want me to see her calf. Maybe she knew I was a serial killer.

It was probably neither, because she went back to grazing after less than a minute, acting like I wasn't even there.

On the road behind me, a car passed, going no faster than walking speed. I turned and saw an elderly couple in their 1980-something Buick, slowing down to get a look at the buffalo. An old couple in an old-couple car. The husband was driving while the wife held a cell phone out the passenger window, taking a picture.

I didn't consider killing one of them, even though it would have been easy to do. But since there were two of them and I needed only one body, I left them alone. Besides, it would have been hard to kill one of them and keep the other from calling the cops on me, so I didn't bother. I was more concerned about seeing my first real, live buffalo. Plus, I had nearly a full week to get my next victim. I had plenty of time.

A low, distant growl made me turn back around to the buffalo herd. A hundred yards away, one of them was walking straight towards me. It didn't have a calf tagging along, and it was absolutely huge. The hump above its shoulders must have been six feet high. No doubt about it, this was a male. The alpha male.

And he was coming to check me out. He had to make sure I didn't pose a threat to his cows and calves, no matter what side of the fence I was on.

Every few steps he let out another growl. He didn't sound mad or aggressive, but there was no doubt he meant business. My gut became a nervous knot as he got closer, but I didn't move away from the fence. I was going to hold my ground to show I wasn't afraid of him, even if I was actually terrified.

It took a few minutes for the lumbering bull to reach me. He stopped ten feet from the fence, sniffing at the air and blowing huge wads of buffalo snot onto the ground. He pawed at the dirt and growled again. I couldn't tell if he was challenging me, or if this was normal behavior for a male buffalo.

On the road behind me, another car passed, but I didn't turn around. I kept my eyes on the buffalo as the sound of the car faded. The big guy in front of me didn't pay attention to the car, either. He kept his eyes on me. Every few seconds he would growl, but it sounded more like he was curious rather than aggressive.

I remembered I had a cinnamon bun in the car that I had bought at a convenience store before I left Bismarck, and for some reason I thought it would be fun to feed it to him. My rental car was fifteen feet away, so I backed away from the fence and reached through the passenger window to grab the cinnamon bun from the front seat. I peeled away the wrapper, broke it in half, and held it out for him.

He snorted, looked to his right and then his left, and took a short step forward. He snorted again and stood there looking at me. He was clearly interested in the bun, but it was being offered by a human, and most animals have a natural fear of humans. But something told me this wasn't the first time somebody had offered him food from the other side of the fence.

He growled again, lowered his head, and took three steps forward. I still had the bun in my hand, held out for him to take if he wanted it.

He definitely wanted it.

I've heard that buffalo like sweets. I remember reading that when the movie "Dances With Wolves" was filmed, a pile of cookies was used as bait for a scene where a buffalo charged one of the actors. In the movie, it looked like he was about to attack a young boy, but in reality, the trained buffalo was running full speed toward a pile of cookies.

I imagine that when a buffalo wants something, you'd best get out of the way, or at least have something between you and it.

Like I said, thank goodness for barbed wire fences.

After another brief pause, he walked the rest of the way to my hand. He reached out with his tongue to taste it, realized it was delicious, and pulled it out of my hand and into his mouth. It was almost delicate the way he took it. Because of his size, I thought he would snatch it out of my hand the way a wild dog would. Instead, he grabbed it like he was a mild-mannered dairy cow.

He chewed the bun like it was a cud. A slow, relaxed chew followed by licking all around his mouth with his tongue. Then he looked at me like he wanted more. He didn't growl or snort or blow snot on me or anything like that. He just looked and waited.

On the road behind me, a low rumbling got gradually louder. I had first heard it in the distance, almost on a subconscious level, right after the buffalo took the cinnamon bun from my hand. The closer it got, the more I noticed it, until it was right next to me. I turned and saw a motorcycle rolling to a stop beside my car, its engine idling, sounding like a mechanical version of the buffalo's growl. The noise implied there was a lot more power available if needed.

It was the two-legged buffalo from the riverside park in Bismarck, with his rode-hard-and-put-up-wet girlfriend sitting behind him.

Was this a coincidence? Or was he following me?

He looked at me through a pair of mirrored sunglasses while his girl-friend looked at something on her cell phone. It was like a continuation of the stare down he gave me at the riverside park yesterday. His face had no expression, but it was obvious he had a problem with me. Maybe he didn't like anyone looking at him. Maybe he was the type who considered some-thing like that as a challenge to his manhood.

I guess I could have stared back at him, but I wasn't here to do that. I came to see a buffalo. The four-legged kind. So I turned back to my new friend on the other side of the fence and held out the other half of the cinnamon bun. By now I was confident enough to lean forward, with my head, arms, and torso well past the top strand of barbed wire.

That also told the motorcycle guy that he wasn't worth my time.

People with a certain type of inferiority complex get angry over many things. One thing that eats at them is being ignored. Show a person with this mental condition they're not worth your time, and they'll respond in a way that'll force you to pay attention to them. They may have a tantrum where they throw things, or they might resort to violence. Or they will create some type of loud noise to focus attention on themselves.

As the buffalo reached out with his tongue to lick the cinnamon bun, the guy gunned the engine. The motorcycle roared like a prehistoric dragon. The sudden blast of noise startled me, and I flinched hard, but the buffalo flinched harder.

Buffalo have a dual arsenal of horns and hooves to fight off a threat. If they can't gore something with those short, hook-shaped horns, they will spin and kick the hell out of it with their rear legs. And when they're running away from something, their horns aren't available, but their hooves are.

The buffalo bolted away, and he lashed out at the noise with his feet. Since I was leaning across the fence, it put my upper body in the line of fire. My head was turned toward the motorcycle as a huge hoof slammed into my ear. It might as well have been a sledgehammer, because it certainly felt like it. The blow knocked me five feet backwards, but not before a barb on the fence dragged across my ribcage.

I should have been knocked unconscious, but for some reason, I wasn't. Everything turned sideways, and I backpedaled and teetered and stumbled until my legs buckled. I wound up on my knees and right hand, with my left hand covering my ear.

I heard the guy and his girlfriend cackling over the high-pitched ringing in my head. Then the prehistoric dragon roared again, and they sped away. I don't know if he laughed because he thought it was funny or because he caused it. Either way, it pissed me off that he drove away after he knew I was hurt.

I crawled to my car and used it to steady myself while I rose to my feet. I was out of breath. It's amazing how a blow to the head can knock the wind out of you as easily as a kick to the stomach.

After several hard blinks, I could see well enough to take inventory of my condition. I wobbled to the door and sat down in the passenger seat. The visor had a mirror on it, and I could see a trickle of blood from a two-inch-long cut just above the earlobe. I guess I was hurt too badly to get sick from the sight of blood, because my stomach didn't get queasy like I thought it would.

I also had a combination of mud and buffalo shit matted in my hair and stuck to my jaw.

I flipped the visor up and got out of the car. With one hand pressed to my ear I braced myself against the door as I assessed my situation. I was hurt, probably with a concussion, with a lacerated ear that needed stitches, and there was nobody around. After a minute or two I realized that I had to drive myself to help, because help wasn't coming to me.

After I sat down in the driver's seat, I felt a sting from the cut across my abdomen. I looked down to make sure I wasn't bleeding to death, and I saw that my shirt had a long gash across it, and that made me even madder.

My damn shirt was ripped. The son of a bitch made me rip my shirt. I couldn't believe it. Wasn't it enough that I nearly got killed by the animal version of an army tank? Hell no. This was literally adding insult to injury.

Right then and there, I made up my mind. The motorcycle guy was going to be one of my victims, no matter what it took. I was as mad as I had been in a long time. This guy was going to pay with his life.

And I was going to tear his shirt to shreds.

Chapter Twelve

Believe it or not, there are actually things called "serial killer gods." That's why killers have lucky coincidences that help them find victims or help them get out of a jam.

I sat in my car trying to find an emergency number, but it's hard to do when you've got a headache, an old man's eyesight, and only one available hand to navigate the internet on your phone. My left hand stayed pressed against my ear because I was afraid if I pulled it away, the ear would fall off.

I suppose I should add "irrationality" to the headache, bad-eyesight, and one-available-hand list.

Less than ten minutes after the buffalo kicked me, the gods sent a thirty-something couple and their minivan full of kids to help me. The wife used baby wipes to clean the blood off me, and she kept a tissue pressed against my ear while her husband called a park ranger on his cell phone. Twenty minutes later, an EMT showed up and put butterfly strips on my ear. He said I probably had a concussion, and I should go to a hospital, but I shouldn't drive.

The husband volunteered to drive me in my car to a clinic not far from us while the wife followed in their van. That floored me. Who does that these days? We need more people like that in this world. That's a good reason not to kill them. The fact they had kids is another good reason. The world is full of people who never knew their parents, and I don't see any need to add to the problem.

Maybe if more people treated others with empathy and kindness, there might not be any serial killers. Maybe kids wouldn't grow up to be asshole adults who gave less than a damn about everybody but themselves. Maybe we wouldn't have a world full of people who laugh when somebody gets kicked in the head by a buffalo.

Then again, maybe I'm oversimplifying things. The world is more complicated than that. Despite this couple's best efforts, one of those kids in the van might end up being the next Charles Manson. You never know.

"I'm Dan," he said as he offered his hand. I gave him a firm handshake.

"Jon," I said.

"I'm really sorry this happened to you, Jon," he said as he steered my car onto the road.

"Well, I can't believe I'm lucky enough to have people like you stop and help me. I don't know that I'll ever be able to repay you."

"Don't you even worry about that. There's nothing to repay. We'll get you all stitched up, and you'll be fine. I just hope you don't have a skull fracture."

I managed a small laugh. "I just hope that buffalo doesn't have a cracked hoof," I said.

He smiled and nodded but didn't say anything. We rode along for a few miles in silence before he asked a question I didn't want to answer.

"Got any kids?"

I thought about lying, saying that I never married and had no kids. But why would I do that to this guy? He seemed sincerely interested in finding out more about me, or maybe he was just a bullshit artist who could talk to anybody about anything. Didn't matter to me. I made my mind up about him and his wife the minute they stopped their van.

"Yeah, I've got a thirty-year-old son. He lives in Oregon."

"Really? Oregon? That's where we're headed. We're taking a cross-country trip with the kids. We figured we'd show them there's more to the world than a ten-mile radius around Pittsburgh."

"You're from Pittsburgh?"

"Yeah, been there all my life. I told my wife we should take this trip for the kids, but it's actually more for me."

"Nothing wrong with that," I said. "I'm doing kinda the same thing. I plan on going to all the lower forty-eight states this year. I'm actually going to be in Oregon in about a month if my schedule keeps up. And if I survive."

He laughed. He thought I was making a joke about getting kicked in the head, but I meant it in the literal sense. If some biker doesn't stab me to death, or if the cops don't shoot me, or if I don't decide to end it all before the year is over.

"You going to see your son?"

"Hopefully, yeah."

"Hopefully? You mean you might not see him? How long has it been since you've seen him?"

"I don't know," I said. I couldn't look at Dan, so I stared through the windshield at the road. "It's been way too long. Years, I guess."

"Hey, Jon, look...I'm sorry. I didn't mean to pry too much," Dan said.

"No, no. It's okay," I said with a wave of my hand. "You didn't know. It's just that sometimes it hits me how much of his life I've missed."

In my peripheral vision, I saw him nod, but he didn't say anything.

We drove the rest of the way to the clinic in silence. I'm sure he felt guilty about bringing up a painful subject, and I couldn't think of anything to talk about.

We pulled into the clinic's parking lot, and he helped me inside while his wife waited in their van with the kids. After a receptionist told me it would be about ten minutes before a doctor could see me, I thanked Dan again for helping me, and told him I'd be fine. They could leave.

I followed him outside to the van. His wife got out, and I thanked her for being so nice to a total stranger. I offered to shake her hand, but instead she wrapped her arms around my neck and gave me a hug. A warm embrace, like a daughter saying goodbye to her father the day she leaves for college. The suddenness of it surprised me. As she hugged me, I looked at their kids in the van. Four of them, two boys and two girls, between five and twelve years old.

Tears blurred my eyes, and I blinked them away as she stepped back from me and smiled. "Take care of yourself," she said, and she walked around to the passenger side of the van.

I turned to Dan and shook his hand. "Listen to what she said," he told me. "She's a smart lady." I nodded. He tried to release my hand, but I held on and pulled him a little closer so I could tell him something that only the two of us could hear.

"You take care of those kids," I said. "Don't let the demons get them like they got mine."

He gave my shoulder a squeeze with his left hand as he gave the handshake one final pump. "Good luck to you, Jon. I'm glad we were able to help you."

He climbed in and they drove away, the kids waving at me through the van windows. I waved back. Yeah, there are actually good people in the world, and there went a van full of them.

Two hours later, I checked into a hotel to do nothing but relax and sleep for a couple of days. Doctor's orders. No driving other than to get to the hotel. I didn't have a concussion, but I still took a pretty hard jolt to the side of my head. Eight stitches in my ear. He said it probably wouldn't look normal ever again. The only thing the scratch across my stomach needed was some antiseptic.

Five minutes after walking into the hotel room, I was asleep.

———

By the time I checked out Wednesday, my headache was gone. The cut on my ear was still tender, but at least it wasn't oozing blood any longer. I also learned during the past two days that sleeping on the same side as an injury results in bloody pillowcases.

It looked to be a gorgeous day. The sun beamed down from a cloudless sky, temperatures were predicted to be in the low eighties, and there was a zero percent chance of rain. A perfect day for driving to my next town with the windows down and the radio blasting.

And then I saw something that threw a wet blanket over my day.

Miss Rode-hard-and-put-up-wet walked out of the hotel's vending area carrying a bucket of ice. She had her back to me, so she didn't notice me. I looked across the parking lot in the direction she was walking, and there was the loud Harley leaning on its kickstand at the very end of a block of rooms.

I mean, what the hell? Were these two following me? What were the odds we would end up in the same place at the same time, on three different occasions? Either it was the most bizarre of coincidences or they were looking to pick a fight with me.

Normally, I would stick around to give the motorcycle guy the fight he wanted. Not saying I wouldn't be scared, but I promised myself that someday one of my victims was going to be a lot bigger than me, just so I could prove that to myself. Plus, he ripped my shirt, and I was still pissed off about that.

But my circumstances changed the instant that buffalo kicked me in the head. I was nowhere near one-hundred percent healthy, and I would need to be if I attacked this guy. If I wasn't, he'd rip me apart.

Instead, I decided to be smart rather than tough. I had a brand-new computer in the car, and I could use it to figure out what to do about him. There had to be a thousand websites with info I could use.

I got in my rental and drove past the motorcycle. I committed its license plate number to memory, and then pulled onto the highway and headed south. I planned on making Denver my next stop. It was getting late in the week, which meant I had about four days to drive there, find a victim somewhere along the way, kill them, dispose of their body, get a new rental car, have my Sunday breakfast, then head to my next town.

Sometimes people work better under pressure. I was going to find out if I could do it, too.

My route to Denver would take two days, with a stop in a small town somewhere along the way. Once again, I planned on taking only the back roads, avoiding the interstates. In my opinion, the real way to see the country is from the small roads that led through small towns. Interstates are all about speed and efficiency, and that causes people to miss the little nooks and crannies that make this country unique.

It's like looking at a picture of an old, worn-down-by-life farmer. If the picture is taken from a distance, you might be able to tell he's an old man, but you won't see any details. A close-up picture shows all the lines and creases in his face, all the things that were put there by a hard life. You can see the man's *character*.

From the interstate, you miss the character of the land. Give me the back roads.

Part Two
ETHAN

Chapter Thirteen

Eugene, Oregon. That's my destination. That's where Ethan's tattoo shop is located, and that's where I hope to reconnect with my son.

The past few weeks since getting kicked in the head have been good for me. I managed to stay focused on my goal of one dead body per week, while at the same time I rehearsed in my head the conversation I hoped to have once I stood face-to-face with Ethan.

My victims gave me no problems at all. I guess I'm either getting better at this, or I'm hitting a lucky streak. It may be a combination of both, but I prefer to think it's because I'm becoming an expert.

A hitchhiker outside Akron, Colorado died one evening when I slammed the trunk lid down on his head as he was putting his backpack in the trunk. It's a good thing my duffel bag and fishing equipment were in the way, because he paused long enough while he was scooting them out of the way for me to crash the lid onto the back of his neck. He fell to his knees with his head half in the trunk and half out. Perfect for the trunk lid to come down two more times on his skull.

There was no traffic within miles of us, so I rolled his body into the ditch and threw his backpack on top of him. By the time he was found, I would be in Denver.

The next victim was in Albuquerque, New Mexico. I've always heard how that town is in the desert and it's always dry there, but don't let anyone kid you. Sometimes it rains hard enough to strangle frogs, like it did the night I spied a late-night shopper exiting a twenty-four-hour grocery store. He had a case of beer over his head to keep the rain off him as he ran for his car in the parking lot.

I got out of my rental and trotted toward him, not caring if I got soaking wet or not. The rain was perfect cover for any sounds or physical evidence. The guy slowed down as he saw me approaching him, probably because he couldn't believe some idiot was walking through the downpour as if it wasn't there. When he stopped ten feet from me, he kept the case of beer over his head, but I continued closing the gap between us.

I smashed him in the nose with a palm-heel strike, which is a quick and easy way to stun someone without risking broken bones in your hand. The impact comes from the heel of the hand striking the nose straight-on and slightly up, which, if done correctly, can rip the cartilage of the nose loose from the bone and knock them unconscious.

Or, as in his case, it can make them fall down and drop the case of beer on the pavement. A rapid twist of his head as he struggled to sit up finished the job. I found his car keys in his pants pocket, then I laid his body across the front seat, put the keys in the ignition, and locked the doors.

The *bad* thing about the rain is that it soaked his clothes and made him harder to move. A dead limp body is difficult to move, anyway, but if you add another five or ten pounds of water to the equation, it makes a huge difference.

The *good* thing is that the rain muffled any noise I might have made, and it washed away any physical evidence I might have left at the scene. Just to make sure, though, I took the case of beer and put it in my front seat. I figured there was no sense in letting a perfectly good case of beer go to waste.

I slept really late the next day because I was drunk. When I got up sometime after noon, there were six beers left in the case.

A week after that, a Catholic priest in Salt Lake City became my next victim. He was gullible enough to allow me in the church, and after I confirmed we were alone, I kicked him in the groin, then turned his head to the side as I jerked it downwards into a knee thrust to the temple. I dragged him into the confessional booth and left the church through a side door. He became victim number twenty-two. I couldn't feel too sorry for him, either, because Roman Catholic isn't anywhere near the first religion that comes to mind when you think of Salt Lake City. Had he been a Mormon, he might not have ever stood out from the crowd, and I might not have noticed him.

You know the old saying. When in Salt Lake City, do as the Mormons do.

Only a couple of days ago, I killed victim number twenty-three in Caldwell, Idaho. As I drove down an old country road, I happened upon a woman chopping at the ground with a hoe in the middle of a patch of sunflowers behind her unpainted, broken-down house. It's a wonder I saw her, because she was no taller than five feet, and the sunflowers towered at least two feet over her head.

I parked in her driveway and walked toward her, hoping to look like someone who was lost and needed directions. Between her flower patch and the driveway was a big shade tree, and leaning against the tree was a shovel. It was old and dirty, with a handle wrapped with duct tape.

I grabbed it as I walked past. When I reached the edge of the sunflower patch, she looked up and smiled. She must have been eighty-years-old. White thinning hair, wrinkles on her face, liver spots on her hands, and varicose veins in her legs. She was completely surrounded by the flowers.

"Excuse me, ma'am," I said. Then I swung the shovel like a sledgehammer and cracked her skull with the flat underside of the blade. Grains of dirt flew off the shovel and sprayed against the flowers with a sound like rain falling. She fell without a sound, dead as the pile of compost on the other side of the flower patch.

Her final act in life was giving a smile to a stranger. Good for her. We need more people like her in this world.

I buried her in the compost pile with the shovel I used to kill her. Then I put it back against the tree and drove away. Two days later I arrived in Bend, Oregon, where I am now.

Eugene was due west of Bend, a fairly short trip that would take me through the Willamette National Forest. I'd have to take a zig-zag route, but that wasn't a problem. I sorta looked forward to it, because this was an area of the country where Bigfoot had been spotted a bunch of times. Wouldn't it be awesome if I could have added a Bigfoot to my list? I think I could've ended my hobby right then and there, because that would have given me more notoriety than killing fifty-two people. Weird, ain't it? You kill a bunch of people, and you're labeled as a serial killer. But kill just one Bigfoot, and all of a sudden, you're a hero to the entire conspiracy theory crowd.

Let's just say I didn't plan on killing a Bigfoot, but I would've jumped at the opportunity if I got it.

The more important thing was finding Ethan. The past few weeks hadn't been focused only on killing. I had lots of downtime, and I used it to get familiar with my new computer. With a little practice, I managed to find Ethan's tattoo shop, *The Body Canvas*. He had a website and everything. He even had his picture there.

I looked at his face for a long time. It was the same as I remember it, but several years older. Tattoos covered his neck all the way to his jawline. His hair was the same color, but shorter, and his eyes looked darker, as if he wore eyeliner.

And he was smiling. That's what made me pause for so long. I hadn't seen him smile since he was a little kid. No matter what his mother and I did, we simply weren't able to make him happy, but it looks like he found happiness somewhere between there and here.

I had mixed feelings about that. I was glad that my son had found peace in his life, but it also bothered me that he didn't find it until he got away from his mother and me. Were we the cause of his unhappiness? Were our parenting skills that horrible?

I convinced myself that we did the best we could, and that it really didn't matter now, because all that was in the past. I need to be focused on the future, on getting to know my son again, on being his father again.

The first step had to be getting in touch with him before I went to see him. It would be a bad idea to show up at his shop unannounced. Surprises like that often don't end well. This is something both of us need to be prepared for. When the moment comes that we look into each other's eyes, there needs to be some sort of understanding between us. We need to act like two grown men, not like a withdrawn teenager and his distant dad. We both need to understand that maybe neither one of us is at fault for the divide between us, that sometimes the world makes it hard to do the right thing, and makes it even harder to make things right after everything has gone wrong.

No matter how hard it was going to be, it still had to be done. I found the phone number on Ethan's website, then I grabbed the phone off the bedside table. I held the receiver close to my ear, the dial tone humming like a slow, steady air raid siren. My finger hovered over the number nine button, ready to access an outside line. I sat like that for nearly a full minute, until the dial tone started beeping at me.

Then I put the receiver back onto its cradle. I wasn't ready for this just yet.

I packed my bag, threw it into my rental car, and pointed the headlights west. I needed a few more miles of highway therapy before I would be ready for a phone conversation with my son.

A few hours later, I had a new hotel room in Eugene, a different rental car in the parking lot, and a whole week before I needed to find my next victim. Tomorrow morning I'll have my regular Sunday breakfast and I'll mark an X on my calendar for the little old lady buried beneath her sunflower compost pile. Victim number twenty-three. I'll spend the rest of the day driving around Eugene, seeing the sights and basically nothing else. Then on Monday I'll face the moment of truth. That's when I'll call Ethan and ask to meet him.

This was going to work.

This *had* to work.

Chapter Fourteen

It was the least-satisfying breakfast all year. I didn't feel any elation from marking the twenty-third X on my calendar. The pancakes had no taste, and the coffee might as well have been tap water.

I couldn't enjoy the accomplishment of another victim because my stomach was in knots. I felt more nervous than a nerdy high school kid before asking the cheerleader to prom. What was I so afraid of? He's my son, for crying out loud. A dad shouldn't feel this way about his son. He should be confident that his son will want to talk to him, to see him.

But not me. Noooooo. I had to be worried I would get rejected by him. I was concerned he wouldn't even recognize my voice. I was concerned I wouldn't even recognize *his* voice.

After sitting on the bed in my hotel room and staring at the phone for half an hour, I finally found enough nerve. "Screw it," I told myself, and I picked up the receiver and started pressing buttons. A hammer was banging away at the inside of my chest.

After three rings, there was a voice on the other end.

"The Body Canvas. How may I help you?"

It was him. The voice was still the same, except now it seemed to have more life than the last time we spoke. It was like his soul had been revived after all this time, and it was coming through loud and clear.

The clarity and enthusiasm of his voice caught me off guard, and I couldn't speak for a few seconds. Not only did I not know what to say, I had no idea how to say it. The hammer beat even harder in my chest.

"Hellooo?" he said. There was no hint of irritation in his voice, no impatience. In years past he might have hung up on me, but he was an adult now, both mentally and physically, and he reacted to my silence like an adult should react. Maybe he thought we had a bad connection. Maybe I was calling from a cell phone somewhere between cell towers. Maybe I had accidentally dialed the wrong number.

No matter the reason, he waited for me to speak.

"Hi...uh...Ethan," I squawked. I must have sounded like a chicken with laryngitis. I cleared my throat and was about to repeat myself, but I couldn't get anything out. I cleared my throat again. Then again.

After the third time, I felt like giving up. I was just too nervous to do this.

"Dad?" Ethan said.

I stopped everything I was doing and sat there in silence for a few seconds. I was sitting in a nearly empty room with drab furnishings and wood paneling on the walls, but I didn't notice any of that. I didn't notice anything around me. I hung my attention on that one word.

Dad.

Name a man whose heart doesn't leap at least a little bit every time he hears that word spoken by his children, and I'll show you someone who isn't really a father. When Ethan said it, a warmth started spreading across my body that's hard to describe. If you're a father, you understand. If you're not a father, then you're missing out on one of life's little miracles. My posture went from a semi-slump to steady upright, with my shoulders back and my chin lifted a little.

Dad.

That word coming from a son on good terms with his father is special enough, but when it comes from a son who was thought to be gone forever, it takes on a magical quality. I realized I didn't need to clear my throat any longer.

"How are you, son?" I said.

"Wow. I'm...could you...hold on for a second?" he asked.

"Of course."

I heard a click, then silence. He must have put me on hold so he could switch phones. There was no soft music playing on the hold line. I guess something like that would be out of place for a tattoo shop. Unless they played heavy metal music, maybe.

After ten seconds, the line clicked again, and Ethan said, "Sorry, Dad. I had to switch phones. I'm using the office phone now." He was slightly out of breath. He must have run to the office. That was a nice thought.

"I'm, uh…I'm in town, believe it or not," I said.

He hesitated a second, but no more than that. "Wha…really? You're in Eugene? What brings you out here?"

I couldn't tell him the whole truth about why I was here. And in this instance, a little white lie wasn't going to hurt anybody.

"I'm out here to see you, son. I finally retired, and I decided to take a cross-country trip and maybe surprise you."

"You're retired now?" he asked. "That's good, Dad. You deserve it. You worked in that place for way too long."

"You know, I'd like to come see you if I could," I told him. "If that's okay."

"Uh…yeah, of course. Uh, hold on a second."

He didn't put the phone down because I could still hear him breathing. It sounded like he was looking at something. In the background, I heard a series of soft clicks. He was looking on his computer.

"How long are you in town?" he asked after several seconds.

"How long do you need me to be?"

"Well, I'd like to see you as soon as possible, but we have appointments booked for the rest of the day and part of the day tomorrow. Since there's only two of us here, I don't want you to come here when I'm not able to spend some time with you."

"How about if I came to see you today after you close?" I asked.

"Well…listen, Dad." He paused again, as if he was searching for the right thing to say. "I think I might need a few extra hours to wrap my brain around everything. It's been a long time since we've seen each other, and I want to have the right mindset before we do. I don't want to have things go bad for us."

I didn't say anything.

"Life's too short. You know?" he added.

"Yes. Yes, it is. I'm finding that out every day."

"How about if you come to the shop tomorrow around mid-afternoon? We don't open until eleven."

"How about 2:30?"

"Yeah, that'll work great. I won't book any appointments after then, and we can have the rest of the day together. How's that sound?"

Man, his voice. There was no way this was the same sullen, angry teenager who refused to talk to me years ago. He was happy now. His life had purpose and a sense of direction. Getting out from under my roof was the best thing that ever happened to him.

"That sounds great, son. I can't wait."

"Hey...uh, listen," he said. He sounded hesitant. I braced myself for him to tell me not to expect much, to not be encouraged by this conversation, to not have high hopes for a grand reunion.

"I've got a pretty good life now, Dad. Things are going pretty well here," he said.

I didn't say anything, but the hammer started hitting my chest again.

"But, you know...when I heard your voice...it was..." he stopped, because his voice had started to tremble. I still didn't say anything, but I probably couldn't have spoken if I had tried.

"It was by far the best thing that's happened to me in a long time," he said with a rush. He had to get the words out of his mouth before his quivering vocal cords tore them to shreds.

The warmth that began spreading over me a few minutes ago now fully enveloped my body. See? There was never anything to be nervous about.

"I feel the same way, Ethan. Thank you. I'll see you tomorrow."

"Bye, Dad," he said, and he hung up.

Dad.

I sat on the bed for another couple of minutes without putting the receiver back on the cradle. I was too dumbfounded to move.

What do you bring with you when you're about to visit the son you haven't seen in years? Do you bring him a gift? An old photograph?

I thought about this for hours after we talked, and I decided to bring him nothing but a hug. To be honest, that's all I really had to offer him, anyway. I didn't want to bring him something to remind him of the past. I wanted to open the door to our future relationship.

The bad thing is, if my plan ends up the way I think it will, with me on death row somewhere, he wouldn't consider this a good memory. I would be an embarrassment to him.

But I can't steer away from my plan at this point. I have to stay true to myself and live my own life, no matter what consequences happen later. It's like the old saying. Sometimes it's better to beg forgiveness than to ask permission.

So, I loaded myself and the hug I was going to give him into my rental car, typed the tattoo shop's address into my phone for directions, and headed out. It was five miles away, enough time to calm myself down, and to plan the first words out of my mouth when I saw him.

It was a nice drive. Traffic wasn't too bad for a mid-afternoon, and the sun had broken through the clouds. It was so bright I had to wear my sunglasses, which I rarely did. That's probably one reason why I have so many wrinkles around my eyes. That and old age.

Ten minutes after I left, my phone told me I was nearing the tattoo shop.

In one thousand feet, your destination is on the right.

I searched both sides of the street for a parking spot. Just as I reached the front of the shop, somebody ran out the door and across the street. I slammed on my brakes to keep from hitting him. The guy looked about twenty or twenty-five, wearing a black T-shirt, his neck and arms covered with tattoos. He ran with an awkward gait because his right hand was shoving something into his pants pocket. He never looked to see if traffic was coming. He simply ran across the road, as if he didn't care whether he lived or died.

Stupid damn kids today. I swear. One of these days that kid was going to get killed doing that.

I found a parking spot a few yards past the shop. I did my best imitation of parallel parking, locked the doors, and gathered my thoughts before walking in. I decided not to say a word to him. I was just going to walk up and give him a big hug.

The shop was empty as I walked in. There was a couch on the left, with a coffee table covered with magazines in front of it. At the back of the shop were two chairs that reminded me of something you would see in an old-time barber shop. They were designed to recline nearly flat. Beside each chair was a multi-drawer, roll-around toolbox.

Mirrors covered most of the walls, along with posters displaying different tattoo patterns. To the right, near the back, was a counter with a computer monitor mounted on it.

But I didn't see Ethan or anyone else.

I stood there for a few moments, looking around, and I noticed a funny smell in the air. I had smelled it before, but it had been a long time ago. What was it?

Then it came to me. Gunpowder. Why would a tattoo parlor smell like gunpowder?

I walked further into the shop, looking left and right for Ethan. Or for anyone, for that matter. As I neared the counter, I saw a set of legs sticking out from behind it. Black lace-up military boots, black pants.

I stepped around the end of the counter, and there was Ethan, lying on his back, with a small pool of blood under his left shoulder and side, and a bullet hole in his chest.

Chapter Fifteen

His right arm was propped against his side, his elbow on the floor and his hand hanging from his wrist like a wet flag on a windless day. His fingers twitched every couple of seconds, every time his dying heart pumped a dwindling supply of blood to his extremities.

And his eyes were open, staring at the ceiling.

I screamed out his name and fell to his side. As I reached down to prop up his head, his eyes were glazed over. Unfocused.

"Ethan!" I yelled. "Ethan! No! Wake up!"

I pressed my hand against the bullet hole, hoping to somehow heal it. But the hole in his back was where the blood came from, and it trickled out in a thin, steady stream.

I sat on the floor with his head in my lap, cradling him, begging him to wake up, tears filling my eyes.

"Come on, Ethan. You gotta wake up. Please wake up," I said. I blinked away a tear that fell onto his neck. I shook him and said his name again, but he didn't respond. His eyes remained fixed on the ceiling, unfocused. His mouth was slacked open just a little, as if he was asleep. I did everything I could think of to wake him up. I didn't know CPR. Was it something I should try, anyway? If I did try, would it be worse than doing nothing?

Instead, I held him and gave him the hug I had saved. I rocked back and forth with him in my arms, and I cried the most honest tears I could remember. There is no greater pain than losing a child, especially when that child is coming back into your life after being absent for years. The sense of loss is overwhelming. The regret of not staying involved in his life and then not taking the effort to reconnect with him for years is more than a sane mind can bear.

Then a sound came from his lips. It sounded like a cross between a groan and a slight cough. I stopped rocking and pulled back so I could see his face. His eyes were half closed, but they weren't glazed over. He was looking right into my eyes.

"Dad," he said. His voice was barely a whisper, and it seemed to take everything he had left in his body to say it.

He gave me a little smile. And then his eyes lost their focus, and he was gone.

I felt for a pulse in his neck. The same way I had felt for life in many of my victims. Except this time I wanted to feel a sign of life instead of a sign of death. But there was nothing.

Ethan. My son.

My son was dead. The only part of me I had left in this world was gone.

"Dad." The last word he ever uttered.

I held his head in my hands, looking at his face, not knowing what to do. This wasn't like he had a terminal disease and there was time to prepare for the end. This was sudden. Unexpected. A total shock. This ripped my emotions down from the high I felt a few moments ago to the mental wastelands of despair that now gripped me. It felt like my heart had been torn from my chest.

I used my fingertips to close his eyes, and I laid him back down. I was crossing his arms over his chest when someone screamed.

A young woman stood on the other side of the counter, her face twisted by anguish and fear. She had tattoos on her arms, and her eyebrow was pierced with a small silver hoop.

"What happened? Ethan!"

She ran around the counter, dropping a small rectangular box to the floor. She tried to shove me out of the way, but I held firm and told her to call 911. She screamed his name over and over, trying to get to him. I finally grabbed her arm and forced her to look at me.

"Call the police. Right now. Go."

Hours later, after the crime scene specialists had gathered evidence, the coroner had taken Ethan's body, and the police had questioned me, I managed to sit down on the couch and gather my thoughts. While I was sitting there, the young woman approached me. Her eyes were bloodshot from crying. She held a wadded-up tissue that she used to dab her nose.

"You're Ethan's dad," she said. It was more a statement than a question. "He couldn't stop talking about you last night."

I looked up and gave a weak smile. I patted the couch cushion beside me, inviting her to have a seat. She sat on the forward edge of the couch, half turned to me so she could talk to me easier. We sat in awkward silence for a few moments, neither of us knowing what needed to be said.

Finally, she dabbed her nose and cleared her throat. "I'm Sara, by the way. I'm Ethan's fiancée," she said.

"Jon," I said.

We sat there for a long time, well into the small hours of the morning, talking about Ethan. She told me she had never seen him as excited as he had been after talking with me on the phone. He hardly slept that night. She said he was almost like a young kid on Christmas Eve.

They had lived together for three years, building their business and planning their life. The past six months had been a blur of a surge in business, a new location for their shop, and a new place to live. They had moved out of the basement of a friend's house to a small apartment. They had bought a car. Things were looking up for them.

The best thing of all happened a little over a month ago. Sara found out she was pregnant.

"I thought nothing could top that for making Ethan happy. Nothing. But when he got off the phone with you he was ten feet off the ground, and that night he told me about how he was angry with you and his mom all the time, but he couldn't remember why. I think after all these years he realized that he had grown into a man, and he didn't have any reason to be mad anymore," she said.

"I'm sure some of that anger at me was justified. I wasn't the best parent in the world," I said. "I didn't know how to reach him."

"He knows...he *knew* that," she said, correcting herself. "He said that maybe nobody is to blame for what happened. Maybe life in general is to blame."

"I wonder why he didn't contact me for so long?" I said.

"He said he wondered the same thing about you."

I didn't have an answer for that. I just sat there staring at the floor. So many of my problems in life were caused by nothing but my own actions.

"He had me buy a gift for you," she said. "That's why I wasn't in here when...when everything happened. It might have been different if I had been here."

"Or both of you might be dead," I told her.

She nodded, then looked at the counter across the room. "See that box?"

The rectangular box she dropped when she saw Ethan on the floor had been picked up and set beside the computer monitor.

"It's for you," she told me. "Go open it."

I walked over to the counter and picked it up. It didn't feel heavy, but something slid back and forth inside it. Something solid.

I opened up one end of the box and poured the contents out into my hand. It was a long, slender knife. A fillet knife meant for cleaning fish. The blade was about seven inches long, with a wooden handle. It was inside a leather scabbard.

"He knew you love to fish," Sara said. "This was the best thing he could get you on short notice."

I didn't say anything. I couldn't. I don't know if Ethan ever gave me a present, except for those times when he was four or five years old, and my ex-wife would buy something for me. She would allow him to give it to me, so that it seemed the gift was from him. But after he got old enough to buy his own gifts, he never made the effort.

He sure changed over the years.

"I know who shot him," Sara said.

"Did you tell the police?"

"Yes. It's this drug addict who owes us money. He's been owing us for over a year, and Ethan finally called a debt collection service on him. The guy has been in and out of jail his whole life."

"How do you know it's him?"

"He's threatened us before. A week ago, he came in here with a knife, and Ethan just laughed at him. I think it embarrassed him, and he ran out before anything else happened. Ethan told me this guy would probably be back, maybe to rob us."

"He didn't rob you this time, did he?"

"Yeah, he did. He robbed me of the love of my life. He robbed this baby of its father."

I pulled the knife out of the leather scabbard and looked at the shine of the blade. I never was a fan of knives because of all the blood they caused. But maybe, just maybe, this punk deserved a bloody death.

"He robbed me, too," I said.

"Yeah."

"Do you know where I can find this asshole?"

"I bet the cops have already arrested him. Everybody in town knows him."

We buried Ethan three days later, on a rainy, dreary day. I paid for the funeral, even though it put a dent in my traveling money. I also put a large down payment on a small headstone. I couldn't stand the thought of his body lying in an unmarked grave, a mound of earth piled over him with nothing to tell people who was beneath it. To me, it's one of the most undignified things that can happen to a person.

The coroner said he died from massive blood loss and internal trauma. He was shot with a 9mm, and it tore a large hole through his body. His left lung and a couple of arteries were cut to pieces.

I had two days before the funeral to do nothing but think. It was hard to reminisce about the good times with Ethan because there weren't very many of them. There were some good times when he was really young, and a few when he first became a teenager, but when the zits and the growth spurts hit, it was all over between us.

But not all of the two days were spent thinking about him. I also started thinking about me and my so-called hobby.

The thing that struck me most about the day Ethan died is that I didn't get sick at the sight of blood. Was it because of the rush of adrenaline from seeing my son wounded? Was it because the blood was one of the last things I noticed? I couldn't figure it out.

I also wondered why I was thinking about this when I should have been mourning my son. Was I simply a selfish bastard with no regard for human life, including my own son's life? What was I feeling right now? Anguish? Regret? Loneliness? Anger?

How about all the above? There was no doubt I was in deep despair. Ethan was gone. He left behind a pregnant girlfriend who was carrying my grandchild. I didn't get to reconnect with him. I was lonely, because I still had no one to share my life. That's the main reason I came to Oregon, because of my loneliness.

And yeah, I was angry. Ten thousand times more than pissed off. My son was no longer a part of my life because of a decision neither one of us made. He was gone because some punk-ass thug couldn't pay his bills and took it out on Ethan. He handled his problems with violence, like most people in this country.

And then I thought, hell, that's exactly what I'm doing, too. I'm handling my lack of accomplishments in life by creating violence, by killing people, by injecting anguish, regret, loneliness, and anger into the lives of people I would never know.

I guess I'm as American as apple pie and the electric chair.

What was I going to do now? Was I going to quit my hobby, maybe buy a house in Oregon, and watch my grandchild grow up? Was I going to continue down this path of murder for the sole reason of gaining fame? Was I going to be true to myself, or faithful to Ethan?

Sometimes overthinking things makes the brain tie itself in knots. I've heard it called "paralysis from analysis." You think and think instead of acting, and before you know it, you haven't done anything.

My first inclination was to hunt down the guy who shot Ethan and cut his throat from ear to ear, but the police put a stop to that thought when they arrested him the day before the funeral. He confessed to the murder when ballistics tests matched his pistol with the bullet that killed Ethan, and when his fingerprints were all over the counter, door, and floor beside Ethan. It didn't help him when they found gunpowder residue on his hands, too. I guess the scumbag never took a shower.

There was no way for me to get access to this guy, so I decided to leave town and continue with my hobby. But now, I had a new focus, a new weapon, and I seemed to no longer get sick at the sight of blood. Now, it didn't seem like a hobby any longer. It was more like a driving force.

I said my goodbyes to Sara and promised I would stay in touch, even though I didn't mean a word of it. I knew I would probably never see her again, and I would never lay eyes on her baby. But I had to make her feel reassured. She had just experienced one of the most horrible things a person can experience, and it was the least I could do for her at the moment.

I pulled my tackle box from the trunk of my rental car and put it in the front seat with me. The knife Ethan gave me lay beside it. Maybe this was some form of destiny. Maybe he gave me this knife and removed my nausea from the sight of blood at the same time because of some weird force of nature, because I was running out of non-bloody ways to kill people. I know a lot of people who would say it was because of God, even though the God they believe in would never lend a hand to something like this. Maybe it was all a coincidence. I don't know. It didn't really matter, anyway. A dead person is still dead whether they die screaming or peacefully in their sleep.

I mapped out my next destination, and within an hour I was headed for Carson City, Nevada. I was running out of time to find victim number twenty-four.

Part Three

SUMMER HEAT

Chapter Sixteen

Hitchhikers make easy victims.

Especially those who are walking through a driving rainstorm. All they want is to get out of the rain, and if you offer them shelter, they'll almost always take it.

That's how victim number twenty-four happened. I stopped twenty feet past him as he walked along the highway, his head down, slogging through the muck on the shoulder of the road. He trotted up to the car, I leaned over and opened the passenger door, and he climbed inside.

Five seconds later, I had him in a choke hold. He clawed and kicked and twisted for nearly a full minute, but he finally fell asleep. After that, breaking his neck was easy. I left him on the side of the highway behind some boulders. I had to clean the mud from the inside of my car where his feet had scraped against the door and the dashboard while I choked him, but that didn't take long.

After a few days in Carson City, I decided I needed some dry air. I thought that's what I was going to get when I headed for Nevada, but all I got was rain. After Ethan's death, several cloudy days in a row were enough to make me feel depressed. Dry air and sunshine would be enough to bring me out of it. That's how I ended up outside Phoenix, in a town called Surprise.

Now there's a perfect name if I ever saw one.

"Surprise! I'm a serial killer!"
"Surprise! You're my next victim!"

Victim twenty-five was certainly surprised when I killed her. Three days after I arrived, I saw her alone behind the counter of a fast-food restaurant. Because of her white shirt, and she appeared older than your typical burger flipper, I figured she was the manager, and the only car at the back of the parking lot was hers. Slicing her front tire was easy. As she came out and saw her ruined tire, I pretended to be walking past the restaurant and asked if she needed help. She hesitated a second, then said she did.

Two minutes later I stuffed her into her own trunk with a broken neck.

The next day, I went to a backpacking store and bought a tent small enough to pack into a pocket. The support rods for it collapsed small enough to fit inside the tackle box.

After paying for Ethan's funeral and headstone, I had to save money one way or another. I decided to pitch a tent whenever I could, at least until my funds caught up. City parks, deep woods, roadside rest areas, places like that. The only thing I might miss would be internet access, but I could use my phone for that. I might miss a bath, too, but truck stops and convenience store bathrooms would be good enough.

After leaving Arizona, I stopped for three days at a campground in Las Cruces, New Mexico. Victim number twenty-six was the campground manager. After swapping cars and spending a couple of days in San Antonio, Texas, I found number twenty-seven in New Orleans. I was there nearly a week before I killed him because the Big Easy is a fun town, and I was enjoying myself. He died when I pushed him over the rail of a stairwell eight stories high inside an old hotel, as he stumbled back to his room from the hotel bar. The steps circled around a column of empty air that didn't stop until the bottom floor. The fact his blood-alcohol level was three times the drunk limit made it easy to believe he fell on his own and not because he was pushed.

I had my celebration breakfast in a little café just outside town before hitting the road, and the next day I enjoyed the 4th of July at a campground near the beach in Biloxi, Mississippi. I sipped a beer while I watched families play in the surf during the day. I felt a little jealousy towards them, because we never took Ethan to the beach. It would have been easy for that same cloudy-day depression to set in again, but I told myself that he had forgiven me for being a shitty father, and my focus now was to prove to him, and myself, that I wasn't some run-of-the-mill loser.

After darkness fell, even though the mosquitos were a problem, the reflection of the fireworks off the ocean was beautiful. I was so overwhelmed with patriotic pride that I didn't consider killing anyone that night.

That would happen three nights later in Memphis.

There would come a time when I'd test myself by attacking some huge monster who stands a foot taller than me, or a human buffalo with oversized muscles, but that night wasn't the time. A drunk pissing on a dumpster at two a.m. in an alley behind a bar was low-hanging fruit, and it would have been stupid to let an opportunity like that pass me by. He was too lost in his drunk fog to hear me as I walked up behind him, and there was nobody around to hear what I was about to do to him.

A brick to the head, and crushed windpipe, a check for pulse, and victim number twenty-eight was in the books. I lifted him into the dumpster and covered him with trash. There was a chance he would never be found until after his body reached the landfill.

I hung around Memphis for a few more days, listening to blues on Beale Street, eating barbecue, seeing the sights. I even took time to visit Graceland and pay my respects to Elvis. It was neat seeing where he lived, but it was also sad, because it had been turned into a big tourist trap. The souvenir shop across the street from his mansion even sold tiny plastic vials containing a clear liquid. They claimed it was his sweat. Yeah, right. I'm sure somebody grabbed his socks after one of his late-night racquetball games and wrung the perspiration out of them because they wanted to sell it.

One thing I learned about being in the South during July was that I should be somewhere else. It was hot as a furnace, and three times as humid. Thirty minutes outside in this weather, and I looked like I had been drenched by a salty rainstorm.

I decided I needed to be in the mountains during hot weather, so I mapped out a route that would keep me cool. The day I marked victim number twenty-eight on my calendar, I headed east for the other end of Tennessee. Two days later, I was camping out in the Great Smoky Mountains. My rental car had been swapped for a rental SUV, and I used my fishing gear to catch some trout in one of the streams that coursed throughout the park.

Life was good. I was camping under the stars at night, the area was full of potential victims, and I was saving money by using my tent and fishing gear. Now all I needed was an easy victim.

Even though the nausea from the sight of blood seemed to be cured, I still preferred to use other methods to kill. Bloody murders leave a shitload of evidence, and I didn't feel like buying new clothes and burning my blood-spattered ones every week. But I needed to know how to stab someone to death, or sever an artery, or whatever, even though the odds of me using that tactic were slim.

At the campground, it was impossible to get internet reception. Despite all the cars, RVs, and paved roads, sometimes it felt like civilization was hundreds of miles away. If I wanted to research ways to kill someone, it would have to wait until I stayed at a place with wi-fi. For now, I had to kill victim number twenty-nine with primitive measures.

In the mountains, potential victims aren't as plentiful as they are in cities. It's rare to find a drunk pissing on a dumpster while you're camping in the woods. You're more likely to cross paths with a bear or a herd of raccoons raiding a campsite trash can, and they don't make good victims. Plus, I couldn't add them to my list since they don't officially qualify as "people."

It would be too risky to pick one of the campers, also. Camps can become tight-knit communities, and someone missing for even a few hours would set off a ton of alarms. Once the body was found, who would everyone consider the prime suspect? That's right. The creepy old guy camping by himself, that's who.

So, I needed to find someone who was just passing through the park. I thought about it for a couple of days, turning it over and over in my brain while I fished, napped in my tent, and strolled around the campground. Campers were obviously out. Tourists often stayed in nearby Gatlinburg and drove through the park, then circled back to the safety and warm showers of their hotels.

Who would be passing through the park and be nearly anonymous at the same time? I found my answer on a Saturday, as I was starting to panic because my weekly deadline was fast approaching and I still hadn't claimed a victim.

I decided to visit Clingman's Dome, which is the highest mountain in the Smoky Mountains, and it has a tall observation tower at the end of a steep half-mile-long path. A sign at the beginning of the path showed the distance to the Appalachian Trail. Then it hit me.

Hikers often travel alone, and they're just passing through the park. They're almost completely anonymous. If their family members didn't hear from them for several days, they would have no way of knowing where on the Appalachian Trail to look for them, because it stretches over 2,000 miles from Springer Mountain in north Georgia to Mount Katahdin in north-central Maine.

I once suggested to my ex-wife that we should try to complete a thru-hike, which is completing the entire length of the trail without interruption. Once she did a little research and saw how long it was, she shot the idea down in a hurry. After we divorced, I briefly considered trying to hike it, but I shot the idea down in a hurry when I figured out that I didn't want to. It would have been a more noble hobby than becoming a serial killer, but thousands of people complete the trail every year. I would have done something remarkable and nobody would have noticed.

I knew I was likely to find a hiker all by himself on the trail. All I had to do was find a place to wait, then figure out how to kill him.

After looking at a map of the area in the souvenir shop at the bottom of the path, I decided to get on the trail and follow it to a tall cliff a couple of miles away. Then I would wait.

Chapter Seventeen

The air is definitely thinner at higher elevations. After I made the two-mile walk to the cliff, I tried inhaling huge breaths of oxygen, but it didn't help much. I was more out of breath than a four-hundred-pound, three-pack-a-day lung transplant patient with emphysema. Good thing I decided I didn't want to hike this trail, because I wouldn't have made it more than five miles before deciding it was too hard, and sitting in a fishing boat was a much better option.

It took me about thirty minutes to get my breathing right. It's a good thing, too, because if someone had come along while I struggled for breath, I wouldn't have been able to kill them. This had to be done today. Sunday was less than half a day away, and I needed a victim to keep my streak going.

There was a thick tree branch lying next to the trail, about a foot longer than a normal baseball bat, and maybe a little larger in diameter. It would be perfect for cracking someone's skull. I sat on a boulder with the branch leaning against it, looking across the horizon at the haze that slightly covered the mountains as far as the eye could see. The valley floor was at least three hundred feet down a nearly vertical cliff.

My choices were to either bash someone's skull in and dispose of their body by throwing it over the cliff into the trees and weeds below, or to simply throw them off the cliff with the hope they would die from sudden impact after a hundred-yard nosedive. Hitting them with the stick seemed to be a better choice, because there was no guarantee someone would die from falling off a cliff, and I wouldn't be able to verify they were dead.

Be honest, would you scale down a huge cliff just to see if someone was dead? I know I wouldn't. So I waited with the branch handy.

It was about an hour before dark when I heard someone walking toward me. Their steps sounded heavy, like they were either a large person, or they were carrying a heavy load. I picked up the branch and stepped off the boulder to be in a better position to hit them. The steps got louder each second, until the hiker was undoubtedly within fifty yards of where I stood. I tightened my grip on the branch, squeezing it near one end, holding it like it was a baseball bat and I was Babe Ruth. I wasn't going to give him any warning. I was just going to smack him across his teeth to knock him down, then I would finish him off and dump him over the cliff.

As he rounded a bend in the trail, I saw him.

He appeared to be in his thirties, with dark, sweaty, matted hair, and a week-old beard. He had an oversized backpack, which added to his heavy footsteps. He was breathing hard, laboring along with a trekking pole in each hand. Even though we were more than a mile above sea level, the July air was hot. His sleeveless T-shirt was probably originally light gray, but now it was a dark charcoal color.

And his arms and neck were covered with tattoos.

When I saw the designs covering his skin, something shot through me like an electric jolt. It was like I had stepped on a live wire. Although his tattoos were different than Ethan's, they covered the same areas. The similarity caused me to act in a way I wasn't ready for. I felt a wave of sadness start to wash over me, gripping at my heart until I felt actual pain in my chest.

I dropped the end of the stick to the ground, but I held on to the opposite so it looked like a makeshift walking stick. I tried to make it look like I was some lost sightseer. The hiker got closer and closer, until I could see the color of his eyes and hear his lungs wheeze. He didn't seem to notice me until he got within ten yards, but he didn't slow down or pause. He just kept trudging on. As he passed me, I gave him a little wave and said, "How ya doin'?"

He didn't answer, but he acknowledged me with a quick nod and continued on. I think he was too out of breath to say anything, but he was probably raised by parents who taught him to be courteous to strangers, especially old strangers he might encounter on a hiking trail deep in the mountains.

After he passed, I was shaking so bad that I had to sit down on a rock. My chest still hurt, and I felt a bit out of breath. Then the tears came.

I wondered why this young man decided to hike such a demanding trail. He didn't seem to be the type who hiked very often. To the contrary, he gave me the impression he was on a quest to shed himself of demons. People tend to do that. When they're burdened by emotional pain they can't shake, they'll do something far out of character in order to shed that pain. Sometimes they sail around the world, or change jobs, or move to another town, or completely change their hairstyle.

Or take up a hobby where they kill people.

What kind of pain drove this young man? Did he lose a girlfriend or wife? Is he a soldier trying to rid himself of the horrors of war? Is he trying to forget a father who never gave him the time of day?

I leaned forward and let my tears drop to the dust. I hadn't really grieved over losing Ethan, and for some reason my soul decided now was the right time. Why it waited this long, I'll never know. Maybe I had to get to a certain place in my life before I could let my feelings loose. Maybe watching all those families play on the beach in Biloxi several days ago started a chain reaction that ended with me crying my eyeballs out because I saw a hiker who reminded me of my dead son.

After a long time, my sobs stopped and my tears dried up. I sat up and gave a look around me, and I noticed I couldn't see as well as I could when the hiker passed because it was starting to get dark. The sun had already gone behind the mountains to the west, but the sky still had some light left.

I've done a lot of things in my life that were idiotic, but this may have been the worst. I was a couple of miles from the Clingman's Dome parking lot with no shelter, food, water, or flashlight. Walking back along the trail in the dark was out of the question. I couldn't see rocks or roots that might trip me and cause me to break an ankle. I couldn't avoid rattlesnakes or copperheads. And possibly worst of all, I wouldn't see any bears until they ripped my face off with their claws.

Then again, staying out in the elements wasn't smart, either. I could have built a little shelter, but I had no way to start a fire, and I wasn't one of those outdoorsy magicians who could start a bonfire in a rainstorm with sparks from banging two rocks together. I didn't have a cigarette lighter.

I didn't know what to do, but one thing was sure. I wasn't ever going to let myself get trapped like this again. It was stupid of me to do this in the first place. I guess my success at killing people somehow made me think I was invincible, that I could do whatever I wanted and I wouldn't fail. I don't know why I would ever think that, because I had been nothing but a failure in my life up to this point. Why would I think my fortune had changed all of a sudden?

I was about to start looking for somewhere to hole up for the night when I heard more rustling on the trail, heading my way.

Great. Probably a bear. Not only was I going to get my face clawed off, but I was going to be supper for some mama bear and her cubs. But she wasn't going to take me without a fight.

The only weapon I had, other than rocks, was my baseball-bat tree branch. I still had my fingers wrapped around it, so I stood up and got myself ready to fight this thing to the death. I was surprisingly calm about it, too. It's like I had made peace with my life, and I wasn't afraid of dying. If anything, I felt a surge of adrenaline and a strength in my body equal to five men. This bear might get the best of me, but she was going to be too beaten up to enjoy her meal.

I hid behind a huge boulder and waited. My pulse raced and my breath grew quicker. I imagined giving this tree branch the hardest swing I could muster. Hard enough to break this bear's teeth. I could hear it getting closer by the second, coming slowly up the trail, scuffing its paws along the ground with each step. I gauged its distance from me by the sound, since I didn't dare poke my head around the boulder and let it see me before I could surprise it.

It was ten yards from me. Then seven. Then five.

Three.

Two.

I sprang forward and swung the branch with all my might. I braced my front leg and pushed with my rear leg, just like a baseball power hitter. I rotated my hips for extra force and snapped my wrists at impact.

I caught the bear right in the face, and it let out a yelp before it fell to the ground. It lay there in the near-darkness, motionless in the dust. I couldn't believe it. I had killed a bear with a stick. I bet Davy Crockett never did anything that badass in his life.

Except it wasn't a bear. It was a man.

I had hit a solo hiker in the mouth and knocked out a bunch of his teeth. I could see a small trickle of blood running out of his mouth and pooling in the dirt. He had more blood seeping out of his ears. I had hit him so hard one of his eyeballs hung from its socket by strings.

The guy didn't move, so I reached down and checked for a pulse. I checked his neck and his wrists to make sure, but I felt nothing. I had killed him with a blow to the head.

I looked back down the trail from the direction he had come in case he had someone with him farther back, but I didn't see anybody or hear any footsteps. Most hikers usually had their tents up by now. Why was this guy still walking when he should have been building a campfire?

It really didn't matter. He was gone, and I had to focus on the task at hand, which was disposing of his body.

I tried to roll him to the cliff's edge, but his backpack wouldn't let me. I unbuckled all his straps and managed to get the pack off him after a whole bunch of grunting and pulling. Since he wouldn't need his equipment any longer, I decided to commandeer it.

I set the pack aside and rolled him to the edge of the cliff. I pushed and kicked at his body until it fell into space and disappeared into the darkness. A moment later I heard something hit the ground far below me.

The backpack had a tent, a sleeping bag, a mess kit, a little propane burner, some water, some food, and a headband light, plus a bunch of other gadgets. I carried it along the trail until I found a spot good enough to pitch a tent for the night. Fifteen minutes later, I was gathering wood for a campfire. I found a lighter in the backpack, and I had a nice little fire going in no time at all.

I used his propane burner and mess kit to heat up some ramen noodles, and I ate two meals' worth. I drank all but a little of his water, then I got inside his sleeping bag and watched the fire burn itself out. I slept like a baby until a half-hour before first light the next morning.

Then I got up, stuffed all his gear back into the backpack, and threw it over the side of the cliff so it would appear it came off him as he fell.

A few hours later, I was bathing in the freezing water of a mountain stream. I shaved with no shaving foam and no mirror, but I wanted to make sure I looked somewhat presentable. After I packed up my tent and fishing gear into the rental SUV, I drove into Gatlinburg, sat down in a restaurant, and had my usual breakfast. For some reason, this one felt more satisfying than any so far. I had killed a bear last night, and I dumped his carcass over a cliff.

After I marked the twenty-ninth X on my calendar and finished my third cup of coffee, I drove away from Gatlinburg toward Virginia. A couple of hours later, I pulled into Bristol. I was dead tired, so I decided not to camp out for a few days, and I got a cheap hotel room. I showered with hot water for the first time in a long time, then I crawled into bed and fell immediately to sleep.

Tomorrow would start a new week, and I had to be fresh.

Chapter Eighteen

I HADN'T PLANNED ON STAYING IN BRISTOL, BUT AFTER MY NAP I went to a buffet restaurant a few blocks from my hotel, and I couldn't help but notice the number of old people. The restaurant was full of them. Except for a handful of families with children and parents younger than forty, I was nearly the youngest person in the place.

I never knew that about this area. All I knew was the town straddled the Tennessee and Virginia state lines, and they had a famous NASCAR track.

But this looked like a prime location for victims. Not that I would kill more than one here, because I could never take the chance of committing murder and then hang around to see if I could get a twofer.

Two victims for the price of one. The idea was a bit intriguing, I have to admit, but it would have thrown my goal into chaos. I promised myself I would get only one victim a week, and killing an extra person would be like cheating. Like I was sandbagging my victims so I could get a week off at the end of the year.

Nope, I was going to stick to my plan. One a week. And if I ever got myself into a situation where I had to deal with two people at once, well, I would just have to deal with it. But I couldn't worry about something that would probably never happen, anyway. As my grandfather used to say, "I'll deal with that avalanche when it hits." And he lived on the plains of the Midwest, which means he never had to worry about avalanches.

For a minute, I wondered how easy it would be to shove a steak knife between the ribs of some old woman at the buffet. Just mosey up behind her as if I'm looking at the food, and drive a blade right into her lung, then walk away.

Of course, that was a stupid idea. Blood. People. Security cameras. I would be nabbed before I made it to the door. Plus, I was hungry. I wanted to eat, not commit murder. At least for right now. Maybe the best thing to do was get away from such temptation as fast as I could.

I ate in a corner booth to stay out of the middle of the crowd, then I drove to downtown Bristol.

The town was quiet, with a main street lined by mom-and-pop stores. I found a parking spot and started walking toward a huge sign above the main street at the far end of town. It read *Bristol* in huge letters at the top, and *A Good Place To Live* below it. One side of the sign had *VA* and the other had *TENN*.

A Good Place To Live.

And commit murder.

I guess the street was the actual state line. Every few feet, there were bronze plaques embedded in the street, right between the double yellow lines. I waited on the sidewalk for traffic to clear, then I walked over to look at one of them.

It had a thick line running lengthwise down the middle, with *Tennessee* on one side, and *Virginia* on the other. Sure enough, this town was literally in two states. I don't know about you, but I thought that was pretty cool.

I probably could have stayed in Bristol for a few days, but I had to keep an eye on my finances for a few more weeks. That meant I couldn't stay in a hotel for more than a day or two at a time. I needed to use my camping gear when I could, so I went back to my hotel, packed my duffel bag, and went looking for a place to camp. Somewhere free would be best, if I could find it.

After driving around for a while, I found an old church sitting way off the road, with an overgrown gravel driveway leading to it. The grass was deep all around the church, which allowed me to be hidden even better. I parked my car in the back, stomped the grass down enough to pitch my tent, and basically made myself at home. Just in time for dark.

Kind of ironic, isn't it? A serial killer seeking refuge at a church. But I guess stranger things have happened, like when a mechanic's car breaks down, or a fireman's house burns.

Or when a son forgives his father for being a bad parent.

I slept in fits and starts that night. Around midnight, I woke up with severe cramps in my abdomen. Sharp, slicing pains shot through me, one after another, for at least two minutes. Then they stopped as quickly as they had started. I blamed it on the buffet food, but whatever it was, it felt like nails were passing through my guts.

I somehow managed to go back to sleep and woke up right at dawn the next morning. I packed up my gear and put it in the SUV in case I had to make a quick getaway, then I went for a walk down the road. I didn't have any coffee with me, so I had to do something to get my blood stirring.

A mile later, I passed an old woman walking her dog in the opposite direction. The road didn't have sidewalks, and we were both walking on the shoulder. She had on a bathrobe and pajamas, like her dog had forced her out of bed because it had to go outside. She gave me a smile and nodded at me as she walked by. I let her get twenty yards beyond me, then I turned and ran right at her. I hit my top speed—at my age my top speed isn't very fast—just as I reached her. She heard me coming and turned her head toward me the instant I swung my elbow into her cheekbone. She crumpled to the ground and let go of the dog's leash, and the dog ran off. She landed in a shallow ditch beside the road. It was no more than a foot deep, but her body landed perfectly in it, like she had been carried there by runoff from a heavy storm and came to rest as the water receded.

I stepped on her neck and held my foot there for a minute to make sure she wasn't alive, while at the same time I scanned both directions of the road for anyone driving by. Her pulse was gone when I checked.

Old people make easy victims. They don't run very well, they don't typically have a lot of strength, and they tend to trust people more than they should. This lady thought I was some ordinary guy out for a morning walk. I'm sure all she wanted to do was walk her little dog and go back to her kitchen for a bowl of oatmeal and a cup of coffee.

Coffee. Yeah, that's what I needed. I needed that jolt of caffeine. I glanced around and found thick honeysuckle bushes growing beside a road-side fence, then I picked up her dead body, which couldn't have weighed more than a hundred pounds, and stuffed her beneath them. I checked once again for witnesses, then I headed to the nearest caffeine store.

I found a chain diner near the interstate and sat down to order. No food, just coffee. I wasn't concerned about food at that moment. For some reason, I decided it would be a good time for more of my patented self-evaluation. Despite the clatter of utensils on plates and the drone of conversation all around me, I felt alone with my thoughts as I sipped at my cup.

Six weeks. That's how long it had been since Ethan was killed. Six weeks to the day. During that time, I had traveled more than three-quarters of the way across the continent, and killed six people, including the old woman lying in a ditch at the moment.

But the thing about those six weeks was I could barely remember them. Everything was a blur. It certainly didn't seem like six weeks had passed, that was for sure. Why was that? Why did I have a hard time remembering in detail the last month and a half? Why did I decide to drive so far away from Oregon? Was I running from tragedy? Did I consider those thousands of miles a buffer zone between me and the memory of my son?

I downed the last gulp from my cup and nodded at the waitress for a refill. I could already feel a new sense of alertness coursing through my brain.

There's one bad thing about killing someone so early in the week. That leaves a lot of time to think, a lot of time to reflect, a lot of time to wish things had been done differently.

I thought about how the sight of blood no longer seemed to bother me after Ethan's death, and how that could work out in my favor before this year was over. I guess I was still having a hard time figuring out why I didn't get sick from seeing blood, after having problems with it as far back as I could remember, but this was a situation where I didn't want to look a gift horse in the mouth.

That's another phrase I've heard all my life. It basically means when something good happens to you, don't over-evaluate it. Don't question it. And most importantly, don't turn it away.

Of course, I would have to test it out. I would have to actually kill someone with a knife or something that caused bleeding, and I would need to see how I reacted. If I got sick again, then I could pass it off as a glitch in my programming when I didn't throw up after seeing Ethan lying in a puddle of his own blood.

But if I didn't get sick, then a whole new subset of weapons were at my disposal. Razors. Machetes. Knives. Guns, even though I didn't have one, and I didn't like using them because of the noise.

All of a sudden, I became a much more efficient killer.

Those other questions—whether I was running away from my own personal tragedy and whether I considered distance between me and the west coast as a buffer—would have to wait until later, because my second cup of coffee was empty, and I decided to do some more traveling.

Before I left Bristol, I drove back down the road where I had killed the old lady earlier, and I have no idea why I did. Maybe it was to see if she was really dead and still lying in the ditch, or maybe it was to gloat over another murder. I tried to tell myself the real reason was to check for anything I might have left behind at my campsite behind the church, but I can't fool myself. I know me too well to pull the wool over my own eyes.

As I rounded the last curve before the driveway to the church, I slammed on the brakes and came to a complete stop.

A hundred yards ahead, the road was filled with the flashing lights of an ambulance and three police cars. There were three or four other official-looking cars parked on the side of the road.

And there was a group of people standing in the ditch, looking at something on the ground. There must have been seven or eight of them, all wearing blue latex gloves, pointing at different things on the ground around them. The rear doors of the ambulance were open, and inside was a gurney with a sheet draped over it. Beneath the sheet was a body.

I sat there for a few seconds, not knowing what to do. Should I turn around? Would they find that suspicious? Should I just sit here?

A couple of the people in the ditch stood up and looked at me. Maybe it was paranoia, maybe it was a total absence of rationality, but it seemed to me they looked at me longer than a normal glance would take. To me, they stared a hole through my windshield. I had to do something.

I eased my car forward and stopped a few feet from a uniformed officer blocking traffic. I rolled my window down as he walked over to talk to me.

"Sorry, sir. I can't let you drive past this point. You'll need to turn around and go a different route."

I leaned my face out of the window to look at him, then looked through the windshield at the group in the ditch, then back at the officer.

"Somebody have a wreck?" I asked.

"We have an investigation going on. I need you to turn your car around and go back that way," he told me as he pointed at the road behind me.

"Okay," I said. "Uh, what's the best way to get around this, since I need to go in that direction?" I pointed across the top of the steering wheel through the windshield.

He rattled off a few directions, but they went in one ear and out the other, because I wasn't in the least concerned about driving in that direction. I had seen all I needed to see. The part of me that wouldn't admit I wanted to see if the old woman was really dead would just have to deal with it.

In addition to the two cups of caffeine I drank earlier, I felt a new surge of adrenaline. I think it was the rush a killer gets when the public finds out someone has been killed. I can't say it was a thrill because that's not exactly what it was. It was more like a major sense of accomplishment, like receiving an award for a job well-done.

More than halfway through my year-long hobby, and this was the first time I got to see the result of my handiwork getting discovered by the authorities. It almost made me feel important.

Almost.

Chapter Nineteen

THE NEXT MORNING, I GASSED UP MY RENTAL CAR, GETTING ready to drive up Interstate 81 to Harrisonburg, Virginia. It was only about four hours away. I chose it because I woke up too tired to drive further than that. I don't know if it was the heat, the humidity, or possibly dehydration from too much coffee, but my energy level was way less than usual. As a precaution, I had a fresh container of coffee sitting on the roof of the car, where I could grab it after I filled the tank.

I considered getting a bite to eat, but I didn't have much of an appetite. I hoped a few miles on the road with the windows down would liven me up a little. I needed something to liven me up.

I was screwing the gas cap back on when I heard a voice behind me.

"Hey, are you heading north?"

I turned around, and there stood a young lady, no older than her early twenties, wearing a backpack, cutoff jeans, a tank top, and hiking boots. Her sandy hair barely touched her shoulders, and it looked like it hadn't been touched by a brush in several days. She looked as tired as I felt.

I looked at her for a few seconds before answering. The pause was long and awkward enough that she shifted her weight from one leg to the other and gave a nervous glance around to avoid looking at me.

"Yeah, I'm going north," I said. "Headed to Harrisonburg."

"Um, would you mind giving me a ride? I'm going to Harrisonburg, too," she said, and shifted her weight to the other leg again.

I gave her another long stare, saying nothing. The reason I took so long to answer was because I was kinda pissed off. It was like someone was playing a cruel joke on me. The perfect victim was begging me to let her get in my car, like she was offering herself up as some sort of sacrifice, and I wasn't going to be able to do a damn thing about it.

Why did I have to go and kill that old woman? Why couldn't I have waited an extra day? This young girl would have been my easiest victim yet.

Make no mistake about it. The road to hell may be paved with good intentions, but regrets scoop out the ditches on either side.

I wondered to myself whether I had the energy to talk with her for four hours. Four long hours on the road with a girl less than half my age, listening to her yak on and on about absolutely nothing, and me getting more and more tired with each syllable.

Or, she might lay down in the back seat and sleep.

"Yeah, I'll give you a ride," I said. I might have been pissed off because I couldn't kill her, but I didn't see any reason to be a jerk about it.

She gave me a big grin and tossed her backpack into the back seat, then waited for me to get behind the wheel before she opened the front passenger door.

"I don't mean to be rude, but is it okay if I lean my seat back and nap? I've been awake since yesterday morning."

If I had a passenger I couldn't kill, then the next best thing was a passenger who slept. This girl must have read my mind.

"That's fine," I said as I pulled onto the entrance ramp to Interstate 81. Ten seconds later, she had her seat leaned all the way back, with her eyes closed and her hands folded in her lap.

The quiet ride gave me more opportunity for thinking. I know I probably think too much, and I tend to over-analyze things, but I can't help it. What am I supposed to do when my mind is racing at a hundred miles an hour? It's not my fault I turned out to be the kind of person who pores over every thought a dozen times and gets a dozen different answers. It's just the way my brain is wired.

That, or it's the caffeine.

See? There I go again. I'm a hopeless case.

Was I happy with the way my hobby was going? Did I consider it a success so far?

I don't know if I was happy about things. I think satisfied is a more appropriate word. And yeah, it's been a success because I haven't been caught yet. I've had a few scares, a couple of cuts and bruises, and one gigantic personal tragedy, but overall it's turned out much better than I imagined it would. To be honest, I didn't think I would make it this far without getting caught, but after I killed that railroad yard security guard, everything seemed to come together.

It's like I suddenly became really good at something for the first time in my life, but that feeling disappeared this morning.

Maybe that's why I feel so tired. Maybe this whole fun hobby had run its course, and now it seemed to be more of a job. Maybe I felt that way because of Ethan's death.

I looked over at the girl. She was still sound asleep. Actually, I felt a little jealous, because I probably could have managed another few hours' sleep, too. It was like I had no energy, even though I had felt a rush of adrenaline only a few hours ago when the police found that old woman's body.

That adrenaline rush usually made me hungry, but I realized I hadn't eaten since before I went to bed yesterday. I normally get something for breakfast, even if it's nothing more than a piece of toast, but I simply didn't feel like it today. That made no sense to me. All my life I had eaten like a pig, and now the thought of food had zero appeal to me.

Then my stomach growled, loud enough to be heard over the whine of the tires on the pavement. I felt a small twinge in my gut.

Like it or not, I had to get something to eat.

I gave the girl a light tap on her thigh, and she jerked awake, her eyes wide, her hands help up in a defensive manner, as if she thought I was attacking her. She leaned away from me, as close to the passenger door as she could get, gasping for breath.

After a moment, she relaxed, realizing where she was. She lowered her hands and slowed her breathing.

"I'm sorry. I'm sorry," she said. "I didn't mean that. Just an old habit, I guess."

"I'm going to stop at a convenience store to grab a bite to eat. You hungry?" I asked her.

She thought for a moment. "Actually, yeah."

I watched the road for another mile before I asked her, "You're running from your husband, aren't you?"

"What? No. Of course not."

I glanced over at her, nodded, then looked back at the road. We rode in silence for another minute or two. It's usually easy to tell when somebody doesn't believe you, and I didn't believe her. My silence must have finally gotten to her.

"I'm running from my boyfriend. I'm not married," she said. She turned her head to look out the window, letting me know that was all she wanted to say. That gave me a clear view of her neck.

She had light finger-shaped bruises beneath her ear. Her boyfriend was a choker, one of those "men" who used violence to keep women in line.

"I'm sorry," I told her. She didn't respond.

I bought her a hamburger and soft drink at the next exit. She took them without a word, but she thanked me with her eyes. We ate in silence as we continued toward Harrisonburg.

Three hours later, I dropped her off near James Madison University. She walked away toward a group of apartments without saying a word to me. I imagine she felt she had already said too much.

Or maybe she felt I was just an older version of her boyfriend, someone who got what he wanted by hurting people. She probably felt that way about all men.

And who could blame her?

Part Four
EARTHQUAKE

Chapter Twenty

Something about my attitude changed after I let that girl out of my car in Harrisonburg. I felt sorry for her, and I'm not sure I could have killed her, knowing what I now knew about her. There had been other times in the past several months when I questioned what I was doing, causing such emotional pain for the families of my victims. Whenever those thoughts hit me, I would consider quitting my hobby and return to a normal life.

But that didn't last long. I had to finish what I started. I had to do this for myself.

Still, it usually took me a few days to come out of my self-doubting funk. I spent those days camping, surrounding myself with the peace and quiet of nature, alone with my thoughts. I camped in the Shenandoah National Forest for seven consecutive days after I left Harrisonburg. I drove to a small-town café for my Sunday celebration breakfast in the middle of those seven days, but I returned to the campsite after that.

Eventually, though, I got restless, so I packed up and drove northwest. I changed vehicles in Charleston, West Virginia and continued northward. I stopped for a couple of days in Toledo, Ohio, just long enough to change cars again and to find my thirty-first victim. A college-aged young man asked me to help him move his kayak from his pickup truck to the riverbank, and I obliged. I knocked him in the head with a rock the size of a pineapple, then laid his body in the kayak and set it adrift. By the time somebody could find him, I would be in Michigan.

I drove through the state from south to north, taking the back roads all the way to the Upper Peninsula. I never knew Michigan was such a beautiful place. It was an outdoorsman's dream location.

All I had ever really known about Michigan was images on television about the urban decay of Detroit and Flint, and every once in a while, I would watch the University of Michigan play football, but that was pretty much it.

After I crossed the bridge to the Upper Peninsula, I found a beautiful campsite in the Hiawatha National Forest and stayed there for five more days.

I might have stayed longer, but I choked a fisherman to death on my fifth day, and it's not a good idea for a murderer to hang around his crime scene. So, I headed west into Wisconsin.

I stopped in a small town called Tomahawk, for no other reason than I had to. I was exhausted. I was also suffering from a pretty bad case of, shall we say, intestinal problems.

During all that camping I had done for the past few weeks, I hadn't eaten very well. Other than my regular Sunday breakfasts, I existed on fish I caught or unhealthy snacks from a local convenience store. I'm sure I hadn't cooked the fish long enough, and that caused me to have stomach issues.

While I was in Toledo, I looked up my symptoms on the internet. I probably was suffering from dysentery. That condition is common in developing countries without proper sanitation.

Or, in my case, at campsites in the United States.

To be honest, my stomach had felt nauseous practically non-stop since my severe cramping episode in Bristol. It wasn't always bad, but it was always there on the outer fringes of my consciousness.

Another problem with camping is dehydration. I certainly didn't drink as much water as I should have, and now this diarrhea made things even worse. I've heard of people dying from dehydration caused by diarrhea.

If you don't die from it, you feel tired. No amount of rest would help. You had to get hydrated, and probably some antibiotics to get rid of the bacterial infection that caused this mess in the first place.

I decided to get the antibiotics later, because I was taking this route across the northern states for a reason. I had decided to get my revenge on the two-legged buffalo biker from South Dakota.

I had no idea how I was going to kill him, or where I would find him. I had tried to memorize the license plate on his motorcycle, but my old brain couldn't remember it, so I didn't know where he lived. All I know is I encountered him twice in two days in the Dakotas. That would be my starting point.

But I was in no hurry to get there. I had to get some of my strength back first. I'm not a small guy, but the biker was exactly the opposite of a small guy, with a ton of muscles on top of muscles. And then more muscles on top of that.

This would be the way to test myself, like I promised months ago. He might end up killing me instead, but he would be hurting after it was all over, one way or another. And I was going to rip the hell out of his shirt, like mine was after the buffalo kicked me in the head.

After two days of rest, rehydration, and getting my strength back, I decided to drive to Fargo, North Dakota, to use it as a starting point for finding the two-legged buffalo. All the way across Minnesota.

I changed cars in Minneapolis and arrived in Fargo as the sun was setting. Most of my strength had returned, and I felt much better, even though I still wasn't very hungry. But I thought a beer would taste pretty good after more than eight hours on the road.

A search on my cell phone found several bars, including a couple next door to hotels. I chose a nearby mom-and-pop place, checked in, and walked across the parking lot toward the bar next door. It was a rough-looking place, with neon beer signs flashing in blacked-out windows, pickup trucks, motorcycles, and 500-dollar cars in the parking lot, and the clack of billiard balls seeping through the walls.

The place was about three-quarters full. Every barstool but one was occupied with people sitting with their backs against the bar, watching the action at the four pool tables on the opposite side of the room. I didn't see a jukebox, but classic rock was booming from speakers hidden somewhere.

Nobody turned to look at me when I entered, which was fine with me. All I wanted to do was have a beer or two and chill out for a while.

And maybe find my next victim.

I was dressed about the same as most everybody else in there. Jeans, T-shirt, baseball cap. The best-dressed person was the waitress, who wore shorts two sizes too small and a shiny gold tank top, which was also about two sizes too small.

As I made my way to an empty two-chair table against the far wall, she intercepted me and asked what she could get for me. I ordered a beer and pointed at the table, telling her I planned on sitting there.

When she brought me a frosty mug a couple of minutes later, I asked if I could run a tab.

"We don't normally do that unless we know you," she said.

"Okay, that's fine."

"You new in town?"

"Just passing through, is all," I said. "I'll be here maybe a couple of days and then head on out. I'm on my way to Wyoming."

That part wasn't exactly true, but she didn't need to know that.

She wrote something on her order pad, then asked my name as she flipped a long lock of hair behind her shoulder. She was a brunette, probably in her fifties, but trying her best to look young with her tight outfit and hairdo from the 1980's. She was chewing gum.

I entertained the thought of killing her. That would get me to Sunday, and then the two-legged buffalo would come next. That is, if I could find him.

"Tell you what. If you don't say anything to Jeff, I'll let you run a tab. Just let me know when you're about to leave and I'll total it up for you," she told me.

"Who's Jeff?"

"The bartender," she said as she pointed over her shoulder with the eraser end of her pencil. "He owns the place."

"You've got a deal."

She gave a quick nod and strutted away to another table. I sipped my beer and watched the pool games at the other end of the room. The felt on the tables had holes and beer stains, and the pool cues were as crooked as a tree limb, but it really didn't matter to these guys. They weren't very good players, and no amount of perfect equipment would make their game any better. At least one player at each table smoked, and everybody held a beer bottle or mug when they weren't shooting.

I was without question the oldest person in the bar. The next oldest was probably the waitress. The youngest were two guys shooting pool who looked like the only way they made it inside the bar was with fake ID's.

Sometime within the next few hours, I had to make a decision. Saturday night at midnight was just over four days away. I had to have my next victim by then, and I needed to decide whether to kill someone in Fargo or at my next stop. The problem was that I really didn't know where my next stop would be, and getting there would take hours away from my hobby.

I decided not to get all upset over it at the moment. I needed to drink my beers, chill out, and get a good night's sleep. Except for Ethan's death, everything had worked out fine so far.

The first mug of beer tasted so good I decided I immediately needed another. The brunette waitress was behind the bar, setting a bunch of mugs upside down on a towel where the bar made an "L." I tried to get her attention, but she was focused on the mugs, so I sauntered over to her and sat down on an empty stool at the corner of the bar.

"Hi," I said as I plopped down my empty mug.

She raised her head, saw me sitting there, and her eyes instantly got wide. She glanced around the room as if she wanted to hide from someone.

"You can't sit there," she said in a loud whisper.

I imitated her frantic glances around the room. "Why not?"

She leaned across the bar so I could hear her better, and so she wouldn't have to talk so loud. "Since you're not from here, I guess you wouldn't know."

"Know what?" Something in my head told me I should at least stand up, but I sat there like a dummy. By now, several others in the bar noticed me, and were staring at me.

"Quake," she said. "That's his stool. The last person who sat there spent the night in the hospital."

Chapter Twenty-One

There are a few things in this world that cause me to make a quick decision. One of those things is when the words "Quake" and "hospital" are used together. I told the waitress to get me another beer, and I took it back to my table as fast as I could. There was no way I could finish my hobby if my neck was broken.

I pretended to look at my phone, but I could feel eyes looking at me. Even the click of the pool balls seemed to have stopped. After a few minutes, I realized it was all in my imagination, and nobody was looking at me at all. There was no need to take a chance, though. From that point on I decided to have the waitress bring me a beer instead of going to the bar myself.

Halfway through my third beer, I felt the presence of something huge standing beside me. My eyes followed a set of bulky legs to a massive torso with gigantic arms crossed across the chest. Long hair in a ponytail. Scruffy beard. A scowl on his face.

It was the two-legged buffalo. He looked mad. He also looked like he didn't recognize me. I must have one of those forgettable faces. Either that, or he's an absolute dumbass.

Of all the seedy hotels adjacent to seedy bars throughout the upper Midwest, what were the odds I would run into this guy on my first try? I figured it would have taken me several days to find him, if I managed to find him at all. The serial killer gods must have been looking out for me once again.

"I hear you've been sitting on the wrong stool at the bar," he said.

"Really? Who told you that?" I asked.

He turned his head toward the bar but didn't say anything. He looked at me again, and the scowl was still there. Yeah, he definitely didn't recognize me. I was just some other guy to him. Plus, he's without a doubt a dumbass.

"Look," I said, as I shifted in my chair. "I sat down for half a minute to order a beer. I didn't know it was your stool."

"It ain't my stool," he said. "It's Earthquake's."

"You're not..."—I glanced up and down at him—"...Earthquake?"

"I'm Bison. Quake is my brother."

Bison. The two-legged buffalo. You just can't make this shit up. This whole evening was beginning to turn into a Three Stooges episode.

"You mean your mom named you Earthquake and Bison?"

"No, dumbass. Those are our nicknames. That's what everybody calls us. And if you say one more word about my mother, I'm gonna rip your face off."

He didn't have to say anything else to convince me that he was dumber than a barn full of hay bales. He and his brother were bullies, plain and simple. The type of people who feel they can get what they want out of life by smashing someone's face. Zero intelligence. Their only response when faced with a verbal argument is to threaten violence.

I decided right then and there to kill this guy before I left Fargo.

"If I had known that was Quake's stool, I wouldn't have sat down," I said. "I apologize."

"That ain't good enough."

"Okay, then. What else do you need?"

"Just because I'm feeling nice today, I'm gonna give you a choice. You can either leave now, or you can stay here and get one of your thumbs broke."

I stood up and faced him. He was nearly twice as wide as me, and the top of my head reached barely to his chin. I could easily thrust a knee to his groin from this position, which would drop a normal man. But this guy didn't seem to be a normal man. He was a two-legged buffalo, and knees to the groin probably didn't hurt his kind.

Instead of a fight, I brushed past him and walked to the bar. I wasn't ready to nurse a broken thumb today. I slapped a twenty down and walked out without waiting for my change.

The parking lot was dark, with only one faint security light at the far corner. I glanced around for a motorcycle, knowing if there was one here, it would belong to Bison. There were a bunch of beat-up cars and pickup trucks, but no motorcycle.

But there was a car with a tag hanging from the grille, above the North Dakota license plate, that had a faded picture of a buffalo. Beneath the picture were block letters that spelled "BISON." The tag hung at an angle, held in place with zip ties.

Most of the car was maroon, but the hood and left front fender were white. The mismatched tires were mounted on black steel rims. Rust ate away at the rear fenders like skin cancer. Through the smoke-stained windows I could see ripped upholstery, and an ashtray full of cigarette butts. I had no idea what kind of car it was. Something small, like a Nissan or a Toyota. The thing was so beaten up and trashed, it was too difficult to tell.

It was all I could do to not laugh out loud. This big, tough bully named Bison drove a tiny piece of crap when he wasn't on his Harley. I expected him to drive a pickup truck raised four feet off the ground, or a Hummer, or even a mid-sized sedan, but certainly not this little thing.

I wondered if his brother Earthquake drove a Prius.

The only way I would be able to kill Bison was to catch him on some lonely road, or somewhere away from people. A guy like him would have a bunch of sidekicks who would like nothing better than to help him beat the hell out of somebody like me. So, I needed him away from town, preferably stranded. But how would I pull that off?

I looked around the parking lot for something sharp to put under one of his tires. A slow leak would give him enough time to get away from town before the tire went completely flat. If I followed him, I could pull up behind him just as he eased to a stop on the side of the road.

There was nothing laying on the ground in the lot sharper than a bottle cap, and I was just about to think of an alternative plan when I noticed a truck on the other side of the lot with "Bill's Drywall Services" in hand-painted letters along the side of its bed. In the bed were several pieces of drywall of different sizes, bags of spackling mix, several five-gallon buckets, and at least five boxes of drywall screws.

Perfect.

One of the boxes was open, and I grabbed a few of the inch-and-a-half screws inside. I would have rather had three-inch screws, but I couldn't risk rooting around inside the truck until I found them. That's a great way to end up with a bloody nose from some guy named Bill.

I walked back over to Bison's car, looked all around to ensure there weren't any cars coming down the road, then crouched and wedged a screw against the right rear tire and the pavement. Pointed end pressed into a groove in the nearly-gone tread. Then I moved to the other side of the car and did the same thing on the left rear tire. A flat rear tire was less likely to cause a crash than a flat front tire. I wanted him dead, but not from a wreck. I just wanted him stranded until I could kill him myself.

When he backed out of his parking space, the screws would dig through the tread, and air would slowly escape. If my luck held out, he would have two flat tires within about twenty minutes.

I took one last look at my handiwork, and I retreated to my rental car to wait.

While I sat there waiting for the two-legged buffalo to come out of the bar, I asked myself why I wanted to kill this guy. Sure, it made me mad when he laughed at me after the buffalo kicked me and my shirt got ripped to shreds. But something made me determined to come back and take out some extreme form of revenge on him. What made me want to do that?

I turned it over and over in my brain, trying to figure it out. This guy was a bully, and I hated bullies. But why did I hate bullies so much?

Because they run roughshod over those who are weaker or in no position to put up resistance. They get their way by threats of violence, intimidation, or some other form of punishment.

Bison threatened to break my thumbs, but he didn't threaten to kill me. That's because, as a bully, he's more interested in seeing me suffer. He'd rather see me humiliated. He'd rather see me bow down to him.

And that's exactly the way the management of my former employer acted toward someone like me. I was a no-name grunt on the manufacturing floor for decades, and the top management never knew I existed. They were bullies because they kept the workforce in line with threats of termination, or pay cuts, or moving the facility to another country.

Most of the time it seemed they did those things simply because they enjoyed it. That's why I hated them. They were bullies.

And the two-legged buffalo was a bully. He had to die. Painfully. Slowly, if possible.

I was nearly asleep, slumped down behind the steering wheel, when Bison walked out of the bar two hours after I put the screws under his tires. He was obviously drunk, taking stumbling steps through the parking lot, bumping into other cars. He made it to his vehicle, dug into his jeans pockets for the keys, dropped them, and stumbled a couple of steps backwards before gathering himself enough to bend over and pick them up.

He tried putting the key into the door lock, but dropped the whole bundle again.

"Dammit!"

I could hear him all the way across the parking lot, and my car was over a hundred feet from his.

He finally managed to crawl inside and start the engine. His back-up lights worked, to my surprise, as he put the car in reverse and pulled out of his parking space. By the time he put the transmission in drive, the screws were fully embedded in his tires. Now all I needed was a dark country road, and a few minutes for the screws to work.

My luck held out as he drove away from town, toward the darkness of the country. I let him get a hundred yards down the road before I followed. The way he was weaving all over the road, I was afraid he would be pulled over by a cop. But then again, I'm sure cops around here knew him well enough to leave him alone instead of risking a broken jaw.

Bison and his brother Earthquake probably weren't afraid of anything or anyone. That's one upside to having a body twice as large as normal. It makes people afraid of you. Even the cops.

After a few minutes, we were beyond the illuminated perimeter of Fargo. He was still weaving from centerline to ditch, slowing down, speeding up, driving exactly like a drunk. I stayed an eighth of a mile behind, far enough to not be noticed, but close enough to keep him in sight. The landscape seemed empty in the darkness, except for a few remote houses far off the road. There was no other traffic on the road but the two of us.

During one of Bison's drunken weaves, the rear of his car seemed to wiggle more than it should.

His tires were going flat.

He tried to keep it under control, but even a sober man can't handle a car very well with two flat tires. I slowed to keep pace with his car. He eventually gave in and pulled his car onto the shoulder. His tires had almost completely disintegrated, and were on the verge of turning into heavy rubber hammers that would have torn his rusted fender to shreds had he kept going.

By the time I pulled over behind him, he had stumbled out of his car and was bent over looking at the left rear tire. I stopped about thirty feet behind him, and I left my headlights on bright. I reached under the seat with my left hand and grabbed the tire tool I had taken from the trunk earlier, then pulled my fillet knife out of its sheath with my right.

It was time to see whether or not the sight of blood no longer bothered me. I closed my eyes and visualized a kill technique my instructor had taught me, but made me swear I would never use it unless my life was in danger. Once the technique was done correctly, death was just a few moments away. And Bison was going to be my test subject.

I opened my door and stepped out. Bison was now standing upright, shielding his eyes from my headlights, looking in my direction. I moved between the headlights and his body so I would appear as a silhouette. It's the same tactic that's been used in warfare for centuries. Put the sun in your opponent's eyes. Make them fight you and the bright light. If he couldn't see you clearly, he would literally be flailing at shadows.

"Need some help?" I yelled as I walked toward him.

"Don't need no damn help. I can take care of this." He was still shielding his eyes. I could tell he had no idea who he was talking to.

I closed the distance between us in a matter of a few steps. He couldn't have been a better target. Large body, illuminated by bright lights, with a pitch-black background. I focused on the front of his head, at the spot where his hair stopped and his forehead began. I was going to hit him with the tire tool hard enough to stun him until I could use my knife on him.

"Well, make sure you can take care of this, first," I said as I swung the tire iron in a rapid overhead arc straight at his head. I put as much force behind the blow as I dared without falling off balance.

All my life, I've heard the saying, "Don't judge a book by its cover," which I always thought was another way of saying that things aren't always as they seem. I never thought it would also mean that a drunk, two-legged buffalo can move faster than a cat when he needed to.

He must have seen the tire tool swinging at him at the last instant and managed to dodge a direct blow. I hit him on the right collarbone as he leaned to his left. It's a painful strike in its own right, but not nearly as effective as a hit on the head.

At the same instant, he delivered an uppercut to the right side of my stomach that nearly knocked me off my feet. It certainly knocked the oxygen from my lungs. It felt like I had been smacked with a sledgehammer. Or kicked by a buffalo. I have no idea how I managed to hold onto the tire tool.

Pain shot through my midsection like a lightning bolt. I bent forward, nearly doubling over, and threw a wild swing with my right hand at Bison's face. My hand missed, but the extra length of the blade dragged across his eyebrow and his cheek. He screamed and grabbed at his face, stumbling backwards into the rear of his car.

I managed to catch enough of my breath to stand as upright as I could, which was not all the way. Lightning was still shooting through my body, and I struggled to breathe, but Bison was in worse shape. He leaned against his car with both hands pressed against his eye socket. Blood seeped from between his fingers and trickled down his arms. His scream gradually turned into a growl.

"You son of a bitch! I'm gonna kill you!"

He pulled his hands away from his face and moved toward me. He had an open gash from just above his right eyebrow, across the eye socket, into his right cheek. Blood streamed down his face in wide ribbons. It looked like my knife had, at minimum, nicked his eyeball. It might have even cut right through it. Didn't matter to me, though. He wasn't going to need that eyeball any longer. He would be naked on a stainless-steel morgue table before midnight.

The loss of one eye damaged his depth perception, which meant he couldn't tell exactly how far away I was, or how quickly he could reach me.

He also wouldn't be able to see me delivering another blow with my left hand.

I used that handicap to my advantage. Instead of striking again with a downward angle, I swung the tire tool horizontally. He never saw it coming. The metal bar hit him in the neck just below his jawbone, which interrupted the flow of blood to his brain for an instant. That, combined with a blood-alcohol level that was probably five times the legal limit, dropped him to his knees. Then I hit him in the temple for good measure.

I staggered behind him, snaked my hand over his left shoulder and under his chin, and I pulled his head up and to the left. His neck and shoulder were completely exposed. His blood coated my hand and made his face slick. But that was okay. This was going to be over in a few seconds.

Needles of sharp pain coursed through my guts, and it was all I could do to get a lungful of air. I took a brief moment to suck in as much air as I could, steadying myself so I could finish him off. The technique I planned to use required a good bit of precision, and it was hard to hit a small target when you're blinded by pain and lack of oxygen. After a few breaths, my mind cleared enough to do what I needed to do. The pain in my abdomen was still enough to nearly double me over, but I could put up with it for a little longer.

I ran the knife's blade beneath the collar of his T-shirt and cut the cloth away from the top of his shoulder. My target was wide open.

Collarbones protrude slightly forward from the upper chest and create a little shallow depression behind them. When a long-enough blade is inserted to the hilt, at the right angle into this depression, and waggled back and forth, it severs all kinds of major arteries and lung tissue. This is the kill technique taught by my martial arts instructor. He called it a "bloodless kill," because the blood pools inside the body instead of spurting out of the knife wound to the skin. All you have to do is thrust the blade through the skin, push the handle forward, then back, then around in a quick circle to ensure maximum damage, then pull it out. The victim dies from blood loss in mere moments.

So, I guess Bison wasn't going to die a slow death like I wanted. But he was in a lot of pain, and this knife wound was going to be even more painful. That was good enough for me.

He was woozy from the two strikes from the tire tool, but he was coherent enough to know that he was in a lot of trouble. He just couldn't do anything about it.

I rested the tip of the knife in the depression behind the collarbone, putting enough pressure on it to let Bison feel its sharpness, but not enough pressure to pierce the skin. I closed my eyes and concentrated, blocking out the pain in my stomach, taking another deep breath.

I plunged the blade with all my strength, sinking it until it wouldn't go any deeper.

Bison might have been nearly unconscious, but he became a raging wild man when the pain hit him. He swung his arms, kicked with his legs, and screamed. I had a fairly tight hold on him, but I was no match for his strength. A flailing elbow caught me on my left side, just below my ribcage, opposite where he had punched me earlier. Lightning shot through my body once again. I don't know how, but I managed to keep the blade buried in his body.

He grabbed at the knife, screaming, throwing punches at me as if he was fighting off a swarm of bees. He tried to stand up, but he was too drunk and too brain-damaged. He got only as far as standing on his knees.

I fought off his hands as he reached for the knife. I wasn't going to allow him to kill himself by yanking the blade across a major artery. That was my job.

I slapped his hand away and shoved the knife handle towards his face, then yanked it back towards me. I finished by tracing an imaginary cross with the blade before I pulled it out.

Next thing I knew, everything turned upside down and I landed on my back in front of Bison. Somehow, he had managed enough strength to grab the front of my shirt and threw me over his shoulder like he was some kind of judo master. The impact knocked the air out of me again, and it was all I could do to roll onto my stomach. The pain in my gut was worse than ever.

On top of that, the knife was on the ground between Bison and me.

But he didn't see it. He propped himself up with his right hand on the ground while his left hand squeezed the wound on his shoulder. He sucked in huge, hoarse gulps of air, followed by bloody drool that puddled beneath him.

The top of his right lung had been sliced to ribbons, and each breath became more and more shallow as blood from severed arteries filled it up.

His breathing turned bubbly, almost liquid. Blood poured from his mouth with each exhale.

He raised his head and looked at me. There was no emotion in his eyes. No hatred. No animosity. I'm not even sure he saw me. I stared at him for no more than two seconds, then his eyes lost focus, and he collapsed face down. His breathing stopped.

The only blood around his body was the small amount that leaked from his mouth.

I struggled to my feet, still breathing hard and hurting like hell. I found my knife and tire tool and stumbled back to my car. I sat behind the steering wheel for a couple of minutes to get my shit together, but thinking is hard when you're in pain. I finally decided that I needed to get away from Bison's body as soon as I could.

There was no way I had enough strength to drag that huge slab of meat off the side of the road, so I had to leave him out in the open to be found by the first person who passed by.

I did a slow U-turn in the road and headed back to my hotel in Fargo. I needed a hot bath and ten hours of sleep.

Chapter Twenty-Two

I was jolted awake several hours later when a grenade went off in my room.

Then another grenade went off. Then another.

When the fog of sleep cleared from my head, I realized it wasn't a grenade. Someone was pounding on my hotel room door. Someone very large and very strong.

I worked my way out from under the covers, all sore and stiff from my fight with Bison, and telling myself I was too old to ever fight someone twice my size again, no matter if the odds were on my side.

I eased the door open as wide as the safety chain would allow and squinted out into the night air and the parking lot lights that seemed brighter than necessary. Through the glare, I just could make out the silhouette of a gigantic man, bigger than Bison. He kicked the door out of my hand, and it spun on its hinges and slammed against the opposite wall, the ruined safety chain ticking against the wood paneling.

A hand the size of a steering wheel grabbed a handful of my T-shirt and tossed me toward the bed. I fell short of the mattress and slammed my butt against the hard floor. For the third time that night, oxygen completely evacuated my lungs. I let out a yelp of pain as I heard the door slam shut. The giant man was in the room.

He stood over me with his fists clenched at his sides, breathing deep, angry breaths. He had to be at least six-ten, maybe even seven feet, and probably close to 350 pounds. His boots looked like two suitcases on either side of my outstretched legs.

There was no doubt in my mind who he was.

Earthquake.

"You know why I'm here."

It wasn't a question. It was a statement that didn't require a response. But I responded, anyway.

"Uh-uh. No," I managed, despite the absence of air in my lungs.

"Yeah, you do. You killed my brother. Now I'm gonna kill you."

I didn't say anything immediately. I waited until I could suck in enough air before I answered.

"Mister, I don't know who you are, and I don't know your brother, whoever he is. I've been here in my room nearly all night. I'm sick."

"Bullshit."

It took all the strength I could muster, but I raised my hand to give him a dismissive wave.

"I don't care if you believe me or not. I've been in bed with stomach cramps for no telling how long now." I managed to raise my eyes to look into his. "And do I look like somebody who could kill your brother? Or kill anybody? You know how old I am?"

He didn't say anything. He just stood there with his clenched fists and angry breathing.

I don't know how, but I struggled to my knees and leaned back against the bed. It felt like the air was returning to my lungs one molecule at a time. I reached toward the phone on the nightstand.

"You pick up that phone and I'll break your goddamned hand. And then I'll kill you," he said. I pulled my hand back.

"Okay...look. Whatever happened to your brother, I'm really, really sorry. But I'm telling you, I had nothing to do with it." My last few words sounded weak because I began to feel sick to my stomach. I could feel the nausea welling up.

"Somebody stabbed him on the side of the road," he said. "Ever' body in the bar said they saw him talkin' to you. Said he was gonna break your thumbs, but you ran out of there like a little bitch."

I nodded. "Yeah, that's right. I apparently sat in your seat by accident, and he let me know that was the wrong thing to do. He gave me a choice, and I chose to leave. I actually got sick and threw up in the parking lot right after I left. I came straight here and fell asleep."

The nausea was worse now. Whatever was in my stomach was about to come back up.

He cocked his head a little, as if he was trying to decide whether or not to believe me. While he was thinking, he reached down and pulled me away from the bed, forcing me to stand upright on my knees.

"I think yer lyin'." He cocked his fist as if he was going to punch my teeth out.

I shook my head with the little strength I had left. "No...no...I swear... it's..." The room began to spin, and the floor tilted to the left and right. I couldn't hold back any longer.

My body spasmed, and I puked blood all over the carpet and part of Earthquake's arm. Blood that smelled like sour beer. The room spun faster until the walls and floor became a blur, and that's the last thing I remember.

I don't know how many hours later I woke up, but I heard birds chirping, and it was starting to get light outside. I glanced up at the clock on the bedside table. Just after five a.m. I could see the sky lighten beyond the still-opened door. Earthquake had vanished, probably because he figured some sick old man like me had zero chance against his brother.

The way I felt at that moment, he was absolutely right. My sides were killing me, and I wouldn't have been surprised if some of my ribs were broken. My head hurt, my back hurt, my butt hurt, and my stomach felt like it could generate another round of vomit at any moment.

I somehow managed to stand up and balance myself against the bed. The room was an absolute mess. The door had an Earthquake-sized dent below the doorknob, which made it impossible to close even if I pushed as hard as I could. Earthquake had obviously ransacked my room before he left, because the bedspread was pulled off and all the contents of my backpack were scattered across the room.

Worse than all that, the carpet had a pinkish-brownish stain the size of a garbage can lid, the remains of what had been in my stomach. The smell was horrible.

There was no use checking out of this hotel. I needed to just disappear before the maids came around. If they saw the damage to the room, I'd be charged for it, and they might even call the cops. Getting questioned about why my door was smashed, and why I threw up a bunch of blood, and who beat me up was the last thing I needed.

Yeah, I needed to pack up my things and get as far away from Fargo as I could.

I shuffled into the bathroom to wash my face and brush my teeth. There was a bloody towel lying on the toilet. Earthquake must have wiped his arm off with it after I threw up on him. I turned to the mirror and raised my shirt. I was so sore it took nearly a full minute to get my shirt high enough to see my sides.

Sure enough, I was covered with bruises. I guess that's to be expected when you're hit with sledgehammers. My ribs were already dark gray and black, and taking a deep breath was completely out of the question.

I have no idea why I threw up all that blood, unless Bison hemorrhaged some of my internal organs. It sounds funny, but I'm glad I threw up when I did, because Earthquake probably would have killed me.

I made my way to the open door and checked on my rental car. It was still there, apparently without any damage. Earthquake most likely didn't know which car was mine. If he'd known, he could have turned it upside down all by himself.

After gathering up my things and tossing them into the back seat, I pulled out of the parking lot and drove south. As far as I was concerned, I never wanted to see Fargo again. Still, I managed a little smile to myself as I drove along. I had tested myself against a bigger, stronger opponent, and I won. I paid a heavy price, but I won.

The accomplishment gave me new energy and determination. For a while there, I'd felt like I was just going through the motions, as if it didn't matter whether or not I finished my personal challenge. But now, with a dead guy who was twice my size as proof that I'm good at what I do, I felt more focused than ever. I was going to finish this.

I didn't dare think I was invincible, but it felt damn near like I was.

Can you blame me? I had killed thirty-three people so far, and the closest I came to getting caught was in the railroad yard in Omaha. The odds of me reaching fifty-two kills without any roadblocks or hiccups were now better than ever. If I failed, it would be nobody's fault but my own, because I had nineteen kills to go, and the road ahead looked wide open and clear.

And then I accidentally coughed and sprayed bloody mist onto my car's dashboard and windshield. Man, talk about bringing me back to Earth.

Twenty miles south of Fargo, I pulled into a convenience store to clean up the mess. I needed gas, anyway, and I needed a cup of coffee even though my insides wouldn't like the sudden rush of caffeine.

After the car was full of gas and the blood wiped away, I leaned against the trunk, coffee in one hand, and studied a road map I had bought inside the store. I needed to get a new rental car fairly soon, but it had to be in a town large enough so that I would be somewhat anonymous. The last thing I needed was to be the only customer in more than a week at some mom-and-pop car rental place in some town no bigger than a wide spot in the road.

Welcome to Jerry's Family Restaurant and Car Rental.

I had already spent more than a few hours in places with names like Earl's Bar and Grill and Transmission Repair during this hobby of mine, so I knew those places were everywhere.

As I swallowed my last sip of coffee, I found my next destination on the map. I pushed away from the trunk to stand upright, every muscle in my body screaming at me. I leaned my head left and right to loosen my neck muscles, then leaned to each side to work out the kinks in my ribs. I tried to bend over to touch my feet, but my back had other things in mind. After about five minutes of attempted stretching, I eased myself behind the steering wheel of my car. Before I closed the door, I saw myself in the rear-view mirror. My hair looked like it had been combed with dynamite, gray stubble coated my cheeks, my eyes had more bags beneath them than a Greyhound bus, and my T-shirt had dirt and blood on it.

What I needed was a new car, a hot shower, a shave, and about twelve hours sleep. Once I got to my next town, those would be the first things on my agenda. I backed out of the store's parking lot, and began heading south and east to Cedar Rapids, Iowa.

Chapter Twenty-Three

I spent nearly four days in Cedar Rapids, resting, healing, planning, and thinking. It was four days I needed without realizing it. My Sunday breakfast tasted better than it had for months. The red X on my calendar was the most satisfying of them all so far. Even the coffee tasted better than usual.

That shouldn't imply that I was no longer sore from the beating I received from Bison, because everything was still bruised and tender, although getting better by the day. I wore the soreness like a badge of honor, like it was proof I could enter a valley of darkness and come out the other side still standing. It felt like I was practically invincible.

To me, I held all the cards for success in my hands. I no longer got sick at the sight of blood, which opened up many more options for killing. I had proven to myself that I could handle any victim, from the smallest old woman to the largest, strongest man. With the right circumstances, *everybody* was now a potential target. I was a moving target for the cops, which made me more difficult to find.

And the best part of all? I was more fired up than ever about finishing my task.

The biggest thing I did during my time in Cedar Rapids was buy new clothes. I threw my grimy jeans and dirty, blood-stained T-shirt in the trashcan beside my hotel room bed. I also found out what traveling across the country for months on end can do to an old man's body. Since I didn't have time to eat very often, I'd lost weight. I bought 38-inch waist jeans, which I'd worn for years. They used to fit a bit snug, but now they were loose. And because they kept dropping off my butt, I had to tighten my belt another notch. I still had two pair of my old jeans, but I wouldn't be wearing those unless there was some kind of emergency. Like being unable to find a laundromat.

Despite having a new sense of energy for my hobby, I still felt tired. Most people feel livelier when they lose weight, but for some reason, I didn't feel that way. At least, not yet. Maybe it takes several days before the metabolism catches up with the weight loss. Maybe all the sitting and driving sapped my energy. I don't know.

Whatever the reason, once my body caught up to my mental state, I would be practically unstoppable.

My plan for the next several weeks would take me across the northern tier of states, since the weather was still warm. Once late September rolled around, though, I would finish the last three months of my hobby through the southern states, to take advantage of milder temperatures. I don't do cold weather very well, and it's harder to move and react in a dangerous situation when you're wearing a heavy parka and snow boots.

The next stop would be Evansville, Indiana, down at the southern tip of the state. It would take me a full day to get there, and I planned to spend a few days sightseeing before killing my next victim. Then I would get a new car and head eastward.

Traveling across the flat plains of Iowa and Illinois is interesting. There are lots of small towns, surrounded by acres and acres of farmland. The dirt here is almost jet black, which makes it perfect for growing crops. No wonder there are corn and wheat fields everywhere.

The lack of hills and mountains also allows you to see towns several miles away, making them look closer than they actually are. The people are friendly, too. Most people I saw when I passed through those small towns waved at me. You don't see that enough these days. Kinda makes it hard to consider killing them.

But I can't think about stuff like that. A victim is a victim, no matter their circumstances. The most important thing to me is my hobby, and all my victims play a part in getting to my goal.

And then I thought about something. What was my plan after I reached fifty-two victims? Would I stop? Would I be *able* to stop? Would I keep going, resetting my goal to a hundred and four victims in two years? What if I decided to keep killing people until I died or got caught?

Was this new-found energy turning me into a grotesque monster? I mean, I know I'm a monster by definition, but not the kind who collects trophies from his victims, or kills for some kind of perverse sexual gratification. This was about nothing more than getting noticed, after years of invisibility and being ignored by the rest of the world.

Except for Bison, I had nothing personal against any of my victims. Sometimes they were nothing more than in the wrong place at the wrong time. An opportunity.

That's not to say I haven't been tempted to kill somebody because of anger or revenge. There's no telling how many times I wanted to kill my ex-wife and her new husband, but that would amount to shooting myself in the foot. I would be the first suspect, and it's hard to kill somebody when you're in police custody.

By the time I reached Effingham, Illinois, I had promised myself to stop at fifty-two victims. After that, I planned on retiring to some lakeside cabin and spend the rest of my life fishing. That is, if I survived all the way to fifty-two victims, and beyond.

As I pulled into a convenience store parking lot to get coffee and a snack, I also admitted to myself that even though the odds of completing my hobby were now greater than ever, so were the odds of getting caught before it was done. My odds were better because I was becoming more proficient at killing, and I had proven I could take on the most dangerous of victims, but the odds were also against me because every crime scene has physical evidence, and the longer I continued to kill, the more physical evidence the authorities would have.

I decided to focus on the better odds right after I focused on coffee and something to eat.

As I shut my car door, a pain shot through my abdomen like a lightning bolt. It hurt so bad it nearly doubled me over. I leaned against the door for a moment until it subsided, then I took a deep breath and went inside the store.

I put my coffee and a pastry on the counter and fished out my wallet. The slight twisting motion must have pulled something loose in my side, because I got hit with the lightning bolt again. I let out an involuntary grunt and hugged my arm against my stomach. It felt like a knife impaled to the hilt, twisting just below my ribs.

The store clerk was a little old lady who looked about seventy-five years old. She paused with my pastry hovered over a small plastic bag, looking at me with concern.

"You okay, hon?"

I couldn't say anything at the moment, so I just nodded, one hand propped against the counter and the other clutching at my guts.

"Want me to call an ambulance?"

I shook my head, and as I did, beads of sweat dropped from my forehead to the floor. I've heard of pain so intense it causes people to break out in a cold sweat, but I've never had it happen to me. Until now.

It took nearly a full minute, but the spasms faded enough for me to stand a little straighter and gather my breath. As I made it all the way upright, I glanced around the store. Thank goodness nobody else was in there but the two of us.

"You gonna be okay?" she asked.

"Yeah, I think so. I fell the other day and cracked a couple of ribs, and sometimes they really hurt when I move a particular way," I said.

"Like when you twist or something?"

"Yeah. Sometimes."

"Maybe you ought to start putting your wallet in your front pocket. You wouldn't have to reach behind you."

"Good idea. I think I'll try that," I said as I handed her a five-dollar bill.

She handed me my change. "Hope you get to feeling better, hon."

I gave her a smile and eased my way back to the car. The twisting knife in my side was gone, but I had a bruised feeling deep in my abdomen, like an invisible hand had grabbed a random internal organ and squeezed as hard as it could. Bison must have done more damage than I thought.

I sat behind the wheel and opened the center console. I tossed my wallet inside. I wasn't about to stuff that thing in the front pocket of my jeans. To hell with that shit.

A huge sip of hot coffee and a mouthful of pastry felt like heaven, and I closed my eyes and laid my head against the headrest to let the caffeine and sugar course through my body. One thing is for sure. Without coffee, I probably wouldn't have made it past ten victims.

The cold sweat had dried from my forehead and arms, even though my T-shirt was damp in the front and back. I began to feel better. Or at least, good enough to drive.

I put the car in gear and continued on towards Evansville.

I didn't kill anyone in Evansville, or in La Grange, Kentucky the next day, or Maysville, Kentucky the day after that. There was plenty of time to find a victim, and I was enjoying the drive through the Ohio Valley. One day at each town, that's all I needed. I didn't need to stay several days in one place so I could rest. My energy was back where it needed to be.

It's just that every once in a while, I had to fight off those sharp pains in my abdomen.

Those pains didn't bother me enough to keep from killing a hitchhiker in Wheeling, West Virginia. His body is now at the bottom of the Ohio River, weighed down with some rope and concrete blocks. By the time several giant catfish get done with him, there won't be anything left but a scattering of bones, and I'll be hundreds of miles away.

The last two weeks of August and all of September took me through Pennsylvania, upper New York state, Vermont, New Hampshire, Maine, Rhode Island, and Connecticut. My victims ranged from a farmer mending a fence along the side of the road, to a drunk college student trying to walk home on wobbly legs, to a factory worker who picked the wrong time to take a lunch break on third shift.

I kept them all impersonal. They weren't real people to me. They were the next notch on my belt, that's all.

In order to keep investigators from finding a pattern, I used different ways of killing them. A couple of them I stabbed, a few others I bashed them in the head with whatever I could find. There was at least one I smothered to death.

In order to save money, I camped when I could. I stayed in fleabag motels when I had to. I switched cars after every murder, using a different name and credit card each time. Sure, some genius detective might be able to figure things out, but I intended to make it as difficult as I could.

But seriously, how many detectives would be able to find a serial killer who killed in a different town by using a different method each time? If they did manage to figure out all these murders are connected, it would then be turned over to the FBI, and to the best of my knowledge, Elliot Ness died before I was born.

Odds are, I would never be caught, unless I was stupid enough to kill someone where I could be seen. Call it hubris, call it arrogance, call it confidence. Call it whatever you like, but the more I thought about it, the more satisfied I became with my plan and how it had worked so far. It was well-designed, with a minimal potential for failure, if I say so myself.

The possibility of getting caught was always there, no matter how small the odds. I'm smart enough to realize that. There's always the thought in the back of my head that I may not reach my goal, and I might not live to see the end of the year. I'm not stupid. Playing a dangerous game like this can take some tragic, surprising turns.

By September 30, I had been in New York City four days, and a homeless man lay dead behind a dumpster.

Victim number forty. Twelve more to go.

The nights in this part of the country had started to get chilly. It was time to head back south for the final three months. The light at the end of the tunnel was getting brighter.

Chapter Twenty-Four

It would be awfully tempting to stay in New York. Man, talk about your target-rich environments. This town has a potential victim every fifteen feet. And a lot of people didn't pay attention to what others did. They just walked along with their heads down, not looking at anyone. It seemed like it would be a snap to find fifty-two victims here. But that wasn't my plan, and I would be setting myself up for certain capture if I stayed.

So, I headed south. The night before, I had picked Dover, Delaware as my next stop. In a way, I would miss the vibrance and energy of New York. I was raised in a small town, the exact opposite of the Big Apple, and I was a bit of a fish out of water there. But I couldn't help but fall in love with that town just a little. I was there nearly five days, and I bet I heard no less than a dozen different languages on the streets, buses, and subways.

I wouldn't miss the traffic, though. I'm not the best driver in the world, but I'm not the worst, either. Still, I must have been given the finger twenty times. And that was just during my way out of town.

Dover wouldn't be like New York, that was for sure. But then again, what town is like New York?

One thing I noticed about being on the east coast is how close the towns are to each other. My trips consisted of short jaunts of no more than a few hours. When I was in the plains and mountain areas in the middle of the country, towns were further apart, and my trips sometimes lasted an entire day. That gave me more time for thinking and self-evaluation. But on the eastern part of the country, things seemed to happen much faster, which left me less time to think about my situation. I really only had enough time to get my job done, then move on.

I was going to be in the south in a few days, and things moved much slower there. I would resume my psychoanalysis once I got down there.

My stomach pains had hit me a few times in the past six weeks, but nothing as severe as they were before I arrived in Evansville. Whatever Bison had damaged inside of me was apparently beginning to heal. I guess internal damage takes longer to mend. The important thing is that I learned a lot about myself from facing Bison. I could survive a beating from a man twice my size, and my confidence grew tenfold as a result.

Not only has my mental health improved during these past few weeks, I've also gotten in better physical shape. I tightened my belt another notch a few weeks ago, and my blue jeans were definitely looser than they were when I started. The only downside is that I would eventually need to buy new pants.

I arrived in Dover on a beautiful sunny afternoon, although the wind nearly blew my rental car off the road several times. I forgot to check the weather forecast before I left New York, and the gusts caught me completely off guard. The next morning, I woke to the sound of rain tapping on my motel room window. I dressed and made my way across the parking lot to the café next door, my hood covering my head and my hands shoved into my pockets to protect them from the cold. What a difference a day makes. One day it's gorgeous, and the next it's a cold rain that's about five degrees away from turning to snow. Good thing I decided to head south instead of hanging around the northeast for a few more weeks. I've heard of nor'easters and how bad they can get in New England. I didn't know if that's what this storm was or not, but I wasn't going to find out.

I entered the café and stamped my feet on the welcome mat just inside the door to knock the rainwater off my pants and shoes. There weren't many people inside. Ten tables, with two men and a woman at one, and a man alone at another. The only staff I saw was a young waitress, who looked no older than eighteen, and an older lady refilling the sausage tray on the breakfast buffet.

"Hi. Just sit anywhere you want. I'll be with you in a minute," the waitress said to me before she disappeared into the kitchen.

I chose a small table and turned my coffee cup right side up. I was about to mark an X on week number forty of my calendar as she walked up with a full pot of coffee and filled my cup.

"What can I get you, sir? Care for the breakfast buffet this morning?"

I laid my calendar aside, squinted my eyes, and looked at the ceiling as if I was thinking.

"Hmmm. Let's see. How about a big ol' stack of pancakes? That's a good way to start a cold, rainy day, isn't it?"

"It sure is," she said as she wrote on her pad. "Would you like anything else? Water, maybe?" She had an easy smile, just like most waitresses in most small cafes. I never get tired of people like her. They somehow manage to make a bleak day a little brighter.

"Nope. Coffee is just fine, thanks. And I won't need the buffet. Just pancakes."

"Sounds good. I'll have these out to you in a few minutes." She gave me a quick grin and left to deliver my order to the kitchen.

I picked up my calendar, pulled my red pen from my pocket, and drew an X through Sunday, October 2. Three months left to go. I was getting closer and closer to the finish line.

I swallowed a third of my coffee in one huge gulp. It nearly burned my mouth, but it was good stuff. Nothing like a liquid shot of caffeine to start the morning.

I held the cup with both hands and stared at the far wall, not focusing on anything in particular. Just thinking. What if I drove west to the Mississippi river, then drove back east to the Atlantic, and continued that zig-zag pattern until I reached Florida by late November? That would leave me four weeks until the end of my hobby, and I could decide where to find my last four victims when that time came.

There were plenty of large towns scattered all through the southeast where I could find a rental car, and there were enough small towns where I could find an unsuspecting victim.

Plus, it's where I'd lived my whole life, except for the past several months. It's where the seeds of my hobby were planted, where I killed my first victim, and where I hoped to kill my last.

The waitress snapped me out of my daydream as she set the plate of pancakes on the table with one hand and refilled my coffee cup with the other.

"Anything else I can get you?"

I gave her a smile. "No thanks. I think I'm good for awhile. Just don't let me run out of coffee."

"You got it," she said as she left.

I watched as she went to check on the other diners. First the table with three people, then the man eating alone. She said something to him, then walked away. As she left, the guy turned his head and looked at me. I glanced away, pretending to look at nobody in particular as I took my first bite.

As I took my second bite, I looked at him again. He was still looking at me.

I glanced away, then back at him. He continued to stare.

He didn't look intimidating. Average size. Maybe early to mid-forties. Navy blue suit with a white shirt and bland tie. He looked like any average businessman in the United States. I certainly wasn't about to be intimidated by the likes of him. After surviving Bison, I could survive some snooty empty suit like this guy.

To make things worse, he reminded me of the CEO of my former employer, with his hundred-dollar haircut and his thousand-dollar shoes.

I finally had enough, so I clattered my fork down on my plate, sat back in my chair, and crossed my arms. The message was clear. I don't like it when people stare at me, and I wanted to make sure he understood that.

He looked at me for a couple of seconds longer, then returned his attention to his food. I gave it another five seconds before I took another bite of pancakes.

Did the waitress say something to him? Had he asked her to find out something about me? Was it all my imagination? Who the hell was this guy?

For a brief moment, I considered following him when he left, then figuring out how to make him victim number forty-one, but I couldn't see any advantage in getting my next victim this early in the week, in this type of weather. Nothing would feel better than causing this smug asshole a ton of misery and pain, but I would have to stay in town long enough for my clothes to dry before I could leave, and this guy probably had several dozen people attempting to contact him at all times. That increased my chances of getting caught.

The hell with it. He wasn't worth it, and I needed to focus on my goal instead of lashing out at anybody who looked at me the wrong way. If I was a younger man, I might have gotten up in his face, but in this case, the sense of calm that comes with getting older prevailed. If I killed everybody who stared at me, I would have reached fifty-two within a couple of months.

Fifteen minutes after the staring contest, the guy got up to leave. I watched him out of the corner of my eye, hoping he wouldn't force me to do something I didn't want. He paid his bill at the cash register, grabbed a toothpick from the plastic dispenser on the counter, and walked out the door without a word. I felt a cool, wet breeze blow into the cafe as he left.

After the waitress laid my bill on the table, I waited an additional ten minutes before I got up to leave. I wanted to make sure the guy was all the way gone before I ventured out into the rain. I was in no mood for getting wet and getting into a fight at the same time.

I trotted across the parking lot to my room, trying in vain to keep as dry as possible. It was hard enough without any other problems, but I had to grab onto my belt to hold my pants up as I ran. I apparently hadn't tightened my belt enough, and I could feel my pants slipping off my hips. I had to either start eating more or buy new clothes that fit better. I made a promise to myself to buy new pants once I got clear of this rough weather.

Mt. Airy, North Carolina was my next destination, a full day's ride from Dover. That's where I would buy new clothes and ditch my old ones.

Chapter Twenty-Five

On my way to Mt. Airy, I traveled through some of the same areas I'd already been to, and it brought back some memories. I passed near Harrisonburg, Virginia, where I dropped off the hitchhiker I picked up before I left Bristol, Tennessee. I wondered where she was now, and whether she managed to completely get away from her abusive boyfriend. I wondered if she was happy.

I wondered if the police in Bristol found any clues in the ditch where I had killed the old woman walking her dog. I don't know of anything they would have found except for possibly a footprint, but that's not likely because of all the grass in the ditch. But you never know. Cops can be pretty observant at times. Did they find the place I had camped behind the church across the road from her?

I wondered if the old woman's family was still grieving, or if she had any family at all. What if she had a bed-ridden husband at home?

The feeling that my murders had ripple effects was always present in the back of my mind, and sometimes I couldn't help but feel I was no better than Charles Manson or Ted Bundy. I was killing people to reach my own selfish goal, without regard to how others would be affected. Even a big, tough guy like Earthquake had been impacted by Bison's death. When he kicked down my door, he was clearly pissed off, but he was also in pain, and I can't think of anybody bigger or tougher than him.

I'll admit that killing Bison was based on revenge. That was my own selfishness controlling me. But that's okay. I spent years—decades actually —putting someone or something else first, whether it was my wife, my son, or my job. My time in this life grows shorter every day, and I no longer have the luxury of waiting.

A psychiatrist would have a field day with me. I'm definitely bipolar, or something. One minute I'm all fired up about my hobby, and the next minute I have feelings of regret and contemplation. I'm up, then I'm down. I'm energetic, then I'm tired. One minute I have a plan, and the next minute I'm winging it.

All I know is that I have to kill one person a week until the end of the year. Once I finish my goal, well...I guess I'll worry about what comes after that after I get there. For now, I had my next three stops planned. Mt. Airy, North Carolina, then Crossville, Tennessee, and then Union City, Tennessee. My forty-first victim would be somewhere along the way.

In Mt. Airy, I picked out different sizes of pants to try on. I used to wear a thirty-eight waist, but that obviously wasn't the case anymore, so I chose jeans with thirty-six, thirty-four, and thirty-two waists. The thirty-two-waist pair was too tight, without question. I could barely button them, so I tossed them aside. The thirty-fours were a little snug, but not too bad. I decided against them because I needed pants that allowed me to move when I needed to.

The thirty-six pair fit the best. They were a tiny bit loose, but they gave me to best options for kicking and running and moving fast when I needed.

I pulled my belt from my old baggy pair of pants and held it up in front of my face. It was down to the last notch, with dark lines next to the other holes where the buckle had rubbed, sometimes for years. I decided it was time for a new belt, too, so I bought a good leather one, along with two pair of jeans.

Back at my hotel, I took all my old baggy pants, rolled them into a ball, and tossed them into the dumpster behind the building. In a couple of days, they would be in a landfill somewhere, just like a few of the people I had killed.

I tucked my shirt into my new pants and put on my new belt, then gave myself a look in the mirror. I was definitely thinner than I had been in years. Most of my adult life, I weighed over two-hundred pounds, but I was well below that now. Maybe one-eighty-five.

Another ten pounds and I would be about the same size Ethan had...

Ethan.

I hadn't thought of him in weeks. Not since I saw that tattoo-covered hiker in the Smoky Mountains.

What is it about a simple electrical impulse darting through your brain that can cause your whole body to stop what it was doing and begin trembling? That's all the thought of him was. A tiny, fleeting bit of memory. A small firing of neurons that shot through me as powerful as a lightning bolt.

My legs turned rubbery, and my stomach flip-flopped like I had sped over a tiny hill in a car. I had to sit down.

Sometimes you miss someone without even realizing it, and it hit me that I missed my son. Even though we grew apart over the years, our reconnection in Oregon had held so much promise. We were going to be father and son once again. I was going to be a proud grandpa. He had welcomed me back into his world despite our past. He had grown into a man.

And all that was taken away by a bullet hole through his chest. Watching my son die as I held him is something I will never be able to get over. It may slip to the back of my mind from time to time, but I'll never forget it.

And what about Ethan's wife, Sara? I had never attempted to contact her after I left Oregon. She was carrying my grandchild, and I hadn't checked on her to see how she was doing. Sometimes I'm an utter piece of shit, and other times I think I'm a decent person.

Lately, I've been jumping back and forth between the two so fast I can't keep up with myself.

See what I mean? Bi-polar. Up one minute and down the next.

After sitting there for nearly twenty minutes, grieving and feeling melancholy, I got mad at myself. I had a mission to complete, and things that gave me second thoughts threatened to derail the whole operation. I took stock of my life, at where I stood at the moment, and my goal to become infamous was the only thing that made me get out of bed in the morning. I didn't know it years ago, but back then, Ethan was the reason I decided to face each day. I realized that now. But Ethan was gone, and all that I had left of him was his memory.

At that moment, the most important thing in my life was my hobby. It was the only way I could feel proud of myself, since everything else I had done before fell short of that.

I decided to stand up and do some shadow boxing. Something—anything—to get my mind out of its funk.

A few punches, some bobbing and weaving, a little bit of footwork, and before long my blood was stirring enough to cause a light sheen of sweat on my skin. My mind cleared. The negative thoughts faded to the background. Five minutes was enough to make me feel much better.

That is, until I decided to test my mobility while wearing my new jeans. I made the mistake of attempting a kick.

Most martial art kicks require the kicker to "chamber" his leg. That means he has to pull his leg tight to his body, sort of like a snake that coils before it strikes. This is one reason martial artists work on their flexibility so much. It's nearly impossible to chamber your leg if you're not flexible. You use a combination of flexibility, your thigh muscles, your hip flexors, and your abdominal muscles to do it.

People who have never practiced martial arts sometimes believe the object of a good kick is to get the foot up in the air, but actually, the object is to get the knee pulled high, toward the stomach. You get your knee up, the foot will automatically follow. Unless you have the anatomy of a space alien or something.

So, that's what I did. I chambered my knee, ready to throw a shadow kick at an imaginary opponent. Just as my knee got to its highest point, somebody stabbed me in the stomach with a hot flaming spear. Pain and cramps hit me so hard I was knocked to the floor. I laid on my side, curled into a ball, my arms folded across my abdomen. It must have taken me two full minutes before I could draw a breath.

After I sucked in a lungful of air, I managed to roll over onto my knees and elbows. The cramping had stopped, but the stabbing pain was still there. The light coating of sweat from shadowboxing was replaced with a cold, clammy sweat. After a few deep breaths, I felt sick. Whatever I had in my stomach was about to come back up.

I crawled as fast as I could on all fours to the bathroom. The toilet seemed to be a mile away. I made it with less than a second to spare before everything in my stomach poured out of me.

Coffee, pancakes, junk food.

And blood.

Everything in the toilet was tinged red. The toilet water was dark pink. There were even a few clumps of what looked like blood clots embedded in the chunks of pancake.

I thought I had nearly healed from my fight with Bison, but apparently I was wrong. Something inside of me was torn, and it was going to be a long time before it got better. The thing is, I didn't have a long time. I had less than three months to kill twelve more people. The way it now looked, I probably wouldn't be better by the end of December, but I had to keep going.

I had to finish this, even if it killed me.

I sat back against the tub, gasping for air, sweating that same cold sweat. My stomach felt better, now that it was empty, but now my throat was sore from all that food coming back up.

At least my new jeans fit me, and they had enough room to let me kick when I needed to. After tonight, though, I decided not to rely on kicking anymore. Punching, choking, stabbing, and running would do just fine.

Four days later, I was on my way to Memphis, heading south from Union City, Tennessee. Victim number forty-one was in the books, lying at the bottom of Reelfoot Lake, weighed down by concrete blocks. The guy picked the wrong lonely boat dock at the wrong time of night to go fishing by himself. His small boat was sent idling to the middle of the lake to make it look like he fell overboard and drowned. It would be a long time before they found his body beneath the dock.

Forty-one down, eleven more to go.

I planned to switch cars in Memphis, eat my Sunday breakfast, mark my calendar, and head back to the east coast. I wasn't very hungry, but I had to keep to my routine.

Huntsville, Alabama would be my next stop.

Chapter Twenty-Six

The reason I chose Huntsville is because it's a good halfway point between Memphis and Atlanta. I didn't feel like driving nearly eight hours to Atlanta, and I was in no hurry to get to the east coast. Besides, Huntsville had a couple of places I wanted to visit.

I saw the first place as I pulled into town. A huge, full-scale replica of the Apollo rocket used in the moon program in the 1960s. I was fascinated by the space program when I was a kid, but I had never seen anything related to it other than the grainy images broadcast on TV. And now, here it was, sitting only a few yards off the highway, aimed at the heavens like a giant black and white dart. It looked like it was part of a large compound that also contained Space Camp, an SR-71 spy plane, and a replica of the space shuttle.

Oh, yeah. I definitely had to visit this place. I might have appeared to be a thousand years old to some people, but things like this made me feel like a young boy again.

Less than fifteen minutes after I checked into a small hotel, I headed back to the museum.

As I passed through the gift shop at the entrance and paid my admission, my mind was focused on two things. I wanted to soak up everything about NASA and astronauts and rockets while I was there, and I planned on keeping my eyes peeled for a potential victim. I soon discovered it would be a tough task to do both, because being inside the largest space museum on Earth was worse than a kid in a candy store. Every time I tried to focus on someone who stood a good chance to be victim number forty-two, I would pass by an exhibit of an Apollo space suit, or a history of nearby Redstone Arsenal, or Werner Von Braun's office as it appeared when he headed NASA's rocket program.

Oh well. I didn't have to find someone to kill today. I had nearly a full week to get that done. So, after a dozen distractions, I finally decided to forget about finding a victim and just enjoy my time at the museum. This would probably be a once-in-a-lifetime experience for me, and I wanted to make the most of it.

I spent nearly five hours there, and by the time I finished, I was tired, hungry, and thirsty. I could have eaten at the museum's cafeteria, but they didn't serve beer, and I was in the mood for a couple.

One of the clerks in the gift shop gave me a few options for places that served food and beer nearby, and I picked the closest. It was a restaurant-slash-bar in a hotel a couple of miles away, which seemed perfect to me. I was there in ten minutes.

There was no one to seat me when I walked in, so I picked an empty seat at the bar. The place wasn't very busy, probably due to the fact it was a Monday afternoon. There was one other man sitting at the bar, and a few booths held two or three diners each.

A man stood behind the bar, talking to the waitress while he set mugs of beer on her tray, which she would then deliver to one of the booths. After he finished that, he came over to me to take my order. I looked up at the menu handwritten in chalk on a blackboard on the wall behind him. After nearly a full minute, I couldn't decide what I wanted to eat.

"Well, how about if I order my drink first? I'm having trouble making up my mind here," I said to him.

"That'll work," he said. He didn't seem bothered by my indecision. If the bar had been full, I might have received a different reaction, but no hurries, so no worries.

I ordered a draft beer, and he turned away to grab an empty mug from the shelf.

The waitress came walking past my stool right then.

"Get the ribeye," she said as she breezed by. She didn't pause to wait for my answer. It was as if she knew my thoughts. That, or she had seen hundreds of people who sat on this very stool and couldn't decide what to eat.

The bartender pulled a coaster from a stack at the end of the bar and plopped it on the bar in front of me before setting the mug full of beer on top of it.

"Did you make up your mind yet?" he asked.

"Uh, yeah. She told me I should get the ribeye steak." I pointed my thumb over my shoulder in the direction where the waitress was taking the orders of two more people who had sat down in a booth.

The bartender laughed. "Yeah. She kinda has a knack for reading minds."

"Does she own a steak business on the side?"

"Nah. But she definitely knows the best things to order. She's never been wrong yet, and she's been doing this for years."

"Then I guess I'll have the ribeye. Medium well."

"Okay," he said as he wrote it on a small pad of paper. "What kind of side do you want?"

I looked up at the blackboard menu again. There were lots of sides to choose from.

"Uh...."

The bartender looked past me and yelled, "Hey, Cheryl."

The waitress was still with the diners who had entered a few minutes before, writing on the order pad on her tray. She turned her head toward us, but kept her eyes focused on her pad as she wrote.

"Baked potato," she yelled back.

I looked at the bartender and grinned. "I guess I'll have a baked potato," I said.

"I'm telling you, she knows what she's talking about," he said as he disappeared through a door into the kitchen.

I sat there for a few minutes, drinking my beer and thinking about nothing. My mind usually ran at a hundred miles an hour, but I was too tired and hungry for that now. All I felt like doing was to sit still for a while, eat my food, and then lay down for a long night's sleep.

The restaurant was not busy, and the only noise was the usual restaurant sounds. Feet shuffling, muted words spoken, the buzz of a wooden chair as it was pulled away from the table, the faint clack of its legs as someone sat down and scooted forward, silverware rattling against plates.

The bartender kept busy by walking back and forth between the bar and the kitchen, but I didn't pay him much attention. I was pretty much lost in my own little world.

Then Cheryl, the waitress, plopped her tray onto the bar, leaned back against it, and let out a huff of air. She must have noticed me looking at her, because she turned to face me, one arm propped against the bar.

"What brings you to town?" she asked.

"How do you know I'm from out of town?"

"I know almost everybody who comes in here," she said. "If I don't know a customer, it's pretty safe to assume they're from out of town."

"Well, yeah, I'm from out of town. I'm just passing through."

"You on vacation?" she asked.

"I guess you could say that. I'm retired. I decided to do a little traveling and see some places I've never been."

"Yeah? Where all have you been?"

I hesitated before I answered, but I hid my hesitation by looking at the ceiling and wiggling my head back and forth, as if I was thinking. Should I tell her where I'd been? Where I started? How long I had been traveling?

"Mainly around the south," I finally said. "Columbia, South Carolina. Atlanta. Memphis. Places like that."

"Oh, so the bigger cities, then?"

"Yeah, mainly. I wouldn't mind going to the small towns, but they don't tend to have good hotels."

The bartender walked out of the kitchen with my food on a plate and slid it in front of me. The steak was still sizzling and the baked potato was steaming. I nodded a thank you at him and started cutting my steak.

"Well, you'd be surprised at what you're missing," Cheryl said. "Some of the best places to see are in the smaller towns. Sometimes they're literally in the middle of nowhere." I grinned and nodded as I took a big bite of the steak. It practically melted in my mouth.

She picked up her tray and started to walk away, but she stopped as if a sudden thought hit her.

"Oh, and you need to be careful. Apparently, there's a serial killer on the loose. I heard it on the news this morning."

Right then, a chunk of food got stuck in my throat, and I started coughing. Cheryl looked at me for a second before she stepped closer and patted me on the back a few times. I coughed for a full minute before the food cleared out of my windpipe. I wiped my watery eyes and mouth with a napkin and did my best to catch my breath.

"You okay?" she asked.

I nodded and cleared my throat again. "Yeah, but mostly embarrassed. I guess something went down the wrong way."

"Probably. It's either that or you weren't expecting to hear about a serial killer on the loose."

"Where's this killer at? Where do I need to avoid?"

She squinted an eye as she thought for a moment, trying to recall the town. "Hmm. I don't quite remember, to be honest. I just heard a quick mention of it on the radio when I was coming to work today. Seems like it might have been several places. Enjoy your meal."

She walked away to check on the other customers, while I caught my breath and thought about getting the hell out of there. Was it just a coincidence she mentioned a serial killer to me? I hadn't paid attention to the news for several days, and I did it was just the local news in whatever town I happened to be.

All of a sudden, I didn't feel like sitting at a bar in public any longer. I felt like I wanted to hide.

I waved the bartender over and asked for a to-go box. He gave me a puzzled look, but he reached under the bar and pulled out a Styrofoam container without saying anything. I couldn't concern myself with what he thought, because I needed to get back to my hotel room and check the news online. If the feds know about my murders, then there was a possibility they have evidence and a few suspects. Or maybe a "person of interest."

As I drove back to the hotel, my mind raced at a thousand miles an hour. What did they know? Which bodies had been found? Did Earthquake turn me in after I killed his brother? Which of my fake identities did I need to throw away?

I felt sick to my stomach, and if there had been any food in it, I would have thrown up all over myself.

I burst into my hotel room, tossed the food container on the bed, and opened my laptop. It took a few moments to connect to the hotel wi-fi. Once I was online, I searched for national news of a serial killer.

The first link that came up was a story about an FBI manhunt for the killer of a fast-food manager, who was found in the trunk of her car in Arizona this past June. They had no physical evidence, but they had footage from a surveillance camera above the back door of the restaurant that showed someone slicing her tire, then breaking her neck much later. The killer in the video resembled the person who killed a man in an alley behind a bar in Memphis a couple of weeks later. That murder was also caught by surveillance camera. They were looking into other unsolved murders to see if there was a connection to these two.

Dammit. I forgot about security cameras. How in the world could I not remember that? I must have been so hopped up on adrenaline that I never gave them the first thought. I felt like kicking myself. I might as well have hung a sign around my neck with my name on it.

The footage of both murders was grainy and a bit out of focus, which was in my favor. The FBI couldn't get a complete physical description of the killer, but they assumed it was a man. Unknown age. Undetermined height. Unknown hair color. But they were looking for *somebody*. They put out an advisory to all police districts nationwide suggesting people avoid certain places at night, such as rest areas, dimly-lit parking lots, rural roads, and abandoned buildings.

It wouldn't take long for them to identify me. Not with the technology they used.

Well, that did it. Giving up isn't an option, so I had to be more careful with my last few victims. I had to make sure and avoid buildings and alleys. The only places I could trust were deserted roads at night. That cut down my potential victims by two-thirds, at least.

I closed my laptop and began to think of a plan for the next eleven victims. I was so close to my finish line I could taste it. But I was also tired all the time, spitting up blood every now and then, and running out of places to look for victims. My hobby just became a lot harder.

This was a test. A test of my resolve. A test of my endurance. A test of my intellect. I had to pass the test.

I *had* to.

I sat down on the hotel room bed and tried to come up with a game plan. Should I leave? Should I stay put for several days? What were the advantages and disadvantages of each? Where did I need to go next?

My mind was too tired to think. It was all too much to wrap my brain around, and before long, it overwhelmed me to the point that I fell over onto my pillow and squinted my eyes shut. The next thing I knew, it was the next morning. I had fallen asleep and slept all night. I still had my clothes and shoes on, and there are fewer things more uncomfortable than sleeping all night while dressed in jeans and fully-laced shoes. My feet felt swollen and pinched, and my belt cut into my waist. My shirt was twisted around my torso from all the rolling I did in my sleep.

But the real reason I woke up was a cramp in my stomach. It wasn't a sharp pain, but it was enough to make me sit up and wrap my arms around my abdomen until it eased.

This was getting ridiculous. I definitely had some kind of damage from the fight with Bison. I couldn't tell if he'd broken a rib, or ruptured a stomach muscle, or what. He certainly did something bad to me, that was for sure.

Then a thought hit me. What if I was just hungry?

I looked over at the food container on the desk. Still unopened. I didn't need to open it, either, because I knew there was a cold steak and a soggy baked potato inside, and I had no intention of eating that for breakfast. I may be someone who lives off convenience store food and coffee most of the time, but I still had my limits.

Twelve bucks down the drain, and I got one bite out of it. I wasn't exactly broke, but I sure couldn't continue to throw money away like that.

According to the bedside clock, it was 8:23. I pulled the curtains open to look outside and was smacked in the face by bright sunlight. It looked like a beautiful day. October in this part of the country always seemed to have the most perfect weather. The days are warm and the nights are cool. The sunshine beckoned like a siren, urging me to go outside.

That's all it took for me. I tossed off my shoes and clothes, pulled out a clean set of pants, and turned on the shower. Just because I felt like shit was no reason I had to look like it.

Chapter Twenty-Seven

Two days later, I was worn out from driving all around Huntsville and seeing the sights. I rarely ate, except for a bit of junk food and coffee, which certainly was one reason I was so tired. Any thought of my next victim had been pushed to the back burner. It was still several days before the deadline to kill victim number forty-two.

The pain in my stomach had disappeared once again. There was no rhyme or reason for why it came and went from time to time. Maybe it had something to do with internal bleeding, or gas, or just plain old nerves.

I convinced myself it was nerves. I was eleven victims away from my goal, and I had a steeper hill to climb now because of the FBI's focus on finding a serial killer. Personally, I think anyone's stomach would be tied up in knots if they were in my situation. This goal meant everything to me. It was basically the only thing worth living for, and I could see the finish line. But the finish line was now clouded by the very real possibility of getting caught.

There were now more frequent moments when I just wanted the whole thing to be over and done with. I wasn't nearly as gung-ho as I was at the beginning of the year, when the idea of infamy was so fresh in my thinking. There were times lately when it felt like I was just going through the motions, like a beaten-down field hand who trudged through his day without feeling, without thinking, because that's all there was left in his life, and that's all he had ever known. All that mattered was getting to the end of the day.

I thought back on some of my first murders, and I had to admit I no longer had the passion I felt back then. Maybe it was because of months on the road. Maybe it was because I had nobody in my life. Maybe it was because of the injury from Bison that was taking too long to heal. Maybe it was because I was an old man who worried too much about why things happened the way they did, like Ethan dying. I should have just let things roll off my back and not concern myself with issues that do nothing but muddy the waters.

My calendar sat on the hotel room's desk beside my laptop, wallet, keys, and a small pile of coins. I picked it up to give myself encouragement that I was nearly finished, that my goal was within easy reach despite my own self-doubt.

It was wrinkled and curved from all the days it had stayed rolled up in my pocket. There were coffee stains on it, and one corner of the front page was torn off. I flipped through the pages, giving each month a quick scan as the red X's snapped past. The last two pages were empty, as was half of the third-to-last page. I tossed the calendar on the bed, and it curled halfway into a tube, wobbling back and forth, until it settled with some of its pages curved upward like praying hands calling out to the heavens.

That calendar was a perfect metaphor for me. A tired, worn-out collection of images and places bundled into a package that hardly anyone paid attention to, but still with something to offer if anyone would simply bother to look.

Just after dark, I decided to get out of town, but not before I claimed my next victim. Three days was long enough here, and the longer I stayed, the better my chances of getting caught. I decided to cruise around in the outskirts of town, looking for a lone jogger, or a dog walker, or someone who would be an easy victim. My deadline was still a few days away, but I didn't want to wait until I was desperate, especially with the way I'd been feeling lately. I definitely didn't need a stress ulcer to go along with whatever damage Bison had done to me.

There were lots of suburban neighborhoods to choose from, some with small ranch-style houses, others with huge, three-story mansions. I couldn't attack someone on a residential street with houses everywhere, though. People have security cameras all around their house, even in the doorbell, and somebody would certainly catch me on video.

The feds were probably going to catch me before all this was over, but I wasn't going to help them do it. And if they never catch me and wind up empty-handed, oh well. I worked for more than three decades and still wound up with nearly nothing. My heart ain't gonna bleed for them.

I drove around for over an hour before I found someone alone in an area without cameras. A young woman, probably no older than twenty-five, was kneeling beside her bicycle on the shoulder of the road. The bike was upside down, and she was fiddling with the chain, as if it had slipped off the sprocket. She was wearing a bicycle helmet and the typical clothes cyclists wear. Spandex shorts, tight zippered top, running shoes. She had a frown on her face as she slapped and tugged at the chain.

I pulled over a few yards beyond her and got out of my car. I didn't have any weapons on me except for my fists and feet, but I figured I could offer to help her and break her neck when she least expected it.

"Can I give you a hand?" I said to her as I approached.

She held up a grease-stained palm. "No thanks," she said. "I'm good."

"You don't look like it," I said. I was fifteen feet from her. "Let me help you. I used to own a bicycle shop, and I bet I can have you fixed up in less than a minute."

"No, really. I'm fine."

She stood up as I reached her. She was no more than five feet tall, but her legs were rippled with muscle, and she didn't have an ounce of fat on her body. I would rather pick someone who looked more like a couch potato, but sometimes beggars can't be choosers. It was too dark to see her eyes very well, but her body language spoke volumes. She was wary of me.

"Sir, please," she said as she unzipped her shirt pocket and reached inside. She either had a small gun or a bottle of pepper spray, but she didn't pull it out.

I ignored her and looked at the upside-down bicycle. The chain hung like a dead snake around the bike's frame, curled into a loop in the middle, with bits of long grass stems caught in the links.

"Kinda looks like you got a bunch of grass hung up in the chain and it jumped off the sprocket," I said.

"Yeah, I got a little too close to the roadside," she said without looking away from me. She kept her hand in her pocket, still holding the gun, or pepper spray, or whatever it was. My bet was on pepper spray. Or maybe nothing at all.

We stood no more than six feet apart. Close enough to have a conversation, but far enough away that I couldn't attack her without taking at least two steps to get within reach. This girl was smart.

I knelt down and wiggled the chain a bit, pretending to know what I was doing. In reality, I had no idea how to untangle it, but I wasn't going to let her know that. I ignored her cautious demeanor and did my best to seem like a helpful, friendly, elderly, next door neighbor. If I focused on the bicycle instead of her, she'd be more likely to let down her guard and take her hand out of her pocket.

After about a minute, I had the chain untangled and back on both sprockets. She stayed a safe distance away, but her body language seemed to be more relaxed than before. Maybe she no longer considered me a threat, which meant she had at least loosened her grip on whatever was in her pocket.

But I had to get her closer in order to kill her. I was squatting down, and a man my age can't move fast enough from that position to grab a twenty-something athlete who was standing. I took a gamble that she trusted me enough to lean in close to me, as long as I asked the right questions.

"You have a flashlight on your phone?" I asked. "I need to show you what happened to the chain, and I left my phone in my car."

She hesitated a beat, then pulled her phone from the same pocket where she had her hand. She turned toward me enough to give a brief glance of her side, and I could tell she had nothing else in the pocket. No gun. No pepper spray. Nothing. The shirt hugged her ribcage like a second skin. If anything thicker than a credit card was in there, I would have seen it.

She clicked on the light and aimed it at the bicycle. I pointed to the general area of the front sprocket.

"You see that?" I asked.

"You mean the pedals?"

"No. That," I said, pointing again at nothing specific.

She looked for several seconds, moving her head left and right, up and down, trying to see what I was talking about.

"No, I guess I don't see anything."

"It's really small, but if you don't get it fixed, it'll cause you a lot more problems."

She squinted her eyes and leaned in for a better look, and I pounced.

It felt to me like I exploded out of my crouch faster than a rocket, but to her, I was no quicker than cold molasses pouring from a jar. I reached for her neck with both hands, but she slapped them away with her left hand, still holding her phone. The beam from the flashlight arced across my face and blinded me for an instant. I didn't see the heel of her right hand coming as it smacked me square on the nose. Stars exploded in front of my eyes and I got dizzy for a few seconds. I shook the cobwebs from my brain, blinked hard, and tried to bull-rush her. That was stupid, because I zoomed past her as she turned aside like a matador in a bullfight.

I have heard that during the adrenaline rush of a fight, any martial arts training you might have will sometimes evaporate until you're left with animal fight-or-flight instinct. My teacher warned me dozens of times to keep my arms tucked during a fight, because an extended arm was just like handing your opponent a lever to throw you around like a rag doll.

"A straight arm is a weak arm," he used to tell me.

So, with all that in mind, I acted like an idiot and reached out to grab her as she dodged me. I may as well have handed her my arm and said, "Here, take this and use it to kick my ass." Which she did.

She grabbed my wrist with both hands and made a rapid, violent twist with her entire body in the opposite direction I was charging. The sudden change in direction caused my feet to fly out in front of me. The first part of me that hit the ground was the back of my neck. Not only was I knocked nearly unconscious by the impact, but my arm was on fire from my wrist to my shoulder, as if every muscle, tendon, and ligament had been ripped to shreds.

She stood over me, still holding my wrist with both hands, glowering down at me. She had my hand bent at the wrist as her knee pressed against the outside of my elbow. It felt like my arm was about to snap in two different places, and there was nothing I could do about it.

A straight arm is a weak arm.

My eyes cleared just in time to see the bottom of her shoe before she stomped my face. My vision went black, but I felt the pain from another stomp to my groin, and two to my stomach.

She let go of my arm, and I curled into a fetal position, gasping for breath. I heard the patter of her shoes on the pavement as she hurried to her bike. A metallic scrape, a rustling as her feet found the pedals, a crunch as the tires rolled across the fine gravel on the road, and then nothing but the chirp of crickets.

Chapter Twenty-Eight

Everything happened so fast. I went from a crouch to standing to lying flat on my back to curled up in a ball in less than three seconds. I hadn't felt this much pain in a long time. Every part of my body above my knees hurt. I've made some major mistakes in my life, and picking this particular victim definitely ranks up there with the worst of them. I knew she would be in good physical condition just by the way she looked, but how could I have known she was a self-defense expert?

She must have been a martial arts instructor, or a member of the military, or even worse, an off-duty police officer.

If she was a cop, there was a good chance the police were on their way to find me. She had a phone, so they were probably on their way whether she was a cop or not. That's why I needed to get my ass up off the ground and get out of there.

I tried to roll over onto my stomach so I could get my legs under me and stand up, but every slight movement hurt too much. I probably had broken ribs, a broken nose, and crushed testicles. My insides hurt even more than they had during the past several weeks after my fight with Bison.

But I had to get up. If I stayed on the ground, it would be only a few minutes before I could enjoy a nice ride in the back seat of a police cruiser with my hands cuffed behind my back. That would be the end of my goal. Eleven victims short. The finish line so close I could literally reach out and grab it, but one stupid move resulted in my worthless, broken carcass curled up into a lump of pain and misery.

I guess it was the fear of getting caught that provided enough energy to stand up. I don't know what else it could have been. After the agony of rising to my feet and the long walk back to my car, I nearly felt like quitting. Just giving up. Everything was too hard. I was too old for this. Too old and too tired.

But then I brought myself back to reality and remembered why I started doing this in the first place. I had been a nobody for too long. The world was going to remember me, come hell or high water. Giving up was too easy. If I was going to be known as the most infamous serial killer of all time, I had to get moving.

Suck it up, you loser, and quit your whining.

I inhaled as deep a breath as the pain in my guts would allow and started the car. I had to get far away from Huntsville as fast as I could. First, though, I had to get my stuff out of the hotel room. I just hoped I wouldn't pass out from the pain before I got there.

My reflection in the bathroom mirror was nearly as painful as the beating that girl gave me. My nose was swollen and bleeding, my lip was cut, and my hair had blades of grass tangled through it. Like my dad used to say, I was ugly enough to scare the hell out of daylight. I used toilet paper instead of a washcloth to wipe away the blood and dirt. Paper could be flushed down a toilet to get rid of the evidence. If I left a bloody washcloth for the maids to find, there would be a phone call to the cops within five minutes.

The paper fell apart and shredded across my whisker stubble, but it did its job. I used at least half a roll just on my face and neck. I used the rest on my hands, arms, and shoulders.

After I cleaned up as best I could, I threw my things into the car and headed west toward Interstate 65. I needed to get further south.

I made it five miles before I had to pull over. The pain was too intense. My vision was blurry. I was weaving all over the road. I ran a red light at an intersection. I have no idea what kept me from having a wreck. I wasn't sure what I needed to do, but driving a car at that moment wasn't one of them.

I found a convenience store and pulled in, sliding to a stop in the parking space furthest from the door. I needed to find the bathroom and throw up, because my guts were killing me. I opened the door and managed to force myself to my feet by sheer will. I must have stood up too fast, because everything started spinning.

That's the last thing I remember.

It's strange how you can fall asleep or get knocked unconscious, and when you wake up, it seems like mere seconds have gone by, but in reality, it may have been several minutes or hours.

Or, in my case, days.

I didn't wake up all at once. It was a gradual progression of fuzzy noises followed by the feeling of clean sheets against my body followed by bright images coming into focus through my irritated eyes. It was a full two minutes before I realized I was lying in a hospital bed, in a hospital room, surrounded by beeping and buzzing hospital equipment. I felt like I was waking up from a three-day drunk. My eyelids weighed several pounds each, and all I wanted to do was go back to sleep.

How did I get here? The last thing I recalled was getting out of my car and getting dizzy. Someone, some good Samaritan, must have called an ambulance for me after I passed out.

I had a tube from an IV bag inserted into the back of my hand and held in place with a piece of tape. Other than that, I wasn't connected to anything else. I felt around my body and found I was sore all over, but mainly in my ribcage, stomach, and face. The plastic ID bracelet around my wrist had my name as JOHN DOE. They probably found one of my five driver's licenses in my wallet, even though my real license spelled my first name without the H, like it was supposed to be. The other information on the bracelet for date of birth and allergies had N/A. For my sex there was an M. At least they got that right.

The bracelet also had red stripes on it. I was used to the clear bracelets. I don't think I've ever seen one with stripes. But then again, I haven't been in a hospital in years, so it must be something new.

The window shades were open, and I saw buildings and rolling hills in the distance. From the way it looked, I was four or five stories up. The late afternoon sun lit up the trees and their leaves that were beginning to change colors with the season. But late afternoon of what day? Was it Sunday already? Did I miss the deadline for my latest victim? How long had I been in this hospital?

I needed answers, so I fumbled around until I found the button to call the nurse's station. Less than a minute later a nurse wearing purple scrubs knocked on my door and came in.

"Hey, you're awake. How you feeling?" she asked.

I didn't know whether to lie or tell the truth. I felt like shit, but I doubted she needed to know that at that moment.

"I don't know. Not too bad, I guess," I said.

She moved over to the IV bag and checked the drip rate, then pulled out a blood pressure cuff and wrapped it around my bicep. As she pumped the air bladder to inflate it, the grip felt like a vise on my arm.

"One forty over one-oh-five," she said as she released the air pressure. "You're a little high. Might be because of your pain level. By the way, what's your name?"

I didn't answer. What name was I supposed to give her? She was either testing me to see if I gave the correct name, or she didn't know my name and was genuinely wanting to know. I decided to play it safe and change the subject.

"What town am I in, and what day is it?"

"Huntsville. It's Saturday afternoon. We had you knocked out for quite a while after you were brought in last night. What happened to you? Did you get hit by a car?"

"I don't know. I can't remember. That's why I didn't know what day it was."

"I'll let the doctor know you're awake," she said as she opened the door to leave. "He'll explain everything to you."

That's not what I needed. What I needed was to get out of this hospital and away from Huntsville. The more people knew about me, the greater the chances of getting caught, and I was too close to the finish line to let that happen.

I looked around the room for my clothes and shoes. If I was going to escape this place, I wouldn't be able to get very far by wearing a backwards gown with my ass sticking out. I saw a plastic bag beneath a chair and assumed it contained my stuff.

The IV needle hurt like hell when I jerked it out of my hand, but not nearly as bad as the pain in the rest of my body. I was going to be sore for a long time from the beating I took. I hurt from my face all the way down to my crotch. My ribs were in the most pain. It was hard to take a breath without needles stabbing into me.

I swung my legs over the side of the bed, eased my feet onto the cold tile floor, and tested my leg strength. They were strong enough to get me to a standing position, and probably strong enough to walk, but they were nowhere near strong enough to run.

I was in the process of zipping up my jeans when two doctors walked into the room. A man and a woman. The man was tall, with thinning blond hair and a groomed beard spattered with bits of gray. He had the subdued arrogance of a former athlete, like a star quarterback or pitcher. The woman was average height with dark, shoulder-length hair. She had a smile that gave the impression she didn't have an arrogant bone in her body. They both wore the typical white lab coats most doctors wear. The man had "Dr. McCann" embroidered on his, with something else beneath his name that I couldn't make out. The woman had a name pin with "Dr. Michelle Glover."

I froze, my hands still on my zipper, and nearly panicked. I didn't have a ready explanation for why I was putting my pants on, or why I was out of my bed, for that matter. All I could manage was a blank stare.

"Sir, why are you out of bed?" Dr. McCann asked. "I hope you weren't planning on leaving."

"I've got things I gotta do," I said. I plopped my foot onto the chair seat to tie my shoe. It was true I had a deadline to meet, but something about this doctor's tone of voice rubbed me the wrong way. Too loud. Too authoritative. Too used to people doing whatever he commanded.

"No sir, you can't leave yet. First of all, we don't know your name, and there's something else we need to discuss with you."

"Why do you need my name? I didn't ask to be brought here. It wasn't my decision."

"If somebody hadn't called an ambulance for you, you would probably be dead by now."

I paused tying my shoe long enough to look at his face. He seemed to be telling the truth, but I had no way of knowing, and it didn't matter if he was telling the truth or not. His attitude had already pissed me off. Plus, I was running out of time. There was no way I could afford to miss my goal when I was this close. I looked back down at my shoe as I finished tying it.

"Well, I guess not everyone's a bad person. I got lucky enough for one of the good ones to help me. Either way, I'm not staying. I'll give you my address so you can send the bill to me, if that's what you're worried about," I said.

"No sir, that's not what I'm worried about. You've got several significant injuries that need more attention, and there's also..." He didn't finish what he was saying. He glanced at Dr. Glover, then back at me.

I set my foot back on the floor and turned to face him. "What? There's also what?" I asked them.

"Excuse us just a minute," Dr. Glover said. She pulled Dr. McCann to the door and talked to him in soft, whispered tones that I couldn't hear. After less than a minute, he looked over at me, back at her, then opened the door and walked out.

She pushed the door shut and turned back to me. I was standing with my hands on my hips, a posture of impatience. I wasn't going to talk with her very long before I walked out. If they failed to get any billing information out of me, even if it was fake, it would be their loss. Feeling guilty over a large corporation not getting a few hundred dollars wasn't one of my finer traits.

She sat down in one of the two chairs in the room. She seemed to have an ease and gentleness about her that was opposite of Dr. McCann.

"Why don't you have a seat, Mister..." she said, prompting me to give my name. Without question, she had more people skills and better bedside manner than McCann. She knew how to coax people to give information on their own terms.

I hesitated for a moment. Should I use my real name, or one of the others? At this point in the game, did it really matter?

"Call me Jon," I said. "And I'd rather stand, if that's okay with you."

She cleared her throat and adjusted her position on the chair, then she looked into my eyes. Not at my face, like many doctors would do, but directly into the inner depths of my soul. Her eyes were gentle and kind, just like her smile had been when she first came into the room.

"Okay, Jon. My name's Michelle. We didn't know your name because your wallet has five different driver's licenses in it. We didn't have a way to contact someone in your family."

My stomach started to knot up all of a sudden. Maybe it was because we were about to wade into uncharted waters for me. I'd never had a doctor sit down with me like this, as if we were about to have a heart-to-heart talk. This couldn't be a good thing. I felt my blood pressure rising.

"When they brought you in, you were in pretty rough shape. You were unconscious. You had been throwing up blood. You were bleeding from your nose and lip, and you had bruises all over your body. Bad bruises, some of them. Your vital signs were unstable. Dr. McCann thought you had been hit by a car from the kinds of injuries you had. I mean, you had a broken rib and a hairline fracture on your cheekbone. He took several X-rays, and in addition to your fractures, he found some other things he didn't like, so he ordered a CAT scan. We had to use heavy sedation on you, because he didn't want you to wake up in the middle of the scan and do something that might hurt yourself even worse. That's one reason why you didn't wake up until today."

The knot in my stomach tightened. It gurgled loud enough for both of us to hear. She was courteous enough to pretend to ignore it.

"What...uh...what other kinds of things did he find? Am I gonna be okay?"

"The X-rays showed some abnormalities, and we focused on them with the CAT scan. You've got a major concussion," she said. She left that last word hanging, like there was something else she needed to tell me, but really didn't want to.

"And...?" I asked.

She took a measured breath and gathered herself before looking into my soul again with those gentle eyes of hers.

"We found a mass and two spots in your abdomen that were abnormal, and we need to do a needle biopsy to determine if they're cancer," she said.

My blood pressure increased even higher than it had been. The knot in my stomach tightened again. I wanted to cover my belly with my hand, an instinctive move whenever I felt discomfort, but my hand was shaking so hard I had to put it in my jeans pocket instead.

"Um...what...uh...what kind of cancer could it be?" My voice shook as hard as my hand.

"The mass is on your pancreas. The spots are on your liver and your stomach. We don't know if it's cancer. It could be nothing to worry about, but if it *is* cancer, and it's metastasized, we need to do something about it quickly."

I had heard of pancreatic cancer, and how difficult it is to treat. Especially if it's spread.

"Metast..." I began. I didn't know how to pronounce that word.

"Metastasized," she said. "That means it's spread to other organs."

I squeezed my eyes shut because I couldn't think of anything else to do. That's when the floor started tilting back and forth, like an earthquake. My legs turned into wet noodles, and I wobbled like I was about to fall over. That wasn't what I wanted to hear. This can't be happening. Not cancer. Not now. Not to me.

She grabbed my shoulders and eased me onto a chair, holding my hand in both of hers as she sat down. I grabbed the back of my chair with my other hand to keep the room from spinning and tilting. A trickle of sweat ran down my forehead, and whatever was left in my stomach wanted to come out.

"Are you okay? Do you want some water?" she asked.

I drew a couple of deep breaths to clear my head. I've never had something like that happen to me before. People have said things to me that upset me, but nothing had ever made me experience a fainting spell. My concussion probably didn't help matters, either.

I shook my head no. I couldn't have swallowed anything, even if my life depended on it.

"That's a lot to wrap your brain around right after you wake up in a hospital," she told me. "I'm sorry you had to be told this way."

I nodded. "Are you a cancer doctor?"

"Yes. I was asked to come in here with Dr. McCann to talk with you about getting a biopsy."

After my heart rate slowed down and my senses came back, I looked up at her.

"So, if I have cancer, and it's spread all over me, how much time would I have? Give me the worst-case scenario."

"It might be something else besides cancer," she said.

"Please, Doctor. Humor me. I need to know what I'm facing here. Any kind of feel-good words right now won't do a damn thing for me if in reality I'm likely to die from this."

She looked away and let out a small sigh. This seemed to be a question she didn't want to answer. She looked back at me, but she didn't say anything.

I raised my eyebrows at her, a non-verbal way of asking the question again.

"Right now, we don't really..."

"How long?" I insisted.

She looked at me for a long, uncomfortable moment before she spoke.

"We won't know for sure until we do a biopsy, but I've seen a lot of cases like yours in my career, and nearly all of them have followed a similar pattern. If this is pancreatic cancer, and it's metastasized, you probably have no more than three months."

I tried to swallow, but I couldn't. "Is that what you think this is? Do you think I have cancer?"

She gave me a tiny nod. "Yes, I do."

Chapter Twenty-Nine

We sat and talked for nearly an hour. I mainly listened as she told me what struggles I faced. She also told me her own story. She became an oncologist after she survived breast cancer several years ago. Her doctors weren't always discreet or sympathetic when they discussed her condition. They talked too loud. They were standoffish. She felt like a number instead of a real person. When she got better, after she had undergone a double mastectomy and chemotherapy, after her hair started growing back and her clothes began to fit her once again, she made up her mind that she was going to become the kind of doctor who actually cared for her patients. It took her several years, but she made it. She was now the head oncologist at this hospital.

She asked me whether I'd lost weight lately, and I said I had. I told her I'd had stomach cramps, and I'd vomited blood once or twice. I said I was tired a lot. When I said I figured it was because of my unhealthy eating habits and my excessive traveling, she gave me a look of doubt, but she didn't tell me I was wrong.

She told me many cancer patients have a lot of pain. Most of them lose weight because they don't feel like eating. Their strength drains away. Sleep comes in fits and starts.

"Okay, let's say I've got pancreatic cancer, and it's spread all over. Is there any way to treat it?" I asked.

"Yes, we can treat it with chemotherapy, but sometimes that can make your quality of life worse than it already is. There has always been a dilemma between treating the cancer and not treating it, especially when it's at stage four. You've got to remember, chemotherapy doesn't just attack the cancer cells. It attacks the good cells, too."

"Sort of like drowning someone in water when they're on fire, so they won't burn to death?"

"Yes. That's probably an appropriate analogy. But sometimes it helps. People have been cured by it. Lots of people, actually."

"I probably don't have much hope, though, do I?"

She didn't answer. She lowered her eyes to her lap as she searched for a way to say the right words.

"When you were sick, did your doctors give you straight answers when you asked them tough questions?" I asked. I wasn't trying to make things difficult for her. I was trying to make things less difficult for me.

"No. Not very often," she said.

"Did you want them to tell you the truth, no matter how bad it was?" She nodded.

"That's all I want. Don't sugarcoat anything for me. I believe I already know the answer, but I need to hear it from you."

"Miracles have been known to happen. I've heard of people surviving advanced pancreatic cancer, but not often. I wish I could tell you that everything is going to be fine, but that wouldn't be honest," she said.

I knew what was going to happen next. She would do her best to convince me to allow a biopsy, then start some kind of treatment, something to slow down the rate of growth of the cancer. She would tell me that I was too injured to leave the hospital, even if I didn't want to undergo any kind of cancer procedures.

But I wasn't going to get a biopsy, and I wasn't going to stay in this hospital. She didn't have to know that, though.

"Believe me, I know what you're going through right now. It's painful, and it's hard to hear, and that's why I hesitated to tell you."

"So, what do I do now?" I asked her.

"It depends on what you want to do. Chemotherapy will extend your life, but only by a few weeks, and your quality of life won't be very good. If you decide to do nothing, you'll have a better quality of life, but you won't live as long."

"If I decided to do chemotherapy, when would we start?"

"I can have all the orders done pretty quick, and you can start as early as later this afternoon," she said. "How does that sound to you?"

"Can we wait until tomorrow morning? I think I need some time to process everything."

She smiled at me and nodded. "Of course we can. That might be the best approach right now."

She stood up to leave, then turned back to me. "Oh, I'll need your full name and date of birth to write the orders."

Since I'd already given my real first name, I decided to give her my real last name, too. Again, what the hell difference did it make now?

"Doe," I told her. "Jon Doe. Jon without the H. My parents had a horrible sense of humor. My birthday is January 1, 1960." I picked that date totally at random. She would never know the difference.

"Thank you, Jon. I'll have a nurse bring you a different bracelet with your name on it in a few minutes."

I nodded, and she nodded, then she walked out. She ignored the fact that my real name matched the name they give anonymous patients. She had enough class to leave that alone.

Time for me to get my act together. I needed to be ready to get the hell out of this place once the nurse brought my new bracelet. I twisted the original one back and forth around my wrist. I should have asked the doctor what the red stripes meant.

I was stuffing my wallet into my pants when the nurse barged in with a new bracelet in one hand and a pair of scissors in the other. She snipped the old one off my arm and clasped the new one on. It had red stripes, too.

"Hey, uh, why does this have stripes on it? I remember back in the old days, they were just clear."

"Well, different hospitals use different color codes for different things," she said before she turned to leave.

"Okay, but in this hospital, what do the red stripes mean?"

"Cancer patient," she said. She opened the door and left.

Cancer. That word stunned me just as hard as it did a few minutes before. No matter how many times I hear it from this point forward, I'll never get over the pain I feel when I know it pertains to me. The doctors must have had enough evidence to convince them the spots on the X-rays and CAT scans were cancer. At least, they planned on treating me as a cancer patient until they were proved wrong.

I eased to the door and peered out. My room was next to the last at the end of the hall, with the nurse's station at least seventy-five feet away to my left. Fifteen feet away to my right was a door with an exit sign above it. A stairwell. That would make it easier to escape without the nurses seeing me.

After that, all I needed to do was figure out the location of the convenience store where I left my car. It most likely had been towed somewhere, and I'd never find it. But only if my luck continued the way it had been all day.

Just as I was about to dart out the door, I heard a soft, muffled moan from the room right beside the exit door. I listened for it again, because it sounded like someone was in pain, but their voice was too weak to carry far enough for anyone to hear. The door to the room was open about a foot, far enough to let sound escape but not enough to see inside.

Then, an idea hit me.

I pulled my phone out of my pocket to check the time. It was nearly 5:30, and it would be dark soon. I had until midnight to kill my next victim, or my self-imposed challenge would be a failure. But, from the sound I thought I heard coming from the room across the hall, my next victim was only a few feet away. If I was going to do this, I would have to make it quick.

I looked to my left to check the nurse's station again. It seemed to be deserted. Maybe it was time for a shift change. I pulled the deepest breath my sore ribs would allow and darted at an angle across the hall. It took less than two seconds to open the door, step inside, and close it.

An elderly man was on the bed, covered with a wrinkled, twisted sheet. His mouth was open, as if he had fallen asleep while gasping for air. A tangle of tubes and wires crisscrossed his bed, connecting his thin body to several machines and sensors. He resembled Gulliver after the people of Lilliput tied him down. His cheeks were covered with gray stubble, and his mouth was a combination of chapped lips and dried saliva. He didn't appear to have any teeth. A bony arm protruded from the side of the bed, through the bedrails. His name was Gerald something. His last name was on the underside of the bracelet, where I couldn't see it. His birthday was sometime in March, but I couldn't make out the day or year.

The bracelet also had red stripes, like mine. A cancer patient.

It looked like he had been dumped here and left to die, like a sack of discarded fast food lying in a ditch, thrown there by assholes who don't care.

The knot in my stomach became a lump in my throat. My bottom lip started to tremble, and I couldn't stop it. I was probably going to be like this poor man in a couple of months. All alone, suffering, with nobody to offer a kind word or a warm touch to make my final moments a little less painful.

I reached to touch his arm, my hand quivering. All I wanted to do was let him know he wasn't alone, that somebody cared, even if that somebody was about to kill him. But I didn't see this as a murder. I saw this as an act of mercy, a gesture to release this man from his pain.

As I touched him, his eyes opened just wide enough to look at me. They had probably been blue at one time, but now they were a milky pale gray. The brightness that was once there during his youth had now faded away, worn down by time and despair, like soft wood against sandpaper. I'm not sure he saw me, because he had the thousand-yard stare of someone whose eyes refused to focus, not entirely conscious, but not unconscious, either. But that didn't matter to me. He reacted to my touch, and it let him know he wasn't alone.

"Sweet dreams, my friend," I said in a soft voice. His eyes closed again for the last time.

I reached for the on/off button on his monitors, then pulled back. What if they sent an alarm to the nurse's station when they were turned off? The nurses would come running down to his room, and I wouldn't be able to escape without being seen. That might wreck my perfect record so far. But there were only a few hours left in the day, and I couldn't see how I was ever going to get a better opportunity than this.

Desperate times call for desperate measures, so I pressed the on/off buttons and waited. If the nurses came into the room, I would try to make up some story about why I was in here. If nothing else, I could pretend to be suffering from confusion caused by my concussion.

The machines wheezed as they shut off. I listened for any kind of commotion in the hallway, and I heard nothing. After nearly two minutes of waiting, I decided I had gotten lucky, and the nurses didn't know the man's machines weren't functioning.

Then I pulled an extra pillow from under the man's head and covered his face with it. He didn't struggle, but I could tell he was laboring for air by the way his abdomen heaved up and down faster and faster. It lasted less than a minute before his breathing stopped. I removed the pillow and looked at his face. He appeared to be asleep. A quick feel of his carotid artery revealed he had no pulse.

He was gone. Victim number forty-two. Ten more to go.

I put the pillow back under his head to make it appear he had died in his sleep, then pressed the on/off buttons on his monitors. They would take a few seconds to boot up and send messages to the nurse's station, but by then I planned to be on my way out of the hospital.

A quick glance down the hallway to make sure no one saw me, then three steps to the stairway door. As I was halfway down the first flight of stairs, before the door closed behind me, I heard the faint beep of an alarm from the other end of the hallway. The nurses would find the dead man in a matter of seconds.

I was out of the hospital a minute later. I'm sure the security cameras saw me leave, but I hoped to be out of Huntsville before anyone decided to look at the video. My movements were slow and painful, and I still felt a little dizzy. I was out of breath from walking down the stairs. After I walked two blocks from the hospital, I turned in a slow circle to get my bearings. I remembered driving west towards the interstate before I pulled into the convenience store parking lot. The sun was now gone from the sky, but it was still light outside, so I started walking in the direction of the light. To the best of my knowledge, the sun would still set in the west.

But only if my luck improved.

Chapter Thirty

I walked for over two hours, well past dark, sometimes with my thumb in the air, sometimes not. No one offered to give me a ride. Back in the old days, a driver would pick up someone walking on the side of the road, but not anymore. Dozens of horror stories about people getting murdered by a hitchhiker had made their way into the psyche of everyone nowadays. If you had car trouble, or didn't have a car, or were trying to find where you passed out before getting taken to the hospital, you were shit out of luck.

My appearance probably had something to do with it, too. I mean, who in their right mind would offer a ride to a man wearing dirty clothes that hung off his body as if they were three sizes too big? Who would want to stop for a hitchhiker who looked like a limping skeleton?

With the darkness came the chilly air. October was a pleasant month in this part of the country, but it also tended to get cool enough for a sweatshirt or light jacket at night. I had neither. My thin T-shirt and baggy jeans didn't provide much warmth, so I compensated by walking as fast as I could, which was not very fast, and by stuffing my hands into my pockets when I wasn't holding my thumb out.

It was times like this I wished I hadn't lost all that weight. The extra layer of fat would have provided a little insulation against the cold.

The lower temperatures also made it difficult to think. At least, that's what I told myself. It couldn't have been the concussion, or the cancer, or my age. Nope, not possible. Not to me.

I tried to recall various landmarks from my attempt to leave town two days ago, but my memory was fuzzy. Every once in a while, I would walk past a building or street that looked somewhat familiar. I wanted to think I was on the right road, but I couldn't be sure. There were a lot of other buildings and streets that felt like I was seeing them for the first time in my life. I told myself to keep walking, keep heading west, and everything would work out fine.

Meanwhile, a steady stream of cars whizzed past me as I marched on with my shuffling, limping, unsteady gait, my hands, ears, and arms nearly numb from the cold. I gave up on getting a ride from someone. I just wanted to find my car, drive to a motel, and sleep for the rest of the night.

Luck was on my side, though, because right about the time I felt I didn't have the strength to go much further, I reached an intersection I recognized.

The one where I ran the red light. I had to be close.

I paused long enough to take a couple of deep breaths, then I marched on. A half-mile down the road, I found the convenience store. The dim fluorescent lights beneath its eave were just enough to illuminate two rusting gasoline pumps. A dented freezer containing bags of ice sat beside the entrance door. An empty cage that once held propane tanks was beyond that. The parking lot was littered with cigarette butts, bits of broken glass, and cracked asphalt. And my car was not in the parking lot.

Dammit.

I decided to check with the cashier. Maybe he knew where my car was.

He was a young kid, probably no older than eighteen, a good chance he was still in high school. He glanced up from his phone, looked back down, then back at me. I'm sure my appearance would cause a lot of people to do a double take. Baggy, dirty clothes. Gaunt appearance. A bruised and cut face. Sweating while also shivering. Out of breath.

"Can I help you, sir?" he asked.

I leaned against the counter, propped up by my arm, breathing hard until I had enough oxygen to speak. I held up my index finger in a silent request for a moment to gather myself. He stuffed his phone in his pocket and waited, his eyes filled with a mixture of concern and discomfort.

After a long moment, my breathing slowed enough to talk. I gave him a sheepish grin.

"Sorry about that." I said.

"Are you okay?"

"Yes, I'm fine, thanks. I've just spent the last two days in the hospital."

His eyes perked up, like a light bulb had turned on in his brain. "Wait, are you..."

"Yeah, I'm one who passed out here the other night," I said, interrupting. "I came back to get my car."

His blank stare told me he didn't know what I was talking about.

"Do you know where my car is?" I asked.

"Well, I..."

"Do you, or not?"

"Uh, hang on a second," he said. He pulled his phone out, pressed a couple of buttons, and held it to his ear. He faced away from me as he spoke in a soft voice with the person on the other end. The call lasted less than a minute. He turned back to me as he put the phone back into his pocket.

"Where's my car?" I asked, before he could say anything.

"That was my manager I called. He was the one on duty the other night. I wasn't here."

My breathing sped up again. Not from exertion, but because I was getting pissed off. I was in no mood for games, not after the things I had been through the past couple of days.

"He didn't know what to do with your car. The cops wouldn't impound it because there wasn't a crime committed. He took the keys out of it and locked it up. He thought you would be back to get it later that night, or maybe somebody you knew would come get it. The next day he hadn't heard anything, and he couldn't leave the car where it was, taking up space."

I looked through the dirty window at the empty parking lot. I doubted if it had been over half-full within the past five years. "Yeah. I can see how hundreds of customers would have trouble finding a place to park here."

"Yeah, well, whatever. Anyway, he dug through the glove compartment and found rental papers, and he called the rental company to see if they would come get it. They're supposed to be here in the morning."

"Look, pal. I'm really tired, really sick, and really fed up with running around in circles with you. For the last time, where's my car?"

"It's behind the store."

"Where are the keys?"

He didn't answer, but he glanced at the counter. I followed his gaze to a set of keys beside the cash register. They were attached to a key ring along with the rental company's logo on a small plastic tag. I had been standing two feet from them this whole time and never saw them.

We reached for them at the same instant, but I got to them first. I pulled them off the counter and stuffed them into my pants pocket.

"I appreciate it," I said, turning to walk out of the store.

"Hey! You can't have those! The rental company is supposed to be here tomorrow," he said.

"Not my problem," I said as I reached for the door. "Call your manager if you want to, but I'll be long gone before he gets here. And you're not going to stop me. I'm in the kind of mood right now that I'd just love to take out some of my frustrations on a skinny young punk like you. That car is still in my name, and it's legally mine until I turn it back in to the rental company."

He pulled out his phone, poised his thumb over the call button, and gave me a look that dared me to stop him.

A sharp pain shot through my stomach, and I did my best not to wince. I disguised the pain by reaching behind me, under my shirt and into my waistband, as if I had a weapon stuffed there. The cashier wasn't streetwise enough to know I was bluffing. At least, I hoped he wasn't.

"Don't test me, boy," I said.

He considered the situation long enough to realize he should let it go. He lowered the phone and gave me dismissive wave of his hand.

"Go," he said.

I nodded and walked out. I waited until the door closed behind me to wrap my free arm across my stomach. I grunted with every step until the pain went away. By that time, I was at the back of the store and in my car. The gravel parking lot had a narrow driveway that connected to a side road, which then connected to the highway that ran in front of the store. Three minutes after I had snatched the keys off the counter, I was once again heading west toward the interstate. The pain in my stomach was intense, and I had a massive headache, but at least I didn't feel like I was about to pass out again.

But I needed sleep, so I looked for the first mom-and-pop motel I could find. I would resume my zig-zag path to the ocean in the morning.

If I didn't die in my sleep.

Chapter Thirty-One

I left Huntsville the next morning without a destination in mind. I just drove. My mind was all over the place, thinking about my situation, what I was going to do, where I would end up, and whether I should change my goals. Doctor Glover admitted my chances of survival were slight if it turned out I had cancer.

If.

Let's be honest here. Everything that happened to me these past few months pretty much verified I was eaten up with it. All the weight loss. All the nausea. All the fatigue. All the blood when I threw up. Cancer was killing me. Ain't no "if" about it.

But let's also be honest about something else. I knew from the time I quit my job and started getting ready to kill people that I wouldn't survive this self-imposed challenge. This was a suicide mission from the beginning. I would be killed by a cop, or a victim who fought back, or by lethal injection. My hobby was my last great hurrah, my last middle finger at society, my last chance to make my mark on this world, and I had to do it before cancer made its final mark on me.

All I had to do was keep going until the end of the year. Ten more weeks. Depending on how you look at it, ten weeks was either an eternity or a blink of an eye. It would be an eternity while I remained disciplined enough to kill only one person per week, but it would be a blink of an eye while I watched my body waste away.

Because I was getting weaker, I had to be selective about my victims. From now on, they had to be older. Didn't matter if they were male or female. The girl with the bicycle proved that by stomping my guts out. I needed to focus on victims like the old woman I hit in the head with a shovel, or the one walking her dog beside the road. No more young, strong, healthy people. In my condition, I probably wouldn't be strong enough to strangle them, and I certainly wouldn't have enough energy or quickness to take them by surprise.

I had to re-think my entire approach.

Once I hit Birmingham, I headed east a few miles before stopping at a diner for my Sunday celebration breakfast. The place was crowded. I stood at the door, looking for somewhere to sit, but I didn't see an available table.

"How you doin', sir?" said a waitress from behind the counter. "We've got one stool left over here." She pointed at the only empty space left. A single stool at the end of the counter. "Unless you want to wait for a table."

"How long is the wait?" I asked.

"Probably at least twenty minutes."

I gave her a little "nope, that's too long" wave and moved to the empty stool. It wasn't the most comfortable place to sit, and it definitely gave me less privacy, but I didn't care. My Sunday breakfasts had become routine, almost like a ritual, and I didn't want to break the cycle.

The waitress filled my coffee cup, and I ordered my usual stack of pancakes. A man beside me glanced over when I pulled out my calendar to mark a red X on today's date, but he looked away after less than a second. I'm glad he did, because I wasn't up to small talk this morning. My stomach hurt, my face hurt, my ribs hurt. I was bruised and cut all over. And to top it all, I was trying to sort this cancer situation through my mind. Talking about the weather was the last thing I wanted to do.

After I made the X on the calendar, I rolled it up and stuffed it into my back pocket. I ignored the man, and he ignored me. Perfect. Now, let me eat my pancakes and I'll be on my way.

A few minutes later, the waitress clattered my plate on the counter in front of me and walked away without a word. The diner was so full, she didn't have time for small talk, either. I buttered the pancakes, poured syrup over them, and stuffed a forkful into my mouth. Swallowing was like a wad of sticky mud going down.

After two additional bites, I couldn't eat any more. It felt like I was throwing firecrackers into a stomach full of acid. It was all I could do to keep everything from coming back up. I squeezed my eyes shut and grimaced, trying to will away the discomfort, trying to keep from puking all over the counter. I gulped down a mouthful of ice water, and it gave me some relief. The soothing, cool rush rinsed and diluted the burn in my throat and stomach. After a few moments, my breathing slowed down and my abdominal muscles relaxed.

I stared at my nearly-full plate with disgust. This damned cancer. It didn't care who it hurt or what kind of damage it caused.

I took another swig of water and thought about finishing my cup of coffee before deciding I'd probably just get sick again. There was no use sitting there like a knot on a log. I might as well get back on the road. The waitress hadn't brought my check, so I slid a ten under my coffee cup and limped out the door.

It wasn't exactly a full meal, but at least I kept my string of forty-two Sunday breakfasts in a row intact, even if some of them couldn't be considered actual breakfasts. It was going to be hard to keep doing this if I got to the point where I couldn't eat. I just needed to remind myself that it was simply what I had to go through to get where I wanted to be.

For somebody like me, life was never easy. It might be for some people, especially those born with a silver spoon in their mouth, but I was born without a spoon of any kind in my mouth. I had to struggle every day of my life, and now, trying to survive cancer made it worse. When you add being a serial killer to that, it becomes more than a struggle. It becomes a war.

I told myself to just keep moving. Keep putting one foot in front of the other. And every once in a while, end someone's life along the way.

I crossed the Georgia state line a little over an hour after I left the diner, then headed southeast until I arrived in Newnan. I got a new rental car, transferred all my bags and fishing gear, and two days later I checked into a motel in Aiken, South Carolina. I slept for nearly two whole days before I had enough energy to find my next victim.

Mile Marker Zero

I was on my way to Charleston, driving the back roads, taking my time. Late in the day I passed through a little community whose name I can't remember, a place no more than a wide spot in the road, with no buildings other than old houses and barns. A mile beyond that, an ancient pickup truck had pulled over on the side of the road, nearly hidden by waist-high weeds that would soon die from frost. An elderly man stood beside a barbed-wire fence, tugging and bending a broken strand back together with a pair of pliers.

He looked like a stereotypical rural farmer. He wore overalls and a baseball cap, both of them worn and faded with age. He was nearly as skinny as me, except he probably didn't have cancer. He was just old. His face was a wrinkled piece of leather, and his hands were bent and knotted with arthritis. It was clear he was struggling to pull the strand tight enough to fix it.

I pulled over a few yards past him and got out. "Can I give you a hand?" I yelled.

He was too old to twist his body around to look at me. Instead, he did an old man's step-pivot-step-pivot-step-pivot until his body faced me. He waved at me with the pliers and said something, but I couldn't hear him. His body language implied he didn't need any help. He did a reverse step-pivot dance and focused on the fence again.

That's the thing I've noticed about people from his generation. They're stubborn and proud, and they don't want some youngster like me helping them do something they can do themselves. He struck me as a man who had mended fences for decades, probably even before I was born, and he wasn't willing to admit it was now beyond his ability.

I looked up and down the road in both directions. We were at least a mile from the nearest house. Perfect for me.

I wouldn't have the strength to struggle with him, despite his age, so I had to figure out how to get him down in a hurry. By the time I was within ten feet of him, I had remembered a technique my martial arts instructor showed me for slamming someone to the ground when they didn't expect it.

He felt me coming up behind him and started to do his step-pivot thing again, but I grabbed the back of his collar with both hands and yanked hard. At the same instant I kicked his feet forward with a sweep of my leg. His clodhopper boots banged against the fence post an instant before the back of his neck hit the ground. His toothless mouth opened in a silent scream because the impact knocked all the air from his lungs.

The fall may have broken his neck. It may have broken something inside him and caused internal bleeding. He might have died right there if I'd walked away at that moment. I don't know.

I didn't have the luxury of depending on maybes and probable outcomes. I had to make sure he was dead before I left.

"I'm sorry, sir," I said to him. "You won't have to worry about fixing your fence. You'll never have to worry about it again." He replied with a hoarse, gagging sound as he struggled to catch his breath, his mouth opening and closing like a fish out of water.

I took a deep breath to ready myself and jumped as high as I could—which wasn't very high—and landed with all my weight on the farmer's face. I felt and heard bones crack beneath the soles of my shoes. I weighed a lot less than I did at the beginning of the year, but I still had enough mass to crush his skull.

I stumbled for a few steps, but I didn't fall. In most cases like this, I would check the victim's pulse to make sure they were dead, but I didn't have to do that with him. He had blood pouring out of his nose and eyes, and his entire head was shaped like a pile of sculptor's clay. I didn't have to see bits of gray matter to know that his brain had been mangled.

Number forty-three. Nine to go.

The road in both directions was still as empty as it had been when I pulled over, and there definitely weren't any cameras around. As I walked back to my car, I realized I was gasping. My lungs couldn't get enough air in them, and a light sheen of sweat covered my arms and face. If something as simple as knocking down an old man made me this tired, these next few weeks were going to be hell.

I barely had enough strength to shut my car door and start the engine. It took another fifteen seconds to lift my arm and put the car into gear.

If I was going to finish this thing, I had to have more energy. Maybe caffeine. Maybe one of those energy drinks kids were addicted to these days. Maybe better food. Maybe more exercise.

Then I came to my senses and realized no short-term answer was going to get me to my finish line. I just had to push through the pain and get there by any means possible. I had to use my brain and the internet to figure out how to kill people in an easy manner that didn't require a lot of time or strength.

I made it to Charleston the next day and stayed until I had my breakfast two days later, even though I again had only a few bites. The next destination in my route was way over in northern Louisiana. I planned on taking about three days to get there, and I figured to find number forty-four along the way.

Part Five

TUNNEL

Chapter Thirty-Two

I wish I had known my life was about change yet again after I reached Shreveport. The past several days had been nothing but a series of life-changing events, and my forty-fourth victim either opened up a huge can of worms or made my goal easier. I guess it depends on how you prefer to look at it.

During an overnight stop in Meridian, Mississippi, I checked my bank account and found I had less than I anticipated at this point. I don't know if it was caused by an increase in gas and hotel room prices, or if I was simply not being thrifty enough. No matter the cause, I realized I had to either spend less or start taking money from my victims.

I could use my camping equipment instead of hotel rooms whenever the weather allowed, but I didn't have the energy to pitch a tent and build a fire every few days. I would probably get better use of the money if I sold the equipment for a few bucks. I could easily get $50 for everything, and that would get me a couple of meals and a night's stay at a cheap motel.

I kicked myself for not rummaging through that farmer's pockets. I'm certain he would have had a bunch of money on him. I've known a lot of people his age, and most of them didn't trust banks. They tended to keep lots of cash in their wallets.

Anyone younger might not carry much cash, but they would probably have credit cards, and I could get by with using a stolen card for a couple of days before anyone noticed.

So, my plan was to check the pockets of the rest of my victims. And that's what changed everything for me.

I had bought a small can of pepper spray from a convenience store before I left Meridian because I would need some way to disable my victims before I killed them. I was too weak to chase them down or struggle with them, but if they were struggling with burning eyes, they would be less likely to focus on fighting me.

And, since I needed to operate mostly at night, I got myself a cheap thin jacket. It helped protect against the chill, and it gave me extra pockets to hide my pepper spray. Total cost for the spray and the jacket was under $30. If I were lucky, I would get that much back from one of my next victims.

Number forty-four was a construction worker. Imagine that, a big, burly guy getting killed by a sickly, weak, wheezing lump of cancer like me. But that's what happened. I was driving around the outskirts of Shreveport, trying to find an easy victim. It was after dark, but not very late. I was about to give up and go back to my hotel room when I saw a five-story office building under construction with a single white pickup truck parked in the dirt beside it. There was a light coming from the second floor. It strobed from bright to dim to bright again. The building had no walls or doors yet. Only a web of steel framework had been completed.

I figured the odds in my head and decided to stop. One truck, one light. That meant one person, maybe two at the most. If there were two, I planned to act like I was lost and ask for directions. If it was just one person, then he'd be dead in a couple of minutes.

I heard the crackling of a welder as I eased my car door shut. That was even better. A welder wouldn't hear me coming, and he would have a helmet covering his face, which meant he wouldn't see me, either.

The makeshift stairs to the second floor were wobbly and steep. By the time I got to the last step, I was gasping for air. The flashing light and noise came from the other side of a group of beams and sheet metal twenty feet away. The person welding couldn't see the stairs from his position. I stayed where I was, hands on my hips like a runner who had just finished a race, until I could catch my breath.

The best way to kill this guy would be a blow to the head with something heavy, but I didn't have anything to use. I scanned the floor for a crowbar or a piece of lumber or something useful. The darkness and the heavy shadows caused by the welder light made it difficult to see, but I finally found a pile of rebar lying against the wall right behind me. The iron bars were half an inch thick and heavy. One blow to the head from one of them was instant death.

The problem was that most of the pieces were at least fifteen feet long, with a few smaller pieces of about eight feet scattered beside the pile. Those were all too long. I needed something shorter, something I could swing like a baseball bat or an axe.

The flashing welder arc continued to throw shadows all over the second floor. I couldn't see the rebar well enough to tell if there were any pieces short enough for a weapon, so I stepped toward the pile with the intention of finding one by feeling for it, like searching for your dropped car keys while you're standing knee-deep in a muddy lake.

On my third step, I kicked a foot-long piece of rebar. It clattered, banged, and rolled for what seemed like a full minute before it came to a stop against a steel beam. If I had set off a pack of firecrackers, it wouldn't have been that loud.

I squatted down in a crouch and sat motionless, my heart hammering in my chest. I don't know why I knelt down, because I was out in the open, and if the welder had looked around the columns in my direction, he would have seen me whether I was standing or not.

The welding light and crackling noise stopped. The area on the other side of the columns was still lit up, probably with a portable industrial light.

My right hand reached for the floor to balance me, and it landed directly on another piece of rebar. I traced my fingers along its length until I found one end, then I felt in the other direction. It was nearly three feet long.

I dragged it closer, inch by loud, scraping inch. It weighed more than I thought it would, but not too heavy to manage.

"You back, Neal?" a man's voice called from the other side of the group of beams.

I sat completely still. I didn't even breathe.

"Neal? Why're you back so quick?"

The guy whispered a curse word. Something metallic dropped to the floor, followed by heavy steps coming toward me around the columns. The impacts of his boot heels were spaced apart, like the steps of a big man.

Great. Just freakin' great. I promised myself to concentrate on old and frail victims, and the first victim I choose is a damn gorilla.

"Neal?"

He emerged from behind the beams, his helmet flipped up, his arms thicker than my legs. His boots were at least size fifteen. With the light behind him, his silhouette looked like a combination of a cave man and a bear.

I stood up, holding the rebar behind my leg, opposite from him, my right hand squeezing it with a death grip. Sweat trickled into my eye. I blinked it away as best I could.

"Sorry, I think I'm lost," I said. "I was looking for my hotel, and my GPS took me to this place."

"Who the hell're you?" he asked. He kept walking toward me.

"Nobody, really. I'm just lost."

"Does this look like a goddamn hotel to you?" He stopped six feet away. His chest was thicker from front to back than my shoulders were from side to side.

I looked left and right. "I don't know if it does or not. I don't know what hotels look like when they're getting built. It doesn't look like *my* hotel."

"You damn right, it ain't your hotel. You need to leave," he said. "Somethin' happens to you, our insurance company ain't gonna be happy. And I don't wanna get fired 'causa you."

"I'm not looking to get anybody fired. I just need to find my hotel."

"What hotel is it?"

I pretended to fumble with my pockets on the side opposite him.

"I don't really remember. I've got my room card here somewhere. Do you have a flashlight?"

"Jesus Christ," he muttered. He looked down at his belt to unclip a small flashlight from his left hip, and I swung the rebar at his face with everything I had. Adrenaline can be a wonderful thing. I wouldn't have had the strength to lift the bar without it. I aimed for his forehead, but the weight of the bar combined with his height caused me to hit him a bit lower. The impact shattered several of his teeth and ripped his mouth open.

He yowled like a scalded dog and reached for the back of his pants as he stumbled sideways a step, but I swung the bar again and caught him on the temple. His arms dropped to his side, but he didn't fall. He stood there swaying like a tall tree in a strong breeze. He was basically out on his feet, but I had to make sure. I swung the bar downward like an axe and split his skull. That got him down. His face made a *splat* sound against the floor. Nobody would let their face hit that hard if they were conscious. Or alive.

His legs twitched for a few seconds before he stopped moving. A puddle of inky blood grew under his head and soaked into his hair.

I let the rebar drop to the floor with a loud *clang* because I didn't have the strength to hold onto it anymore. It felt like it weighed fifty pounds. Three swings of it drained all the energy from me.

I knelt beside his body and checked for a pulse on his wrist. Nothing. He was gone.

Even though I was tired, I had to move in a hurry. He had been expecting someone, and that person could show up any second. I dug his wallet from his hip pocket and pulled out $120, all in twenties. That made up for me not searching the farmer. As I stuffed his wallet back into his pocket, my hand brushed against something attached to his belt.

And that's when everything changed for me.

I couldn't see it very well, but I already knew what it was. A nylon gun holster. That's what he was reaching for after I hit him the first time.

I unsnapped the strap from around it and pulled out a small automatic pistol. It probably held no more than six or seven shots in its magazine. My knowledge of guns is almost zero, so I didn't know what caliber it was.

It felt strange in my hand. I hadn't shot many pistols in my life. I had hunted a bit, but only with shotguns and rifles. The rest of my outdoor activities involved fishing and camping.

This welder guy had presented me with a solution to my increasing weakness by donating his pistol.

The light wasn't bright enough to see where the safety and magazine release were located. A gun lover would find them in his sleep, but not me. I didn't have time to figure it out, either, because Neal, whoever he was, would be pulling up any minute. I shoved the gun into my back pocket and raced down the steps as fast as I could without falling on my face.

I left the guy lying on the floor. I didn't have the strength to move him. Besides, Neal would find him shortly, and then the coroner could move him. I would be long gone by then.

I slid the pistol under my seat and headed back to my hotel. I couldn't believe my luck. I needed a new method for killing people, one that didn't require much physical effort, and it dropped into my lap like a gift from heaven. I originally didn't want to use guns because they were loud and messy, but that was back when I had energy to burn. Now that I could see the light at the end of my year-long tunnel, now that I was too weak to do what I was once able to do, my opinion on guns changed.

This pistol was going to get me to the finish line.

Chapter Thirty-Three

It took several victims before I got used to shooting a gun. I was clumsy with it. I had trouble finding the safety. My hand shook when I tried to hold it in front of me to aim. Steadying it with both hands didn't help much. The only way I found to keep it from shaking was to prop it against something and hold it with both hands. My nerves, adrenaline, and muscle weakness worked against me whenever I shot it, but after my forty-ninth victim, I started to get into a comfort zone.

My forty-fifth victim was a different story.

It was in Lake Charles, Louisiana that I found her. I pulled into town late at night after traveling from Shreveport to Crockett, Texas, then to Austin, back east to Beaumont, then across the Louisiana state line into Lake Charles. She was a convenience store clerk who had struck up a conversation with me when I bought some coffee and diarrhea medicine. I don't know if I have a certain aptitude with convenience store clerks, but some of them, especially the women, seem to want to talk to me. This one was named Renay.

She made a point to emphasize her name was spelled differently than "that other Renee," as she put it. I don't really think she was flirting, because she was at least two decades younger than me. Maybe she was just a big talker. Whatever the reason, she ended up giving me enough information about her to plan her murder.

She told me she got off work at midnight, and she lived in some low-income apartments on the other side of town with her boyfriend, who worked long shifts at one of the numerous chemical plants in the area. Sometimes her car started, sometimes it didn't. On nights when it didn't, she had to walk or hitchhike because she couldn't afford a cab and her boyfriend was either at work or asleep. She always kept her car behind the store because that's where her manager told her to park so that she wouldn't take up parking spaces.

Sounded like she had the same manager as that kid at the convenience store back in Huntsville where I'd left my car.

By the time I managed to pull myself away from her and drive away from the store, it was nearly ten o'clock. I had to find a hotel, get all my stuff in the room, and get back to her store to somehow disable her car.

I made it with fifteen minutes left to spare.

I parked down the block and walked the rest of the way, entering the lot behind the store by wading through a row of worn-out hedges. Before I stepped out of the bushes, I made sure there were no cameras spying on the rear entrance. I didn't see any.

Her car was a beaten-up, thirty-year-old Chevy that had seen better days, and it was unlocked, so I popped the hood and yanked the distributor cap loose. It wouldn't start that way, and I doubted she would have the mechanical smarts to understand why.

I went back to the bushes and waited for midnight.

Two minutes after twelve, she came out of the back door, sipping a can of beer she had probably stolen from the store's cooler. She cranked the engine, but it didn't turn over. She kept cranking for a couple of minutes before she gave up. She beat on the steering wheel and yelled some muffled profanities, stepped out of the car and threw her beer against the store wall.

"Son of a bitch!" she yelled. She stood looking at her car for a moment, hands on her hips, trying to calm down. With a resigned shake of her head, she walked back into the store.

I headed back to my car parked down the street. That would give her enough time to leave the store and walk several hundred yards before I could drive past her and shoot her dead.

By the time I found her, she was on a dark side street with boarded-up houses and weed-covered empty lots. I saw the glow of her cigarette coming towards me, just out of reach of my headlights.

I buzzed down my window and slowed as I reached her. The pistol was in my sweaty right hand, resting in my lap, ready to pull the trigger. Point and shoot. That's all I needed to do. Point and shoot right at her face. Get close enough so that I wouldn't miss. Kill her with one shot and get the hell out of there.

"Need a ride?" I asked her. "You shouldn't be walking through this kind of neighborhood at night."

"No, I'm fine. Thanks," she said. She barely gave me a look as she kept walking. She didn't seem to recognize me from two hours before.

I put the car in reverse and kept pace with her as she walked.

"Oh, come on. It's late, it's dark, and you wouldn't be walking unless you had no other choice. I've got a daughter, and I definitely wouldn't want her walking by herself this time of night."

She stopped, let out a sigh, and started walking toward me. When she was less than ten feet away, I lifted the pistol from my lap, hit the steering wheel with the muzzle, glanced it off the door frame, and pointed it in her direction. She saw the gun and froze in her tracks as she put her hands in front of herself as a shield.

I pulled the trigger. The gun lurched in my hand with an explosion so loud that I couldn't hear anything but a ringing in my ears. The woman screamed and grabbed the top of her shoulder as she went down on her knees. The scream sounded like it came from inside a barrel of pillows. To the rest of the public, it probably sounded like a woman getting murdered. I had to shut her up quick.

I switched the gun to my left hand to put my car in park, and I pressed my fingers against the trigger instead of the trigger guard. The gun barked again, and I nearly dropped it. It was only by dumb luck I had it pointed up in the air and not at myself, but the bang made the ringing in my ears even worse. I literally couldn't hear anything else.

I jumped out of the car and tried to point the gun at the woman's head, but my hand shook so bad that I knew I would miss if I pulled the trigger. She kept screaming, but she didn't try to get up. Maybe she was in too much pain or simply too scared to move. If she had tried to run, I don't know what I would have done.

I grabbed the gun with both hands to steady it the best I could and squeezed off another shot. I tried to aim for her forehead, but the bullet struck her in the throat. She fell over and stopped screaming, but she still wiggled around like a dying roach on its back. I decided four shots were not much worse than three, so I put the gun against her temple and fired again.

This time she stopped moving. I didn't even bother to check if she was dead. I didn't have time. The longer I stayed at the scene, the more likely I was going to get caught.

I tossed the gun into the passenger seat and tried to put the car in gear, but I was trembling so hard that I had to use both hands.

I sped away from there with my headlights off until I was a hundred yards away, hoping the whole time I could manage to stay on the road. It wasn't until I was a mile away that my vision started to get blurry, and I realized I was hyperventilating.

By the time I reached my hotel, I told myself I had a lot to learn about guns. Especially how to operate them. Good lord, I'm a horrible shot. I should have killed her with only one bullet, but due to my inexperience and ignorance, it took four. Sometimes I wonder how I managed to make it ten months without getting caught.

I scrubbed my hands and forearms with soap and hot water for five minutes to wash away the gunpowder, then I opened my laptop to start researching. I had a lot to learn, and not much time to learn it.

Chapter Thirty-Four

It's amazing how much you can learn by watching videos online. There are literally dozens of tutorials for basic handgun use, and I watched all of them two or three times. After I got a basic understanding of the mechanics of my new toy, I spent nearly a full day loading and unloading the magazine into the grip, learning how the trigger safety worked, chambering and ejecting a round, and taking the gun apart and reassembling it.

Eventually, I could do everything with my eyes closed. But watching videos and playing around with a harmless unloaded gun is far different from shooting live ammo. It still felt smaller than I imagined a pistol would feel, like it did when I first grabbed it, but it definitely had killing power. It was a Glock 43, one of the smaller models perfect for concealed carry. It held a total of seven 9mm shots. Six in the magazine and one in the chamber. The welder guy probably chose it because it was reliable, and because he wouldn't need something with a dozen rounds or more while he was on the job. I imagined he had a gun to fit that bill at home.

After a stop in Baton Rouge, Louisiana to buy more bullets and to do a little practice in a deserted backroads field, I continued eastward through Mobile, Alabama. I killed a man wearing a reflective vest picking up trash along a country road in Bay Minette, Alabama, even though it took two shots to finish him off. A week and a half later, victim number forty-seven was a young man on a bicycle with a plastic bag of aluminum cans tied to his handlebars near Rosewood, Florida. I shot him as I drove past and knocked him to the ground, but I had to double back and fire another shot when I saw in my rear-view mirror he was trying to get up. My hand still shook, but not nearly as bad as it did the first time.

Six to go.

I sold my camping equipment to a junk dealer in the parking lot of a seedy motel in Ocala, Florida a couple of days later. I wouldn't need it anymore, and even if I did, I was too weak to set up a tent.

Everything wore me out. And I mean everything. Taking a shower took me forty-five minutes. Shaving took fifteen. After nearly every bit of exertion, no matter how small, I had to stop and catch my breath. And that's only when the abdominal pains didn't hit me.

The spasms came more frequently now. All hours of the day and night, with no regular schedule. I still had to eat, though. Sometimes the food stayed down, and sometimes it didn't. I was also getting severe muscle cramps in my feet and legs. Every joint in my body cracked and popped whenever I moved.

The motel had a set of scales stashed under the sink. Even though I shouldn't have, I stepped on them and found I had lost over seventy pounds since the beginning of the year. That's not a bad thing if you're obese to begin with, but I had been in fair shape for my age. Not lean and trim, but certainly not fat.

Late November, and I was wasting away before my own eyes. Even if I made it to the end of my hobby, I wouldn't live to enjoy the infamy. My strength would dry up before then.

My long drives between towns were a thing of the past, too. I didn't have the energy to sit behind a steering wheel for eight or nine hours a day. Granted, I was already on the Florida peninsula, and the distance between its two coasts wasn't very far, but it was still too far to drive in one long stretch in my condition.

Three hours was pretty much my maximum. After that, I was too tired to keep my eyes open, and my body was sore from sitting still for that long.

I managed to get to Daytona, where I holed up in a motel for a few days. For two days in a row, I was too sick to get out of bed. It felt like I had the flu. Low-grade fever. Body aches. Nausea. I had the "Do Not Disturb" sign hanging on the doorknob so the maids wouldn't bother me, and I did nothing but sleep. I didn't even eat.

When I finally managed to wake up enough to sit up in bed on the third day in Daytona, my fever had gone from low-grade to high. I don't know how high it was because I didn't have a thermometer, but as far as I was concerned, any fever at all wasn't good. I didn't have any medicine, either.

I decided I needed to at least get something in my stomach and take some aspirin, so I forced myself out of bed to take a shower. Maybe the water would cool me off a little. The second I overcame the popping, cracking, and stiffness of my back, a wave of nausea hit me hard. I rushed to the toilet just before I spat out a mouthful of brownish bile. My stomach and sides contracted several more times, but nothing came up. I didn't have anything in my stomach to throw up. When I was a teenager getting drunk on strawberry wine, I would puke until there was nothing left, and my body would still spasm. My friends called it "the dry heaves."

The nausea caused me to break out in a light sweat, which cooled my fever a bit. After I showered and dried off, I felt a little better, but not much. It didn't matter. I had to get something to eat or I wouldn't have enough energy to keep my eyes open. On top of that, I had to find my next victim before midnight.

To make matters even worse, it was raining like crazy outside. The loud tapping on my window and the heavy splatter of water pouring off the roof was all I needed to know. That meant fewer people milling around. Fewer potential victims. The only plus was the noise of the rain would muffle the sound of the pistol. I decided to move on to another town. Maybe I could outrun the rain and find an easy victim in another town.

I got dressed, put on my cap to keep the rain off my head, and hurried as fast as I could through the downpour to my car. You'd think I could walk between the raindrops with all the weight I'd lost, but apparently that isn't the case. I piled into my rental car and threw my belongings into the passenger seat. I was soaked to the skin and out of breath. I sat there long enough for the windows to begin fogging up. By the time I was ready to leave, a set of headlights pulled into the parking lot.

The heavy rain and cloud cover made a normal fall afternoon look like twilight, and I couldn't tell what kind of car it was in the darkness. I rubbed the fog from my window with my sleeve in time to see it pull into the empty space directly in front of the motel office. Two people got out, a man and a woman. But they weren't any ordinary couple.

The woman was a tall blonde with shoulder-length hair, wearing dark slacks and a windbreaker jacket. The man looked somewhat familiar, like I'd seen him somewhere before. He also had on a windbreaker jacket.

The sleeves and back of their jackets had FBI in huge yellow letters.

I don't know if they were looking for me, but I couldn't afford to wait and find out. Time to get out of there.

I drove past the office and saw them talking with the desk clerk. She was pointing in the direction of my room. I barely escaped. Five more minutes, and I probably would have been in federal custody.

Now my situation was worse than ever. I was hungry, sick, pressed for time, and had the FBI right on my heels. I had no idea how this day would turn out, but I didn't have a good feeling about it.

One thing I learned earlier this year was to put false information about my car on my hotel registration. The desk clerks never verified it. They just needed to know who to contact in case the car needed to be moved. I'm sure the FBI agents were asking what kind of car I was driving, and the clerk would tell them I was in a blue Volkswagen Beetle convertible. Meanwhile, I was making my escape in a Ford Taurus.

Just before I drove out of Daytona, it hit me. I remembered where I had seen that FBI agent. He was the man who kept staring at me in the diner in Delaware several weeks ago. It was raining then, too.

He had stared at me like he knew me. The fact that he shows up at my hotel weeks later is not a coincidence. He's on my trail, and he was as close as he could be without catching me.

Thank goodness the light at the end of the tunnel was getting brighter.

I grabbed a small burger at a fast-food place and choked it down with ice water. It tasted like crap, and it was all I could do to keep from throwing it back up, but I had to get some nourishment, even if it was the unhealthy kind. My body probably needed more than a small burger, but that's all I could force down.

Oh, and a block before I got on Interstate 4, I shot a man who was running down the sidewalk with a newspaper shielding his head from the rain. Even though I shot through the passenger window, I somehow managed to hit him in the head. I didn't wait to see if he was dead. He would be in a minute or two. I chalked up the accurate shot to my improving gun skills. Or maybe the serial killer gods were smiling on me again.

Three days later I killed a man on a golf course as he searched through the bushes for his ball. I had pulled over on the side of the road to rest, never intending to shoot anyone, but when opportunity knocks, you have to take it. He appeared all of a sudden, like a deer sneaking out of the woods. He looked like he was at least eighty-five years old. It was time for him to die, anyway. From thirty feet away, I shot him through the heart with a single shot.

Two victims in four days. Numbers forty-eight and forty-nine. Three more to go. The tunnel is getting shorter, and the light at the end is getting brighter.

Chapter Thirty-Five

My back-and-forth course through Florida brought me closer and closer to the Keys. That's where I figured to end my hobby, and where I decided to stay until the day I died.

The Keys are a long string of islands that extend from the southeastern tip of Florida southwestward to Key West. On a map, they look fangs extending from a snake's mouth. You might think something that looked like that would be evil, but to me, the Keys were paradise. I had always wanted to go there, and now I was on my way.

With three weeks to go, I had managed to avoid the FBI, but according to the news reports on the internet, they knew all about me.

After I killed the old golfer, I stayed at a really cheap bed-and-breakfast in Naples to break my typical pattern of hotels. I told the owner I was supposed to meet my daughter and her family later in the week at a resort in Ft. Myers, and I wanted to decompress a few days before I got slammed with all the stress that would come with putting up with her kids. The owner gave me grin that told me she understood the situation and handed me the keys to the room without asking for more information. I went straight to the room and threw up.

I spent the next three days sick in bed. I did nothing but sleep, eat a few potato chips from a bag I had grabbed at a gas station, threw up several times, and surfed the news sites on the internet to learn about the FBI's manhunt for me.

There were tons of articles and videos to be found online. Apparently, my murders had been big national news for several months, but the first time I found out they were well-known was when the waitress in Huntsville told me about them. I guess I'm not like the stereotypical serial killer who has a huge ego to feed. All I wanted was to be known for all this long after the fact.

I was already making headway to that achievement. The FBI had figured out my identity, and I was now number seven on their Ten Most Wanted list. If I could make it to the end of the year, I had a chance to get into the top five.

And there it was. I had accomplished some of what I started out to do nearly a full year ago. I was now infamous. People knew my name and associated it with a string of murders. If I could stay alive for three more victims, I would reach my self-imposed finish line.

The thing is, I was no longer driven by my hobby. I was basically going through the motions, doing whatever I needed to do to click victims off the list until I got to fifty-two. I thought gaining notoriety would give me some kind of emotional rush, like scoring the winning touchdown or hitting a grand slam in the bottom of the ninth inning, but it didn't. I actually felt indifferent about it. It was both kinda cool and not a big deal at the same time.

To be honest, more than anything else, I wanted this whole ordeal to be over. I wasn't going to quit before I got there, but after I killed my fifty-second victim, it would be more of a relief than anything else.

The latest online video about me was a press conference the FBI gave two weeks ago in Daytona, after I had left town. The two agents in charge of the case were named Cooper Kendrick and Rae Miller. Kendrick was the man from the diner in Delaware. Rae Miller was the tall blonde who got out of the car with him during the rainstorm. I'd never seen her before, best I could remember.

They said they had tracked me all over the country, learning my habits and methodology. They knew all of my aliases as well as my real name. They knew my birthday, my hometown, my ex-wife's name, and the name of my dead son. They said I had no surviving family members, but they were wrong about that.

I had a grandchild and daughter-in-law in Oregon. I wondered why they weren't mentioned. Most likely, it was to keep them safe from vigilantes. You never know when some grief-stricken family member will be able to put two and two together and figure out the identities of a serial killer's extended family, and then go kill them.

Agent Miller said they had tracked me into Florida and had missed me by only a few minutes in Daytona. They knew I was heading south and had alerted every law enforcement station in the state. They said I should be considered armed and dangerous.

A reporter asked her what kind of vehicle I was driving, and she said it would vary, depending on when I got another rental. The last car they knew about was a Ford Taurus.

Just like the one I had parked in the lot outside.

She said they made the connection to me from eyewitness accounts and security camera footage of cars in the area of some of the murders. Then they held up my picture. It was an 8x10 of my driver's license photo, and it looked nothing like me now. The version of me in the picture weighed well over two hundred pounds with a roundish face and salt and pepper hair. The man in my mirror weighed less than 150 pounds with gaunt cheeks, sagging eyelids, and a wrinkled face. The salt and pepper hair still looked the same.

I decided I needed to change that.

I went to a small drugstore around the corner from my hotel, wearing my cap pulled low to hide my face, and bought a cheap set of electric clippers and hair coloring for men. That night, I buzzed my head as close as I could, then dyed jet black what remained of my hair. I even added dye to my eyebrows.

When I was finished, my face didn't look at all like the picture from the FBI video. The dark hair combined with a gazillion pounds of weight loss made me into an entirely different person. But let's face it, if I hadn't lost all this weight, if not for cancer eating my body away, I would have looked like the same guy with darker hair.

Gee, thanks, cancer. I guess this was one of the ways the serial killer gods were helping me. Nothing says they're helping me more than giving me cancer just so I'll be harder to find in a manhunt. I guess they work in mysterious ways.

I decided to head back east, but I wanted to kill number fifty before I got to the coast. I managed to do that by sitting on the side of the interstate with my hood up at two o'clock in the morning. Zero traffic. No security cameras within miles. Before long, a young man stopped to offer help and ended up face down in the weeds twenty feet from the side of the road.

Number fifty. Two more to go. I was practically standing at the end of the tunnel. All I had to do now was step out into the light.

I ate one bite of my Sunday breakfast two days later in Ft. Lauderdale, wearing sunglasses the whole time to keep anyone from seeing my blood-shot eyes. People stared, and I don't know if it was because of the sunglasses or my appearance. It's not every day you see someone who looks like they could be knocked over by a stiff breeze while wearing shades and drawing on a tattered calendar. But I didn't care if they stared or not. I had to keep to my schedule of a pancake breakfast every Sunday. These folks would never see me again, anyway.

The weather was warm, with a gentle breeze blowing puffy clouds out to sea and the sun shining. That's the main reason I came to south Florida. I don't like cold weather because it makes my bones hurt. After I paid for my breakfast, I stepped out into the sunshine, closed my eyes, and leaned my head back, basking my face in the warmth.

I could have stayed that way for hours, but I got dizzy after less than a minute. When I straightened up, a pain hit me, and the single bite of pancakes decided it wanted out of my stomach. My car was parked three spaces away, and I sat down behind the steering wheel two seconds before I emptied my guts on the pavement outside the open car door. One bite of pancakes and a whole bunch of brownish-yellowish bile.

"Sir, are you okay?" a woman asked. She was standing at my front bumper on the sidewalk, about to enter the diner.

I couldn't speak, but I nodded, wiped my mouth, and waved at her.

"Can I get you some water or something?" she asked. "Do you want me to call an ambulance?"

I shook my head and managed to spit out a couple of words. I'm not sure what I mumbled, but she finally got the message that I was fine and continued on into the diner.

Yeah, but I wasn't fine. Cramps ravaged my guts so hard that I couldn't sit up straight. They were like a shark eating me from the inside out. All I could do was sit there and wait for the pain to pass. Sometimes it went away after only a few seconds, but this time it kept going. The intensity of it ebbed and flowed, increasing and decreasing, like waves in the ocean, but it never completely disappeared.

I rocked back and forth in the car seat, doing my best to will away the pain. I don't know how long I kept doing that before I opened my eyes and saw a dozen people in the diner looking at me. I must have been putting on quite a show.

I decided they had seen all they needed to see, so I started the car and pulled out of the parking lot.

I drove for nearly three hours, straight down Highway 1, the road that stretches from the northern tip of Maine all the way down the east coast to Key West. Even though I wore sunglasses, I had to squint my eyes against the bright sunshine beaming through my windshield. Despite the pain in my body, the fatigue, the weakness, and the nausea, I couldn't help but smile, because sand, salt water, and tropical trees were everywhere.

But so were thousands of tourists. Traffic crawled along at a snail's pace, which forced me to be on the lookout for somewhere to pull over in case a severe spasm of nausea or diarrhea hit me without warning. Most of the places I saw were souvenir shops and tourist traps. South Florida was snow-bird country, where millions of wealthy residents of northern states flocked every fall and winter to avoid the bitter cold. I wasn't exactly a snowbird by definition, but I certainly understood the appeal of warm weather. If I could have afforded it, I would have moved permanently to the Keys decades ago.

An hour after I crossed the short bridge between Key Largo and Plantation Key, I cruised into Marathon. Traffic thinned a bit, but not a lot. I decided I needed to find a cheap place to stay, but at this time of year, that would be a tall order.

In order to speed up my search, I pulled over on the side of the road at a souvenir T-shirt stand and hunted for a place on my phone. It took quite a while, but I finally found one that was somewhat close to my price range. Everything else ranged from $200 to $1,000 per night.

According to the map, it was right across the road from a small airport, not far from where I was parked.

Fifteen minutes later, I was in a tiny room that smelled like a combination of disinfectant, decaying seaweed, and stagnant air. The hotel had no other cars in its parking lot, and the individual bungalows were covered with peeling paint and spider webs. The lady at the desk told me I was their only guest for this week. I told her I didn't know how long I would stay, but it shouldn't be more than a night or two. She said I could pay when I checked out, which was totally opposite of how hotels operate. Maybe that's how she always conducted business, or maybe she felt sorry for me based on how I looked.

I have to admit, I looked like someone who needed a hole to crawl into and die, so it's a good bet she took pity on me.

When I asked about a beach to visit that wouldn't be crowded, she mentioned Bahia Honda State Park, just across the Seven Mile Bridge. I decided I would go and just lay on the sand, listen to the surf, and soak up some rays. Heck, even serial killers dying of cancer need to relax on the beach every once in a while.

Chapter Thirty-Six

The drive to Bahia Honda was beautiful. Seven Mile Bridge is exactly that, a bridge that crosses nothing but seven miles of open water. I took off my sunglasses while I drove so I could enjoy the full color of the ocean. Incredible various shades of turquoise, deep blue, and bright green. Why would anyone want to live anywhere but here?

When I first started my year-long hobby, I had no idea I would end up in south Florida. I didn't have a plan. I thought I would go wherever the wind blew me, not caring where I landed, just as long as I could check off one victim a week.

Then this cancer bullshit hit me, and everything changed. I had to be somewhere warm, and driving to Hawaii was out of the question. Flying anywhere never entered my mind. It was too expensive. Plus, it leaves a huge paper trail, complete with video evidence and security checks. It wouldn't have been fun trying to explain to Homeland Security why I was flying with one change of clothes, a laptop computer, a knife, and cheap fishing gear.

Renting a car was risky enough, but it didn't pose the problems of flying.

The parking lot at Bahia Honda was maybe half full. License plates were from all over the country, but not many from Florida. Normally, I would have been excited to see this many people because crowds gave me lots of options for my next victim. But I didn't want that today. I had nearly a full week before my next-to-last murder. Today, all I wanted to do was chill. All I wanted was a few hours with no pain, no stress, no nausea, and no worries.

The beach was a narrow strip of sand with random piles of seaweed washed onto it. Tourists, gathered in small groups with a few singles dotted here and there, were scattered for several hundred yards. Some read books, others laid on towels, and a few waded into the water. The ocean was as calm as a mountain lake, with barely a ripple of waves that gave a soft sigh as they touched the sand.

I pulled off my shirt and rolled my jeans up to my knees. Less than two weeks before Christmas, and the temperature was nearly eighty degrees. I hung my shirt across my shoulder along with a towel I had brought from the hotel room.

I must have been one hell of a sight. My skin had gone from pale white to yellowish many weeks ago because of tumors in my liver. My muscle tone had vanished along with nearly all of my body fat. My collarbones looked as prominent as curtain rods between my neck and shoulders. My knobby knees bobbed from beneath my pants cuffs with every step. My skin hugged my ribs.

I had to smile despite the way I looked. I always wanted a washboard stomach, and I ended up with a washboard chest.

Everything about me suggested I was an old, skinny man hobbling his way down the beach. Everything, that is, except for my fake dark crew cut hair, which made me look like an old, skinny man hobbling down the beach with bad hair coloring.

I found a spot, spread out my towel, and laid down on my back. The mid-day sun felt warm on my stomach and shins. I closed my eyes and listened to the sounds. The faint conversations from other people. The sea gulls yelling at each other. The white noise of wind and water. The breeze was the perfect temperature as it tickled the hairs on my body.

It was almost like getting a massage while wearing headphones. I don't think I had ever been that relaxed in my life.

The next thing I knew, everything sounded and felt different. I could sense the changes without opening my eyes.

It took me a moment to get my eyes used to the sunlight, and when I did, I realized it was now late in the afternoon. The sun was sitting low in the sky, and there were now less than half the number of people on the beach compared to when I first arrived.

I checked the time on my phone. I had fallen asleep for nearly four hours, like some drunk college student during spring break.

My mouth felt sticky. I was badly dehydrated and needed water. Like an idiot, I didn't bring any with me, and there were no water fountains around. My car was at least a hundred yards away. A hundred yards walking through sand on weak legs. I'd be lucky if I stayed conscious long enough to get to the driver's seat.

I shook the sand off my towel and shirt and started the long haul back down the beach with short, halting steps. After ten yards, a twinge of pain grew in my right side. It wasn't enough to double me over, but it hurt enough to cause shortness of breath and to make me pause for a minute.

I made it back to my car after nearly a half hour. I was sweating, gasping for air, and about to collapse from exhaustion. My brain was so foggy I couldn't figure out which button to press to lower my window. I kept hitting the door lock. I had a hard time figuring out where the start button for the ignition was located.

The pain in my side got worse. I covered it with my hand and could feel the spasms rippling through my abdomen like earthquake waves. My T-shirt was partially soaked with my sweat, and streams trickled down my face and neck.

All I wanted to do was get back to my little shithole motel room and go to sleep. I felt awful even though I'd been asleep for the past four hours. I could easily sleep for another forty.

The drive back would have been less dangerous if I had walked down the middle of the road. I weaved all over the place. I tailgated people. I drove too fast. I couldn't see well. It would have almost been a blessing if a cop had pulled me over and thrown me in the slammer for reckless driving.

After what seemed like an eternity, I pulled into to parking space in front of my motel room. The front tires tossed gravel as I skidded to a stop. There was nobody around, and my car was still the only one in the lot. I actually would have preferred if someone had been there to offer me help. Instead, I had to haul my crippled ass into my room all by myself.

I landed face-first on the bed, my pants still rolled up to my knees and my T-shirt still wet. Within an instant, I was asleep again.

I woke up at noon the next day, my body burning up. I was wrapped in the bedspread because I was freezing, but I was also sweating. Maybe I had developed another fever in the night and now I was sweating it off.

My mouth still felt like it had a coating of glue, so I forced myself to trudge to the bathroom sink for a gulp of water. I nearly screamed at what I saw in the mirror.

I was sunburned beyond belief. My face, neck, chest, and stomach were red. So were my lower legs. I twisted to the side to give my back a look. It was as white as the room's walls.

The burn hurt like hell. Twisting pulled wrinkles in my skin, setting it afire. I pressed my hand to my washboard chest and pulled it away. A white hand-shaped shadow remained before it began to fade back to red.

Dozens of tiny water blisters were scattered over my chest, shoulders, and neck.

I wet a washcloth and buried my face in it, trying to get some relief. It didn't help. I felt like I had a fever of 105.

My legs got rubbery. The room started to spin.

I plopped down on the floor with my back against the wall. The spasm in my side started again, but this time it brought a wave of nausea with it. There was nothing in my stomach to throw up but bile, but I didn't have the strength to crawl to the toilet. I ended up puking a mouthful onto the linoleum floor right beside me.

On instinct, I felt my wrist, looking for a pulse. I'd certainly had enough practice with all the people I killed. I could feel the beat against my index and middle fingertips, hammering away. I was too mentally wasted to calculate the actual number of beats per minute, but it was without question twice as fast as normal.

That would be my luck. Blessed with cancer, dehydration, and severe sunburn, and I end up dying of a heart attack, right here in some fleabag motel in the Florida Keys. It's a wonder I didn't have dandruff and bad breath to go along with everything else.

Then again, maybe I did.

I stayed on the floor for another three hours. I was too weak to move. Thunderbolts of pain shot through my guts and I didn't have the strength to wince. I sucked on the wet washcloth for water because I couldn't reach the sink.

Finally, after I had summoned all the strength I could muster, I managed to crawl to the bed and lift myself onto the mattress. I stayed there for the next twenty-four hours.

Chapter Thirty-Seven

I had to get something to eat. If I didn't, I would die. Death was a certainty now, given my condition, but I would starve to death before cancer could finish me off if I didn't get a little bit of nourishment in my body. A sandwich. A bottle of water. A freaking candy bar. Anything to put some fuel in my empty tank.

The thing is, I was too sick and too sunburned to get out of bed. But I was also too malnourished and dehydrated not to.

After listening to my stomach growl and rumble for several hours, I forced myself to make a decision. Either get up, no matter how much it hurts, and get something to eat, or lay here and die alone in this musty room, where nobody will find my rotting corpse for several days.

I got up.

I also decided to make my way to Key West. I had no idea where I would stay, and my money was almost gone, but I knew I had no reason to stay in Marathon. I tossed my things into the car, tucked the Glock into my waistband, covered it with my shirt, and hobbled into the motel office.

The same woman who was there when I arrived was sitting at the desk. She was wearing the same clothes, twirling a full key ring around with her finger. She had to have been bored out of her mind.

"Mornin'," she said. "You enjoying your stay?" Then a look of surprise covered her face. "Oh, my goodness. You got burned pretty bad. Does it hurt?"

"No, it feels just like heaven. Why the hell would it hurt?" I said. I was in no mood for pleasantries. All I wanted to do was check out and head further west. "I'm checking out. How much do I owe you?" I asked. My voice was weak and brittle, but full of impatience.

She drew back at my irritated response, embarrassed. "I'm sorry. I didn't mean that as an insult," she said.

"How much do I owe?"

"Do you need some aloe? I've got some right here." She dug into a desk drawer and pulled out a pump bottle with green gel in it. "This stuff works great on a burn."

I sighed. I *really* wasn't in a mood for this. "Ma'am, please," I said.

"You ought to keep lotion on it, too, or it'll peel real bad." She started to giggle. "You oughta seen my husband Dennis several years ago when he got burned real bad fishing. He came home redder'n you are. He didn't want to put anything on it, and two days later he started peeling like a snake." She giggled some more.

That was it. I'd had enough. I pulled the pistol from my waistband and pointed it at her head. It felt so heavy I had to use both hands. I didn't tell her why I was going to kill her. I just pulled the trigger.

She managed to turn her head and get her hand up, palm facing me, like she was trying to stop me, but the bullet went completely through it and slammed into her temple. The impact knocked her backwards and upended her chair, her legs hanging over the seat like wet towels thrown over a shower curtain rod.

She was dead. I didn't need to check. I didn't have the energy, anyway. Not too many people get shot in the temple and live.

Number fifty-one. One more victim to go. I had just taken one step out of the tunnel, halfway into the light.

I considered ransacking the cash register, but I didn't know how to get the drawer open, and I probably had enough money to make it another week.

Actually, since it was Thursday, I might not need another week. I could technically be done with my goal within four days. I could eat my usual breakfast on Sunday and kill somebody that same day. That would be the finish line. I would have done what I set out to do.

If I lived that long.

The way I felt at the moment didn't give me much hope I could make it another four days, though. I had no idea what death feels like, but I had a good idea what its scent smelled like, and the smell was all around me.

I grabbed the wad of keys the woman had lying on her desk. I picked up the bottle of aloe, too, since I needed it worse than she did. I flipped the keys over one by one until I figured out which one worked the lock on the front door, and bolted the door shut as I walked out. I threw the keys into the bushes. That ought to buy me a little time in case anybody came looking for her.

I bought two tacos and a large ice water from a Taco Bell a couple of blocks down the road and forced them down as I drove west on Highway 1. The pain in my stomach almost made me wreck a few times, and it was all I could do to keep the food from coming back up, but eventually the nausea backed away and I could feel a tiny bit of energy easing into my veins. It wasn't much, and it certainly wasn't a huge surge, but it was better than nothing.

I kept the car radio off and let the sound of the breeze through the open windows rumble across my ears. After nearly a full year on the road, I had listened to all the classic rock and talk radio I could stand. I didn't want to hear the news, either. I already knew the feds were closing in. They knew everything about me except my exact location. That was the only news I cared about.

Anybody could have tracked me through Florida just by following the dead bodies. I realized too late that I was painting myself into a corner by driving to Key West. I had bounced around the state like a ball in a pinball machine, rolling its way down to the flippers. Once I got there, I wouldn't have any avenue of escape except to go back the way I'd come. All the FBI had to do was lock down all traffic into and out of the Keys, and they would eventually nail me.

Not long after I left Marathon, I came to a parking area on the side of the road. Three or four cars were there, with a handful of people milling about, stretching their legs after a long drive. A few others were fishing off the bank just past the parking area.

I pulled in because I needed to stop. I had been only a few miles, and I was already exhausted. The energy from the tacos I'd eaten didn't last long.

My fishing gear was in the back floorboard. I thought for a second that it might be nice to try and catch something, but that idea was kicked to the curb just as fast as it entered my mind. If I wanted to finish this thing, if I wanted to get to my fifty-second victim, I didn't need to waste time with a fishing pole.

Besides, I was too sunburned to get back out in it again. The redness on my face and neck were still uncomfortable, and my stomach and washboard chest were starting to itch. I rubbed several portions of the stolen aloe over the worst areas, then I grabbed my gun. I sniffed at its muzzle, taking in the scent of gunpowder and metal. It was still as intoxicating as it had ever been.

I pulled a half-full box of bullets from the glove compartment. I kept them there to reload the gun's magazine whenever I needed. The original box of fifty rounds was now down to fifteen after my last practice session. I inserted two into the magazine to fill it, shoved it back into the gun, and emptied the rest into my hand.

I looked at them for a long moment. I wouldn't need them anymore. The seven bullets in my Glock would be more than enough to finish off my last victim. The extras in my hand were nothing more than excess baggage.

Yeah, excess baggage. I had quite a bit of it I had to get rid of.

I stepped out of the car, poured the bullets into my jeans pocket, and stuffed the gun into my waistband. It felt quite natural there by now. Weeks of carrying it around had gotten me used to it.

I grabbed my fishing gear and walked to an unfinished bridge beyond the fishermen. They didn't even look at me as I passed. It wasn't far, but I was completely out of breath by the time I got there. The pole and tackle box felt like they weighed a million pounds. I set everything down and leaned on my elbows against the bridge railing, looking out at the water and breathing hard. Sweat poured off me. A bitter mixture of aloe and perspiration trickled into the corners of my mouth.

It was a typical beautiful day in the Keys. Brilliant sunshine. No clouds. Barely any wind. The ocean looked like a turquoise mirror, smooth and shiny.

But I didn't have the luxury of hanging around. I had to keep moving.

I pulled the bullets from my pocket and tossed them into the water. The noise from passing cars kept any splashing sound from reaching any of the other fishermen. I did the same with my fishing pole. I didn't drop my tackle box because I thought it would float. I decided to leave it on the ground for somebody else to find.

Before I walked away, I grabbed the knife Ethan had given me from the tackle box. I pulled it from its leather sheath and rotated it back and forth in the sunlight, letting the glare slide across my face. The knife had a tiny trace of dark brown blood on its handle, a remnant from my battle with Bison.

It was also evidence. I needed to throw it away. There was nothing more damning to a defendant than DNA evidence, and this blood stain was nothing but a huge glob of Bison's DNA. I thought I had wiped it all away months ago, but I guess there are some stains that never can be cleaned. Even if a mess is completely cleaned up so there's no trace of it ever existing, things that caused the mess can never be undone.

You can't un-ring a bell. You can't un-see what's already been seen. You can't un-say things that have already been said.

You can't un-kill somebody who's been killed.

This knife was literally the only thing I had left in my possession that tied me to Ethan. I had a daughter-in-law and possibly a grandchild in Oregon, but let's be real; I was never going to see them.

I was never going to get out of the Keys. I was a dead man walking. Or, more accurately, a dead man limping and wheezing.

I held the knife over the railing in order to let it go, but I pulled it back before I could commit. I didn't want to let this one thing, this one physical reminder of my son, drop beneath the waves forever. I repeated the attempt at least three times, torn between getting rid of something that would slow me down and holding on to a precious keepsake.

As I held it out over the railing a fourth time, a sharp, searing spasm tore across my insides, violent enough to make my whole body jerk. I banged my elbow against the railing, and the knife fell from my grasp. I could do nothing but watch as it splashed into the blue water and disappear.

Maybe it was fate. Maybe it was just an accident. Or maybe it was what had to happen for me to get rid of my baggage and move on with what little life I had left.

I stared at the water below me for at least five minutes, not moving, barely breathing, unable to focus my eyes because of the tears.

Finally, I tossed the leather sheath into the water and tore myself away to begin a slow walk back to my car. The world wasn't going to stop because I was sad. It was like a train pulling out of the station. If I wanted to get to my next destination, I had to get on board. Otherwise, I was going to be stranded.

As I climbed back behind the car's steering wheel, I knew what my next move would be. I had to find a cheap place to stay in Key West, and I needed to ditch my car.

Later that afternoon, I found a really cheap hole-in-the-wall hotel, complete with a tiny bed in a tiny room that smelled like the one I'd had in Marathon. I paid for seven days, which nearly wiped out the rest of my money. If I was careful, I could make it to Christmas Day with what I had left. If I didn't have my last victim by then, it would be too late.

I spent the rest of the day looking at a map of Key West and doing research on my computer. I drove to a deserted street after sunset and abandoned my car on the side of the road. Somebody would either steal it or report it to the cops, who would then alert the FBI, who would then start a door-to-door manhunt for me.

They were going to find me. It was just a matter of time. At this point, I didn't really care anymore, as long as I could kill one more person. Had to keep my eye on the prize.

I half walked and half limped back to my hotel. It took me nearly two hours to travel less than a mile. I was so tired, sick, and dehydrated by the time I got back that I fell into bed and slept for two days.

Chapter Thirty-Eight

I PROBABLY WOULD HAVE SLEPT LONGER, BUT THE MAID knocked on my door and woke me up. I was so tired after I abandoned my car that I forgot to hang the *Do Not Disturb* sign on my door. Good thing, too. It was late morning on Sunday, and I still hadn't eaten my breakfast or marked the next-to-last X on my calendar. My sunburn no longer burned, but I felt feverish, like I had a mild case of the flu.

I told the maid I didn't need anything but a small bottle of lotion. She handed me a two-ounce tube from her cart. It wasn't much, but it was better than nothing. My skin was peeling and itching like crazy, and aloe didn't do anything to stop it.

My breakfast consisted of three bites from a muffin and a few sips of water from the complimentary continental breakfast provided in the hotel lobby. I sat at a small table to rest and to mark the X on my calendar, but it fell apart when I pulled it from my pocket. The two staples that bound the pages together had fallen out. The individual pages fell to the floor like leaves in autumn.

It didn't matter. All I needed was the page for December. I tossed the other pages into a trash can. Then I went back to my room and threw up what I'd eaten, along with more bile and dark red, clotted blood.

If there had been some way to inject food directly into my veins, bypassing my stomach, I would have done it. I was so tired of puking several times a day. I was tired of the pain. I was tired of being tired.

But the only way to get nourishment into my veins would be to check into a hospital, and that wasn't an option. The FBI would have walked into my room an hour after I arrived, slapped the handcuffs on me, and dragged me to jail. No more hobby. No more freedom.

Yeah, right. Freedom, my ass. I was no more a free man than someone serving a life sentence in a maximum-security prison. Everything I had done this past year was due to this ball-and-chain hobby of mine. Then, my cancer added more weight to my burden. I couldn't move as fast as I used to. I had to develop a different strategy for killing people. I was wasting away at a rapid pace and there was nothing I could do about it now.

No, I wasn't free. I was a prisoner of my own making. Nobody to blame but me.

Doctor Glover in Huntsville told me I didn't have long to live, and that was more than two months ago. Back when I started this hobby, I felt like I was going to live forever. I felt bulletproof. But I didn't feel that way anymore. I would be lucky if I lived to see Christmas, and that was only a week away.

I could have decided to kill my last victim right away, but I decided to live as much as I could before I fired the last shot. I was going to use every ounce of energy in my body to enjoy these last few days. I was going to force myself to get out of this hotel room. Key West was paradise, for crying out loud.

I also decided to keep the Glock tucked away in my duffel bag. If I had it with me while I toured the town, I figured I would be too tempted to use it.

The hotel desk clerk gave me a free pass for a trolley that zig-zagged all over town, sort of like a bus but with open windows. That probably saved her life, because she would have been an easy final victim when the time came. But because she was nice to me, she got to live.

Key West is an amazing place. I spent two days riding the trolley, going from the public beach to the town's lighthouse, to Ernest Hemingway's house, and several museums. I wore sunglasses and my cap pulled low to conceal my face.

I got to see the most beautiful sunset I could imagine at Mallory

Square, a pier on the town's west side where crowds gathered every evening. It was bustling with tourists buying souvenirs, getting their faces painted, taking pictures, and waving at dozens of boats as they passed.

A man wearing a kilt marched back and forth, playing a bagpipe. A woman twirled a fiery baton. Acrobats juggled various objects while riding a ten-foot-tall unicycle. A funny man with a French accent put on a show with cats he had trained to jump through hoops.

During this whole time, nobody seemed to notice me, and that's just the way I liked it. After a lifetime of getting pissed off because nobody noticed me, it was now working in my favor. It's almost ironic that I didn't want to be noticed while I was killing people in an effort to be noticed, but all it would take is the wrong person recognizing me and telling the cops, and it would be all over for me.

After two full days of being a tourist, I was worn to a frazzle, dehydrated, and barely strong enough to stand. I spent the next day in bed, resting my legs and fighting stomach spasms. In between jolts of pain, I looked up the latest news on the internet.

The FBI knew I was now in Key West. They had found the dead desk clerk in Marathon. The fishing tackle box I left beside the unfinished bridge was at first thought to be a bomb, but after a remote-controlled robot determined it wasn't, the feds found my fingerprints all over it. A day later they found my abandoned car. It had my fingerprints all over it, too, along with some hair samples. It was only a matter of time before they matched my DNA with murder scenes all over the country.

Federal officers were posted at all points of entry into Key West. Every car and bus driving into or leaving from the island by Highway 1 was checked. Everyone flying into or out of the airport was screened. The Coast Guard ramped up their patrols all up and down the Keys, boarding any boats that looked suspicious. The whole area was in lockdown. The news agencies called it a "dragnet."

It was more proof I was now infamous. My name was known all over the country, from coast to coast, and I managed to do it before my fifty-second victim.

That didn't mean I could stop. I still had to prove to myself that I could accomplish a difficult goal without quitting. Life's toughest battles aren't against someone or something else. They're always against yourself. Once I kill my last victim, I will have won that war. After that, the FBI becomes my adversary.

And like the saying goes, the FBI always gets their man.

I was never going to leave this place without wearing handcuffs.

Or a body bag.

Chapter Thirty-Nine

Friday, December 23. Two days before Christmas, and I was still too weak to leave my room. I was also too scared. The FBI had held another televised press conference that was all over the local channels. Agents Rae Miller and Cooper Kendrick said they knew I was somewhere on the island, and it was only a matter of time before they found me. Agent Miller advised everyone not to approach me if they saw me, and that I should be considered armed and extremely dangerous.

Even looking as gaunt and sickly as I did, there was a chance somebody could still recognize me from the pictures that were shown on the news and all over the internet. Key West is only four square miles in size. There aren't many places to hide.

The sand was almost gone from the hourglass. I had the rest of tonight and tomorrow to kill my last victim, but it would take a near-miracle for me to muster enough strength to walk out of the room. But I had to do it. I had to somehow venture out one last time. I couldn't afford to fail when I was this close.

Outside my room, I heard a group of people walking past the hotel. One of them was wearing jingle bells on their shoes. They were laughing and singing a horrible, out-of-key rendition of "Rudolph The Red-Nosed Reindeer." It seemed weird to hear Christmas songs about snow and to see decorations everywhere in the only place in the continental United States that had never seen a frost.

And there I sat on my musty bed, all alone for the second Christmas in a row, with nobody to give me a gift and nobody to give a gift to. I had spent over a year alone. No wife. No girlfriend. No friends. No relatives, except for Ethan.

Ethan. My only blood relative, now nothing but a memory. That's all I had left. The knife he bought for me was now buried in the sand beneath the waves. The memory was good, though, if you don't count the moments after I found him, covered in blood. We had made up. We were on the way to being a *real* father and son. It seemed like all the bad things from our past had been erased, with only a brilliant horizon ahead of us.

And then it vanished.

I didn't even have a picture of him.

I sat on the bed for a long time after the singers passed by, my mind buzzing at a thousand miles per hour. Should I contact Sara to let her know I was about to die of cancer? Has she had her baby yet? Would my grand-baby someday want to know what I looked like? Would it be better to take a picture of myself as I currently looked, or should I take a picture of my driver's license and send that?

What would I have wanted if I'd never met my grandfather? After tossing it around in my mind for nearly an hour, I decided I would have wanted a current picture. A driver's license picture has no emotion, no deep meaning, no personality. It's too...*sterile*.

I decided to get dressed and take a selfie in the bathroom mirror. That's the best I could do. I moved at a snail's pace to the bathroom and held my phone up so my body and face would be inside the picture frame. I clicked the button and looked at the result.

Everything was blurry. I must have wiggled the camera when I pressed the button. I'd never taken a selfie in my life, so I wasn't exactly well-versed on the procedure.

I finally figured out how to hold the phone steady with both hands and still fit my body and face in the frame. I gave my best smile, which probably wasn't very picturesque, but it would have to do. I clicked the button five times in a row before I thought I had one good enough to use.

I sat down on the bed, out of breath, and scanned through the pics.

The first one made me laugh out loud. Well, it wasn't exactly a laugh. It sounded more like a cross between a 100-year-old man with emphysema and someone with a three-day-old case of laryngitis.

The man in the picture looked nothing like me. He had a jet-black crew cut and white stubble on his cheeks. Yeah, that looked real natural. His skin was peeling from his neck and arms, and was a yellowish tan color. He was so skinny he looked like he had anorexia.

My dad told me once about a man he worked with who was so skinny, all the other co-workers would tell him if he turned sideways and stuck out his tongue, he'd look like a zipper.

That's why I laughed. I looked like a zipper.

I picked out the least-unflattering picture and attached it to a text message to Sara. It had been so long since she'd seen me, she probably wouldn't even recognize my number.

The text took a long time to process. After nearly five minutes, a message appeared on my screen saying "Message failed. Retry?"

I tried sending it four more times. It failed on all of them.

The hell with it, I decided. I was going to call her. She might not recognize my number, and she definitely wouldn't recognize my voice, but I had to connect with somebody. I had to hear the sound of a caring voice, something I hadn't heard since Doctor Glover tried to convince me to start cancer treatment.

I needed a human experience. Sara was my only hope for that, and I didn't have much time left. I could feel myself slipping away so fast that I didn't think I could live more than another twenty-four hours.

I found her number on my phone and pressed the call button. It took several seconds before it rang.

It rang once.

The ring was followed by a loud, squealing beep and a recorded woman's voice saying, *"We're sorry. You have reached a number that has been disconnected or is no longer in service"*...blah, blah, blah.

I ended the call. Now what was I going to do? I didn't have a backup number to call her. Then an idea hit me. I actually *did* have a number. I could call the tattoo parlor. Maybe Sara still owned it. At worst, somebody there would know how to reach her.

What was the name of the place? I tied my brain in knots trying to remember, but old-man brain combined with cancer brain doesn't help one's ability to recall names. I flipped open my laptop and did a search for tattoo parlors in Eugene, Oregon. The search engine came back with at least twenty.

I scrolled through the names, looking for one I recognized.

Trendz Tattoos.

The Magic Needle.

Under The Skin.

Then, at the bottom of the list, there it was. *The Body Canvas.* Its address and phone number were listed below the name. My fingers trembled as I entered the number into my phone. As I held the phone to my ear, my hand shook.

Five rings, then a young man's voice answered.

"The Body Canvas. Travis speaking."

"Uh, hi," I said. "I'm looking for Sara."

"Who?"

"Sara. She and her fiancé Ethan..." I began.

"Ohhhh. Yeah, yeah, yeah. Now I remember her. They used to own this place, right?"

"Yes," I said. The guy sounded no older than his late teens.

"Right. Yeah, well...hang on a second," he said. He covered the phone with his hand, and I could hear a muffled conversation. As he pulled his hand away, he told the person he was talking to that he'd be there in a minute.

"Hey, sorry, dude. I had a customer come in. The guy that owns this place had to run out real quick, and I'm pretty swamped."

"That's okay. You said you know Sara?" I asked.

"Yeah. She died, man."

I nearly dropped the phone. My pulse sped up and sweat popped out on my forehead.

"What? What happened?" My hand shook harder.

"I don't know the story. Just what I've heard. Rumor has it she had a miscarriage back in August, and she got all depressed. She sold the tattoo shop, and then she took a whole bunch of pills, like, the very next day. It was sometime around Halloween. But I've only been here about a month, so that was way before my time. That's all I know, dude. Sorry."

I sat there in silence, stunned by the impact of what he'd told me. Words wouldn't come to me. It was hard enough to just breathe.

"Hey, look, I'm pretty covered up. You might want to speak to the owner when he gets back in an hour or so. Thanks for calling," he said as he hung up.

A wave of sadness rolled over me, and my eyes welled up with tears, but I wouldn't allow myself to cry.

Depressed? Yeah, I imagine she was. Her fiancé had been murdered, then she lost her baby, all within a few months of each other. How much heartache can a person stand? Is it unreasonable to think she was in so much emotional pain that she would do anything to make it stop, including something as drastic as suicide? If I had been in her shoes, I don't know whether I could keep living, either.

Now, every connection I had to anyone I cared about was gone. I wasn't a grandfather. I wasn't a father. I wasn't a husband.

Just like when I spent the best years of my life working in a factory, I was nothing anybody cared about. Oh sure, the FBI cared about catching me and putting me away for life, but they didn't care for *me*. They didn't care for anything I felt inside. They damn sure didn't care that I was about to die of cancer.

I checked the time. Nearly midnight. Only a few minutes away from Christmas Eve. If I didn't have my last victim within twenty-four hours, I would be a failure. Midnight Saturday night was the deadline.

I summoned all the strength I had, stood up, and pulled the Glock from the bedside table. I sniffed its gunpowder and metal aroma and tucked it into my waistband. I left the room without locking it. If somebody wanted to take my laptop, they could have it. I didn't need it anymore. I was going to walk through the streets of Key West until my strength completely gave out, then I would shoot the first person I saw. Then I would wait for the cops to arrive. I simply didn't have the strength or desire to stay on the run any longer.

The air outside was warm and humid. That's why I came south, because cold air makes my body hurt. The ironic thing is that my body still ached like hell, only now I was sweaty all over.

Even though it was late, there were still lots of people milling around. Couples, mostly. Some wore red and white Santa hats while others had on ugly Christmas sweaters and sweatshirts. Everybody seemed happy.

It wouldn't be long before somebody was going to be extremely unhappy.

My gait was slow and unsteady, almost as if I'd had too much to drink. In reality, my legs were weaker than a baby's. I had to stop every block or so and lean against something to catch my breath. Most people ignored me, although a few gave me a concerned look without saying anything.

After I'd gone a few blocks, one couple passed by, looked at me, and paused. The woman said something to her husband and pointed at me. He looked over at me, shook his head no, and walked away. The woman turned to give me one last look as they left.

Something in her face made me think she recognized me. If they'd approached me to ask if I was a serial killer, I would have shot one of them on the spot. But they didn't, and that saved their life.

I took a deep breath and limped on down the sidewalk.

I took a meandering course through town, going nowhere in particular. I just went wherever the wind blew me. After over an hour, I was basically dead on my feet. I had no idea where I was, but the crowds had thinned quite a bit. The restaurants and bars were in the process of winding down.

Half a block ahead of me, I saw a small group of people standing on a street corner, taking a picture as they gathered around a metal signpost. If I could make it to them, I would stop there and shoot somebody.

It took me several minutes to get there. I staggered toward the group, sweating, wheezing, coughing, and groaning. They saw me coming and backed away from the signpost well before I reached them. Four guys and four girls, probably college aged.

I fell to my knees as I reached the signpost. It hurt like hell, but I was too tired to see if I was bleeding. All I wanted to do at that moment was catch my breath. I collapsed onto my butt against a fire hydrant and looked up at the post. There were three signs on it. The top one said *End*. Below that was a numeral *1* inside a white shield. Near the bottom of the post was a small green and white rectangle that said *Mile 0.*

Mile marker zero. The end of the road. Literally.

This was as far as I could go. I simply didn't have the strength to take another step.

One of the college-aged guys started to creep towards me. The others stayed back at least thirty feet.

"Hey. Are you okay, sir?" he asked.

I didn't respond. I just sat there breathing and sweating. My legs were splayed out in front of me. They felt as heavy as lead.

He asked me if I needed an ambulance, and I shook my head. I reached behind me, into my waistband, and pulled out the pistol. It clattered against the sidewalk as it cleared my belt. I didn't have the strength to hold it with one hand.

His eyes widened with surprise. He hadn't expected me to pull a gun on him. He held both hands out in front of himself.

"Hey, now. Whoa. I'm here to help, okay?" he said.

I reached across my body with my other hand and pulled the gun up high enough to point it at him. He started backing up.

"Okay. I'm leaving. I'm leaving," he said. His hands were still out in front of him.

The pistol wavered left and right and up and down. Someone on a boat deck in stormy seas would have held it steadier. I pulled the trigger, and a window shattered in a souvenir store across the street.

The girls screamed and took off running. The guys followed them.

I fired two more times, knowing full well there was no chance in hell I would hit them. One bullet flattened the front tire of a parked car, and I don't know where the other one went.

Even though I thought the streets were emptying out, I heard screaming all around me. I fired the gun twice more into the darkness. If I hit someone, I would never know it. I was just shooting at sounds now.

I fired the sixth shot at a car that drove past and missed it by ten feet. A spray of concrete rattled against the side of another parked car as the bullet ricocheted.

I held the gun in my lap and breathed hard. It felt like it weighed a hundred pounds.

Six shots, and I didn't hit a damn thing except for a window and a tire. I had one shot left. I had to make it count.

It wasn't long before I heard sirens coming closer. Lots of them. Way off in the distance, I heard the chopping noise from a helicopter.

At least eight police cars skidded to a stop in a fifty-foot radius around me. Blue lights flashed everywhere. One of the cars was a dark sedan with a suction-cup light on the dash. It was closer to me than all the others. The doors opened, and out stepped FBI agents Rae Miller and Cooper Kendrick with their guns drawn, pointed at me. They shielded themselves behind the doors.

"Jonathan Doe, FBI! You're under arrest! Put your hands on your head!" agent Miller yelled.

Sweat dripped off my eyebrows and landed on the pistol. I was nearly too weak to raise my head and look at her, but I somehow managed. She held her gun steady as a rock, propped against the car's door frame. I gave a weak smile. There was no way to get out of this. I had only one victim left to go, and I was going to come up short.

The story of my life. A failure again.

Only sheer luck would allow me to fire my last remaining shot at random and hit someone. But I knew that wasn't going to happen. Even if I did hit someone, what were the odds I would kill them? The cops would shoot me dead before I could find out.

I would die without knowing if I met my goal or not.

I forced a laugh. This had been a shit show since the beginning.

"Jonathan, drop the gun and put your hands on your head or we will shoot you!" agent Miller yelled.

Yeah, Agent Miller. I know that. You'll kill me before I can kill somebody else. I'd already killed way too many.

Overhead, the helicopter hovered and lit up the entire intersection with its spotlight.

Sometimes, brilliant ideas come during the most urgent situations. Maybe it's because the intensity of the moment causes the brain to hyper-focus. My brain was definitely hyper-focused at that moment. And I had a brilliant idea.

I was going to get out of this. I was going to win.

One more victim. Fifty-two in total. One person a week for an entire year. I wasn't going to be a failure. For the first time in my shitty excuse for a life, I was going to meet my goal. All I needed was the strength to lift the gun one more time.

I looked down at the pistol and stared into its barrel. A long, dark tunnel with no light at the end. What a metaphor for my life. One shot left. I gripped it with both hands to raise it. I needed to be as steady as possible so that I wouldn't miss. A gentle tropical breeze blew the faint scent of gunpowder into my face.

Mile Marker Zero

A gun barrel tastes exactly like it smells.

THE END

I hope you enjoyed Mile Marker Zero. I would be grateful if you took a moment right now to post a quick review wherever you bought your copy, and/or on Goodreads if you have an account there.

Acknowledgments

A writer like me can't be successful all on his own. It took a team of experts to help complete this novel. Many thanks go to:

My cousin Wendy Sims for the medical information.

My cousin John Ray Sims for the weapons guidance.

My former neighbor/honorary wife Cheryl Purtle for being the original beta reader.

All the other beta readers who gave me support and input. There are too many of you to mention. You know who you are.

To Stephanie Candiago, thank you for your invaluable help getting this second edition launched.

About the Author

Benny Sims traces his love for storytelling to reading Jack London's "The Call of The Wild" when he was seven years old and listening to his uncle tell stories of being an artillery cannoneer during World War II. Later, several teachers in high school and college recognized his aptitude for writing and encouraged him to pursue it. He hasn't stopped since.

A native of middle Tennessee, he moved to southern Illinois when he was fourteen. After attending college in Murray, Kentucky, he relocated back to Tennessee to briefly work as a journalist with a small-town newspaper before accepting a job with an aerospace company in Huntsville, Alabama. He retired recently after nearly 34 years with the company and now lives in Foley, Alabama.

His debut novel, "Code Gray," released in 2020, won the prestigious Silver Falchion Award for Best Mystery at the 2021 Killer Nashville writer's conference.